GUY DE MAUPASSANT

37 Short Stories

COMPILED BY
PATRICIA MOORE

UNABRIGED & COMPLETE
LONG READING TEXT

NEW DELHI (INDIA)

GUY DE MAUPASSANT

This English Edition, Published in India

Published by

MG BOOKS

An Imprint of

MAANU GRAPHICS

(PUBLISHERS OF GENERAL BOOKS)

5FF, Ganpati Bhawan, 21 Ansari Road,
Darya Ganj, New Delhi-110002
Ph: 43755225, 9315898404
E-mail : maanugraphics@yahoo.com
mgbooks.maanu@yahoo.com

Printed at

Satyam Enterprises, Delhi

CONTENTS

A DEAD WOMAN'S SECRET

SHE had died painlessly, tranquilly, like a woman whose life was irreproachable, and she now lay on her back in bed, with closed eyes, calm features, her long white hair carefully arranged, as if she had again made her toilet ten minutes before her death. Her pale physiognomy was so composed now that she had passed away, so resigned, that one felt sure a sweet soul had dwelt in that body, that this serene grandmother had spent an untroubled existence, that this virtuous woman had ended her life without any shock, without any remorse.

On his knees beside the bed, her son, a magistrate of inflexible principles, and her daughter Marguerite—in religion, Sister Eulalie—were weeping distractedly. She had from the time of their infancy armed them with an inflexible code of morality, teaching them a religion without weakness and a sense of duty without any compromise. He, the son, had become a magistrate and, wielding the weapon of the law, struck down without pity the feeble and the erring. She, the daughter, quite penetrated with the virtue that had bathed her in this austere family, had become the spouse of God through disgust with men.

They had scarcely known their father; all they knew was that he had made their mother unhappy without learning any further details. The nun passionately kissed one hand of her dead mother, which hung down, a hand of ivory like that of Christ in the large crucifix which lay on the bed. At the opposite side of the prostrate body the other hand seemed still to grasp the rumpled sheet with that wondering movement which is called the fold of the dying and the lines had retained little creases as a memento of those last motions which precede the eternal motionlessness. A few light taps at the door caused the two sobbing heads to look up, and the priest, who had just dined, entered the apartment. He was flushed, a little puffed from the effects of the process of digestion which had just commenced, for he had put a good dash of brandy into his coffee in order to counteract the fatigue caused by the last nights he had remained up and that which he anticipated from the night that was still in store for him. He had put on a look of sadness, that simulated sadness of the priest to whom death is a means of livelihood. He made the sign of the cross and, coming over to them with his professional gestures, said:

"Well, my poor children, I have come to help you to pass these mournful hours."

But Sister Eulalie suddenly rose up.

"Thanks, Father, but my brother and I would like to be left alone with her. These are the last moments that we now have for seeing her, so we want to feel ourselves once more, the three of us, just as we were years ago when we—we— we were only children and our poor—poor mother—" She was unable to finish with the flood of tears that gushed from her eyes and the sobs that were choking her.

But the priest bowed with a mere serene look on his face, for he was thinking of his bed. "Just as you please, my children."

Then he kneeled down, again crossed himself, prayed, rose and softly stole away, murmuring as he went: "She was a saint."

They were left alone, the dead woman and her children. A hidden timepiece kept regularly ticking in its dark comer, and through the open window the soft odours of hay and of woods penetrated with faint gleams of moonlight. No sound in the fields outside, save the wandering croak of toads and now and then the humming of some nocturnal insect darting in like a ball and knocking itself against the wall.

An infinite peace, a divine melancholy, a silent serenity, surrounded this dead woman, seemed to emanate from her, to evaporate from her into the atmosphere outside and to calm Nature herself.

Then the magistrate, still on his knees, his head pressed against the bedclothes, in a far-off, heartbroken voice that pierced through the sheets and the coverlet, exclaimed:

"Mamma, Mamma, Mamma!" And the sister, sinking down on the floor, striking the wood with her forehead fanatically, twisting herself about and quivering like a person in an epileptic fit, groaned: "Jesus, Jesus—Mamma— Jesus!"

And both of them, shaken by a hurricane of grief, panted with a rattling in their throats.

Then the fit gradually subsided, and they now wept in a less violent fashion, like the rainy calm that follows a squall on a storm-beaten sea. Then after some time they rose and fixed their glances on the beloved corpse. And memories, those memories of the past, so sweet, so torturing today, came back to their minds with all those little forgotten details, those little details so intimate and familiar, which make the being who is no more live over again. They recalled circumstances, words, smiles, certain intonations of voice which belonged to one whom they should never hear speaking to them again. They saw her once more happy and calm, and phrases she used in ordinary conversation rose to their lips. They even remembered a little movement of the hand, peculiar to her, as if she were keeping time when she was saying something of importance.

And they loved her as they had never before loved her. And by the depth of their despair they realized how strongly they had been attached to her and how desolate they would find themselves now.

She had been their mainstay, their guide, the best part of their youth, of that happy portion of their lives which had vanished; she had been the bond that united them to existence, the mother, the mamma, the creative flesh, the tie that bound them to their ancestors. They would henceforth be solitary, isolated; they would have nothing on earth to look back upon.

The nun said to her brother:

"You know how Mamma used always to read over her old letters. They are all there in her desk. Suppose we read them in our turn and so revive all her life this night by her side. It would be like a kind of road of the cross, like making the acquaintance of her mother, of grandparents whom we never knew, whose letters are there and of whom she has so often talked to us; you remember?"

******

And they drew forth from the drawer a dozen little packets of yellow paper, carefully tied up and placed close to one another. They flung these relics on the bed and, selecting one of them on which the word "Father" was written, they opened and read what was in it.

It consisted of those very old letters which are to be found in old family writing desks, those letters which have the flavour of another century. The first said, "My darling"; another, "My beautiful little girl"; then others, "My dear child"; and then again, "My dear daughter." And suddenly the nun began reading aloud, reading for the dead her own history, all her tender souvenirs. And the magistrate listened, while he leaned on the bed with his eyes on his mother's face. And the motionless corpse seemed happy.

Sister Eulalie, interrupting herself, said: "We ought to put them into the grave with her, to make a winding sheet of them and bury them with her."

And then she took up another packet on which the descriptive word did not appear.

And in a loud tone she began:

"My adored one, I love you to distraction. Since yesterday I have been suffering like a damned soul burned by the recollection of you. I feel your lips on mine, your eyes under my eyes, your flesh under my flesh. I love you! I love you! You have made me mad! My arms open! 1 pant with an immense desire to possess you again. My whole body calls out to you, wants you. I have kept in my mouth the taste of your kisses."

The magistrate rose up; the nun stopped reading. He snatched the letter from her and sought for the signature. There was none, save under the words, "He who adores you," the name "Henry." Their father's name was René. So then he was not the man.

Then the son, with rapid fingers, fumbled in the packet of letters, took another of them and read:

"I can do without your caresses no longer."

And standing up with the severity of a judge passing sentence, he gazed at the impassive face of the dead woman.

The nun, straight as a statue, with teardrops standing at each comer of her eyes, looked at her brother, waiting to see what he meant to do. Then he crossed the room, slowly reached the window and looked out thoughtfully into the night.

When he turned back Sister Eulalie, her eyes quite dry, still remained standing near the bed with a downcast look.

He went over to the drawer and flung in the letters which he had picked up from the floor. Then he drew the curtain round the bed.

And when the dawn made the candles on the table look pale the son rose from his armchair and, without even a parting glance at the mother whom he had separated from them and condemned, he said slowly:

"Now, my sister, let us leave the room."

MOONLIGHT

MADAME JULIE ROBE'RE was awaiting her elder sister, Madame Henriette Letore, who had just returned after a trip to Switzerland.

The Letore household had left nearly five weeks ago. Madame Henriette had allowed her husband to return alone to their estate in Calvados, where some matters of business required his attention, and came to spend a few days in Paris with her sister. Night came on. In the quiet parlor darkened by twilight shadows, Madame Roubére was reading in an absent-minded fashion, raising her eyes whenever she heard a sound.

At last she heard a ring at the door, and presently her sister appeared, wrapped in a traveling cloak. And immediately, without any formal greeting, they clasped each other ardently, only desisting for a moment to begin embracing each other over again. Then they talked, asking questions about each other's health, about their respective families, and a thousand other things, gossiping, jerking out hurried, M-2broken sentences, and rushing about while Madame Henriette was removing her hat and veil.

It was now quite dark. Madame Roubére rang for a lamp, and as soon as it was brought in, she scanned her sister's face, and was on the point of embracing her once more. But she held back, scared and astonished at the other's appearance. Around her temples, Madame Letore had two long locks of white hair. All the rest of her hair was of a glossy, raven-black hue ; but there alone, at each side of her head, ran, as it were, two silvery streams which were immediately lost in the black mass surrounding them. She was, nevertheless, only twenty-four years old, and this change had come on suddenly since her departure for Switzerland.

Without moving, Madame Roubère gazed at her in amazement, tears rising to her eyes, as she thought that some mysterious and terrible calamity must have fallen on her sister. She asked:

"What is the matter with you, Henriette?"

Smiling with a sad smile, the smile of one who is heartsick, the other replied: "Why, nothing, I assure you. Were you noticing my white hair?"

But Madame Roubère impetuously seized her by the shoulders, and with a searching glance at her, repeated:

"What is the matter with you? Tell me what is the matter with you. And if you tell me a falsehood I'll soon find it out."

They remained face to face, and Madame Henriette, who became so pale that she was near fainting, had two pearly tears at each comer of her drooping eyes.

Her sister went on asking:

"What has happened to you? What is the matter with you? Answer me!"

Then, in a subdued voice, the other murmured :

"I have—I have a lover."

And, hiding her forehead on the shoulder of her younger sister, she sobbed.

Then, when she had grown a little calmer, when the heaving of her breast had subsided, she commenced to unbosom herself, as if to cast forth this secret from herself, to empty this sorrow of hers into a sympathetic heart.

Thereupon, holding each other's hands tightly grasped, the two women went over to a sofa in a dark corner of the room, into which they sank, and the younger sister, passing her arm over the elder one's neck and drawing her close to her heart, listened.

"Oh! I recognize that there was no excuse for one; I do not understand myself, and since that day I feel as if I were mad. Be careful, my child, about yourself-be careful! If you only knew how weak we are, how quickly we yield, a moment of tenderness, one of those sudden fits of melancholy which steal into your soul, one of those longings to open your arms, to love, to embrace, which we all have at certain moments.

"You know my husband, and you know how fond of him I am ; but he is mature and sensible, and cannot even comprehend the tender vibrations of a woman's heart. He is always, always the same, always good, always smiling, always kind, always perfect. Oh! how I sometimes have wished that he would roughly clasp me in his arms, that he would embrace me with those slow, sweet kisses which make two beings intermingle, which are like mute confidences! How I wished that he was self-abandoned and even weak, so that he should have need of me, of my caresses, of my tears!

"This all seems very silly; but we women are made like that. How can we help it?

"And yet the thought of deceiving never came near me. To-day, it has happened, without love, without reason, without anything, simply because the moon shone one night on the Lake of Lucerne.

"During the month when we were traveling together, my husband, with his calm indifference, paralyzed my enthusiasm, extinguished my poetic ardor. When we were descending the mountain paths at sunrise, when as the four horses galloped along with the diligence, we saw, in the transparent mountain haze, valleys, woods, streams, and villages, I clasped my hands with delight, and said to him: 'What a beautiful scene, darling! Kiss me now!' he only answered, with a smile of chilling kindliness. There is no reason why we should kiss each other because you like the landscape.'

"And his words froze me to the heart. It seems to me that when people love each other, they ought to feel more moved by love than ever in the presence of beautiful scenes.

"Indeed, he prevented the effervescent poetry that bubbled up within me from gushing out. How can I express it ? I was almost like a boiler, filled with steam and hermetically sealed.

"One evening (we had been for four days staying in the Hotel de Fluelen), Robert, having got one of his sick headaches, went to bed immediately after dinner, and I went to take a walk all alone along the edge of the lake.

"It was a night such as one might read of in a fairy tale. The full moon showed itself in the middle of the sky; the tall mountains, with their snowy crests, seemed to wear silver crowns; the waters of the lake glittered with tiny rippling motions. The air was mild, with that kind of penetrating freshness which softens us till we seem to be swooning, to be deeply affected without any apparent cause. But how sensitive, how vibrating, the heart is at such moments! How quickly it leaps up, and how intense are its emotions!

"I sat down on the grass, and gazed at that vast lake so melancholy and so fascinating; and a strange thing passed into me; I became possessed with an insatiable need of love, a revolt against the gloomy dullness of my life. What! would it never be my fate to be clasped in the arms of a man whom I loved on a bank like this under the glowing moonlight? Was I never then, to feel on my lips those kisses so deep, delicious, and intoxicating which lovers exchange on nights that seem to have been made by Good for passionate embraces? Was I never to know such ardent, feverish love in the moonlit shadows of a summer's night?

"And I burst out weeping like a woman who has lost her reason. I heard some person stirring behind me. A man was intently gazing at me. When I turned my head round, he recognized me, and, advancing, said:

'You are weeping, Madame ?'

"It was a young barrister who was traveling with his mother, and whom we had often met. His eyes had frequently followed me.

"I was so much confused that I did not know what answer to give or what to think of the situation. I told him I felt ill.

He walked on by my side in a natural and respectful fashion, and began talking to me about what we had seen during our trip. All that I had felt he translated into words; everything that made me thrill he understood perfectly, better even than I did myself. And all of a sudden he recited some verses of Alfred de Musset I felt myself choking, seized with indescribable emotion. It seemed to me that the mountains themselves, the lake, the moonlight, wer singing to me about things ineffably sweet.

"And it happened, I don't know how, I don't know why, in a sort of hallucination.

"As for him, I did not see him again till the morning of his departure.

"He gave me his card!"

******

And, sinking into her sister's arms, Madame Letore broke into groans— almost into shrieks.

Then Madame Roubère, with a self-contained and serious air, said very gently :

"You see, sister, very often it is not a man that we love, but love. And your real lover that night was the moonlight.

A PHILOSOPHER

BLE'ROT had been my most intimate friend from childhood; we had no secrets from each other and were united heart and soul by a brotherly intimacy and a boundless confidence in each other. I had been intrusted with the secret of all his love affairs, as he had been with mine.

When he told me that he was going to get married I was hurt, just as if he had been guilty of a treacherous act with regard to me. I felt that it must interfere with tht cordial and absolute affection which had united us hitherto. His wife would come between us. The intimacy of the marriage bed establishes a kind of complicity, a mysterious alliance between two persons, even when they have ceased to love each other. Man and wife are like two discreet partners who will not let anyone else into their secrets. But that close bond which the conjugal kiss fastens is widely loosened on the day on which the woman takes a lover.

I remember Blérot's wedding as if it were but yesterday. I would not be present at the singing of the marriage contract, as I have no particular liking for such ceremonies. I only went to the civil wedding and to the church.

His wife, whom I had never seen before, was a tall, slight girl with pale hair, pale cheeks, pale hands and eyes to match. She walked with a slightly undulating motion, as if she were on board a ship, and seemed to advance with the succession of long, graceful countries.

Blerot seemed very much in love with her. He looked at her constantly, and I felt a shiver of an immoderate desire for her pass through my frame.

I went to see him in a few days, and he said to me:

"You do not know how happy I am; I am madly in love with her, but then she is-she-is-" He did not finish his entence, but put the tips of his fingers to his lips with a gesture which signified "divine! delicious! prefect!" and a good deal more besides.

I asked laughing, "What? All that?"

"Everything that you can imagine," was his answer.

He introduced me to her. She was very pleasant, on easy terms with me, as was natural, and begged me to look upon their house as my own. I felt that he, Blerot, did not belong to me any more. Our intimacy was altogether checked, and we hardly found a word to say to each other.

I soon took my leave and shortly afterward went to the East, returning by way of Russia, Germany, Sweden and Holland after an absence of eighteen months from Paris.

The morning after my arrival, as I was walking along the boulevards to breathe the air once more, I saw a pale man with sunken cheeks coming toward me, who was as much as like Blerot as it was possible for a physical, emaciated man to resemble a strong, ruddy, rather stout man. I looked at him in surprise and asked myself: "Can it possibly be he?" But he was me and came toward me with outstretched arms, and we embraced in the middle of the boulevard.

After we had gone up and down once or twice fromk the Rue Drouot to the Vaudeville. Theater, just as we were taking leave of each other for he already seemed quite done up with walking-I said to him:

"You don't look at all well. Are you ill?"

"I do not feel rather out of sorts," was all he said'

He looked like a man who was going to die, and I felt a flood of affection for my old friend, the only real one that I had ever had. I squeezed his hands. "What is the matter with you? Are you in pain?"

"A little tired, but it is nothing."

"What does your doctor say?"

"He calls it anemia, and ha ordered me to eat no white meat and to take tincture of iron."

A suspicion flashed across me.

"Are you happy?" I asked him

"Yes, very happy; my wife is charming, and I love her more than ever." But I noticed that he grew rather red and seemed embarrassed, as if he were afraid of any further questions, so I took him by the arm and pushed him into a cafe', which was nearly empty at that time of day. I forced him to sit down and, looking him straight in the face, I said:

"Look here, old fellow, just tell me the exact truth."

"I have nothing to tell you," he stammered.

"That is not true," I replied firmly. "You are ill, mentally, perhaps and you dare not reveal your secret to anyone. Something or other is doing you harm, and I mean you to tell me what it is. Come, I am waiting for you to begin."

Again he got very red, stammered, and turning his read away, he said:

"It is very idotic-but I-I am done for!"

As he did not go on, I said:

"Just tell me what it is."

"Well, I have got a wife who is killing me; that is all," he said abruptly, almost desperately.

I did not understand at first. "Does she make you unhappy? How? What is it?"

"No," he replied in a low voice, as if he were confessing some crime; "I love her too much; that is all."

I was thunder struck at this singular avowal, and then I felt inclined to laugh, but at length I managed to reply:

"But surely, at least so it seems to me, you might manage to—to love her a little less."

He had got very pale again and at length made up his mind to speak to me openly, as he used to do formerly.

"No," he said, "that is impossible, and I am dying from it; I know; it is killing me, and I am really frightened. Some days, like today, I feel inclined to leave her, to go away altogether, to start for the other end of the world, so as to live for a long time; and then when the evening comes I return home in spite of myself, but slowly, and feeling uncomfortable. I go upstairs hesitatingly and ring, and when I go in I see her there, sitting in her easy chair, and she will say, "How late you are." I kiss her, and we sit down to dinner. During the meal I make this resolve: 'i will go directly it is over and take the train for somewhere, no matter where,' but when we get back to the drawing room I am so tired that I have not the courage to get up out of my chair, and so I remain and then-and then-and then-I succumb again."

I could not help smiling again. He saw it and said: "You may laugh, but I assure you it is very horrible."

"Why don't you tell your wife?" I asked him. "Unless she be a regular monster she would understand."

He shrugged his shoulders. "It is all very well for you to talk. I don't tell her because I know her nature. Have you ever heard it said of certain women, 'She has just married a third time?' Well, and that makes you laugh like you did just now, and yet it is true. What is to be done? It is neither her fault nor mine. She is so, because nature has made her so; I assure you, my dear old friend, she has the temperament of a Messalina. She does not know it, but I do; so much the worse for me. She is charming, gentle, tender and thinks that our conjugal intercourse, which is wearing me out and killing me, is natural and quite moderate. She seems like an ignorant schoolgirl, and she really is ignorant, poor child.

"Every day I form energetic resolutions, for you must understand that I am dying. But one look of her eyes, one of those looks in which I can read the ardent desire of her lips, is enough for me, and I succumb at once, saying to myself:

"This is really the end; I will have no more of her death-giving kisses," and then when I have yielded again, like I have today, I go out and walk and walk, thinking of death and saying to myself that I am lost, that all is over.

"I am mentally so ill that I went for a walk to Pe're Lachaise cemetery yesterday. I looked at all the graves, standing in a row like dominoes, and I thought to myself: 'I shall soon be there,' and then I returned home, quite determined to pretend to be ill and so escape, but I could not.

"Oh! You don't know what it is. Ask a smoker who is poisoning himself with nicotine whether he can give up his delicious and deadly habit. He will tell you that he has tried a hundred times without sucess, and he will, perhaps, add: 'So much the worse, but I would rather die than go without tobacco.' That is just the case with me. When once one is in the clutches of such a passion or such a habit, one must give oneself up to it entirely."

He got up and gave me his hand. I felt seized with a tumult of rage and with hatred for this woman, this careless, charming, terrible woman, and as he was buttoning up his coat to go out I said to him, brutally perhaps:

"But in God's name, why don't you let her have a lover, rather than kill yourself like that?"

He shrugged his shoulders without replying and went off.

For six months I did not see him. Every morning I expected a letter of invitation to his funeral, but I would not go to his house from a complicated feeling of contempt for him and for that woman, of anger, of indignation, of a thousand sensations.

One day spring morning I was in the Champs Elyse ès. It was one of those warm days which make our eyes bright an stir up in us a tumultuous feeling of happiness form the mere sense of existence. Someone tapped me OB the shoulder and, turning round, I saw my old friend, looking well, stout and rosy.

He gave me both hands, beaming with pleasure, and exclaimed:

"Here you are, you erratic individual!"

I looked at him, utterly thunderstruck.

"Well, on my word-yes. By jove! I congratulate you; you have indeed changed in the last six months!"

He flushed scarlet and said with an embarrassed laugh:

"One can but do one's best."

I looked at him so obstinately that he evidently felt uncomfortable, so I went on:

"So-now-you are-completely cured?"

He stammered hastily:

"Yes, perfectly, thank you." Then, changing his tone, "How lucky that I should have come across you, old fellow. I hope we shall often meet now."

But I would not give up my idea; I wanted to know how matters really stood, so I asked:

"Don't you remember what you told me six months ago? I suppose-I-eh-suppose you resist now?"

"Please don't talk any more about it," he replied uneasily; "forget that I mentioned it to you; leave me alone. But, you know, I have no intention of letting you go; you must come and dine at my house."

A sudden fancy took me to see for myself how matters stood, so that I might understand all about it, and I accepted.

His wife received me in a most charming manner, and she was, as a matter of fact, a most attractive woman. Her long hands, her neck and cheeks were beautifully white and delicate and marked her breeding, and her walk was undulating and delightful.

Renè gave her a brotherly kiss on the forehead and said:

"Has not Lucien come yet?"

"Not yet," she replied in a clear, soft voice; "you know he is almost always rather late."

At that moment the bell rang, and a tall man was shown in. He was dark, with a thick beard, and looked like a modem Hercules. We were introduced to each other; his name was Lueien Delabarre.

Renè and he shook hands in a most friendly manner, and then we went to dinner.

It was a most enjoyable meal, without the least constraint. My old friend spoke with me constantly in the old, familiar, cordial manner, just as he used to do. It was: "You know, old fellow!" "I say, old fellow!" "Just listen a moment, old fellow !" Suddenly he exclaimed.

"You don't know how glad I am to see you again; it takes me back to old times."

I looked at his wife and the other man. Their attitude was perfectly correct, though I fancied once or twice that they exchanged a rapid and furtive look.

As soon as dinner was over Renè turned to his wife and said:

"My dear, I have just met Pierre again, and I am going to carry him off for a walk and chat along the boulevards to remind us of old times. I am leaving you in very good company."

The young woman smiled and said to me as she shook hands with me:

"Don't keep him too long."

As we went along arm in arm I could not help saying to him, for I was determined to know how matters stood:

"What has happened? Do tell me!"

He, however interrupted me roughly and answered like a man who has been disturbed without any reason.

"Just look here, old fellow; leave one alone with your questions."

Then he added, half aloud, as if talking to himself:

"After all, it would have been too stupid to have let oneself go to perdition like that."

I did not press him. We walked on quickly and began to talk. All of a sudden he whispered in my ear:

"I say, suppose we go and have a bottle of fizz with some girls! Eh?" I could not prevent myself from laughing heartily. "Just as you like; come along, let us go."

AN UNREASONABLE WOMAN

A GREAT wind was whistling outside, an autumn wind, groaning and galloping; one of those winds which kill the last leaves and carry them away to the clouds.

The hunters had finished their dinner and were still booted, red, animated and lighted up. They were those demi-Norman lords, half country squire, half peasant, rich and vigorous, shaped for cutting the horns of beeves when they stopped them in the market.

They had hunted all day on M. Blondel's estate, M. Blondel, the mayor of Eparville, and they were eating now around the great table in a kind of farm-villa of which their host was the proprietor.

They were talking like a whirlwind, laughing like a roar of wild animals and drinking like cisterns, their legs stretched out, their elbows on the cloth, their eyes shining under the flame of the lamps, heated by a hearth fire so formidable as to send to the ceiling its ruddy glow. They chatted of hunting and dogs. But they had come to the hour when other ideas come to men half tipsy, and all eyes followed the strong girl with plump cheeks who carried at the end of her red wrists great platters filled with food.

Suddenly a devil of a fellow, who had become a veterinary after having studied for a priest and who looked after all the animals of the district, by name Sejour, said:

"My eyes! Monsieur Blondel, you have a girl there who is not starved."

And a laugh made the echoes ring. Then an old nobleman, declassed, ruined by alcohol, M. de Varnetot, raised his voice.

"I once had a droll adventure with a girl like that. Wait, I must tell it to you. Every time I think of her it recalls Mirza, my dog which I sold to Count d'Haussonel and which returned every day when she was let out, because she was unable to leave me. Finally I got angry and begged the count to keep her chained. Do you know what the beast did? She died of grief.

"But to return to my maid; here is the story:

"I was then twenty-five years old and lived as a bachelor in my castle at Villebon. You know that when one is young and has an income and makes a beast of himself every evening he has his eye on all sides.

"I discovered a young girl who was in service at the house of Deboultot of Cauville. You know Deboultot well, you, Blondel. To be brief, she pleased me so much, the hussy, that I went one day to her master and made a business proposition to him. He gave me his servant, and I sold him my black mare Cocotte, which he had sought of me for two years. He extended his hand to me and said: 'It is agreed M. de Varnetot.' It was a bargain. The little one came to the castle, and I took my black mare to Cauville myself, and I let him have her for three hundred crowns.

"At first everything went as if on wheels. No one mistrusted anything. Only Rose loved me a little too much for my taste. The child, you see, was not a nobody. She had something out of the common in her veins. She came from some girl who committed some error with her master.

"Briefly, she adored me. There were cajolings, endearments, little pet names and heaps of caresses—enough to make it a matter of reflection.

"I said to myself: 'This cannot last, or I would allow myself to be caught.' But they do not catch me easily. I am not one of those to be taken in with a couple of kisses. So I had my eyes opened when she announced to me that she was large.

"Pif! Pif! It was as if someone had put two shots from a gun into my breast. And she embraced me; she embraced me, I say, and laughed and danced as if she were mad. What? I said nothing the first day, but at night I reasoned with myself; I thought: 'It is just here; it is necessary to parry the blow and cut the thread; it is the only time.' You understand, I had my father and mother at Barneville, and my sister married to the Marquis d' Yspare, at Rollebec, two leagues from Villebon. There must not be any stories.

"But how was I to draw myself out of the affair? If she left the house something would be suspected, and people would talk. If I kept her there the condition would soon be recognized, and then I could not turn her away.

"I spoke to my uncle about it, the Baron de Creteuil, an old buck who has known more than one such case, and asked his advice. He responded tranquilly:

" 'You must marry, my boy.'

"I made a leap. 'Marry, Uncle?' I said. 'Marry whom?'

"He shrugged his shoulders gently as he replied:

" 'Whom you wish; that is your affair, not mine. If one is not stupid there is always somebody to be found.'

"I reflected for two weeks upon this idea and ended by saying to myself: 'My uncle is right.'

"Then I commenced to rack my brain to think of someone, when one evening the justice of the peace, with whom I was dining, said to me:

" 'Mother Paumelle's son is into mischief again; it is true that a good dog shows his race.'

"This Mother Paumelle was a sly old gypsy of whom the youth could have all they desired. For six francs she would certainly have sold her soul, and her rake of a son followed in her footsteps.

"I went and found her and very gently made her understand the state of affairs. As I was somewhat embarrassed in my explanations, she demanded all at once:

" 'Well, how much will you give to this little one?'

"She was malicious, this old woman, but as I was not stupid, I was prepared for business. I owned three pieces of wasteland beyond Sasseville which belong to my three farms in Villebon. The farmers were always complaining that it was too far away; in short, I took back the three fields, six acres in all, and as my farmers found fault, I returned to them, up to the end of each lease, all their rents in poultry. In this way the thing was settled. Then, having bought a piece on one side from my neighbour. Monsieur Aumonte, I had a little house constructed down there, the whole thing for about fifteen hundred francs in all. In this way I had got together a little farm, which had not cost me very much, that I could give to the little girl for a marriage portion.

"The old woman cried out: 'It is not enough, but I will wait; we will leave it without deciding anything.'

"The next day at daybreak the lad came to find me. I could scarcely recall his face, but when I saw him I was reassured; he was not bad for a peasant but had the air of a rude fellow.

"He looked at the affair from a distance, as if he were buying a cow. When we had agreed he wished to see the property, and we set out together over the fields. The scamp kept me going for three hours over the land; he surveyed it, measured it, took up the earth and crumbled it in his hands, as if he were afraid of being deceived in the merchandise. The house was not yet roofed; he exacted slate instead of thatch, because it needed less repairs! Then he said to me:

" 'And the furniture; you must give that.'

"I protested: 'No. It is enough to give you a farm.'

"He sneered: 'Yes, a farm and a child.'

"I coloured in spite of myself. He went on:

" 'Come, now, you must give a bed, a table, the chest of drawers, three chairs and the kitchen dishes, or nothing can be done.'

"I consented to it.

"Then we started to return. He had not yet said a word about the girl. But suddenly, with a sly, constrained air, he asked:

" 'But if she should die who would it go to, this farm?'

"I answered: 'To you, naturally,.'

"That was what he had wanted to know since morning. Immediately he extended his hand to me with a satisfied appearance. We were of one; accord.

"Oh! But I had difficulty in making Rose consent. She dragged herself at my feet, sobbed and kept repeating: 'It was you proposed it to me! It was you! It was you!' For more than a week she resisted in spite of my reasoning and my prayers. They are stupid, these women! As soon as they get love into their heads they understand nothing else. Wisdom is nothing; it is love above all and all for love!

"Finally I got angry and threatened to throw her out. Then

she yielded, little by little, on the condition that I would allow her to come and see me from time to time.

"I myself conducted her to the altar, paid for the ceremony and gave the wedding dinner. I did the thing up grandly, in short. Then, 'Good-by, *my* children!' I went to pass six months with my brother in Touraine.

"When I returned I learned that she had been at the house every week asking for me. And I had scarcely been home an hour before I saw her coming with a baby in her arms. Believe me if you will, but it affected me in some way to see this little monkey. I believe I even embraced it.

"As for the mother, she was a wreck, a skeleton, a shadow. She looked thin and old. Ye gods! It was evident this marriage was not to her liking. I said to her mechanically:

" 'Are you happy?'

"Then she began to weep like a fountain and with hiccups and sobs she cried:

" 'I can never, never leave you now. I would rather die; I cannot.'

"She made a devil of a noise. I consoled her as well as I could and conducted her back to the gate.

"I learned that her husband beat her and that her mother-in-law made life hard for her, the old cabbagehead.

"Two days later she returned. She took me in her arms and dragged herself upon the earth. 'Kill me,' she said, 'but I will never go back down there.'

"This is exactly what Mirza would have said could she have spoken! These stories began to be very tiresome to me, and I went away again for another six months.

"When I returned—when I returned I learned that she had died three weeks before, having visited the castle every Sunday—just like Mirza. The child had also died eight days before.

"As for the husband, the cunning rascal, he inherited the property. He has turned out well since, it appears, and is now municipal counsellor."

M. de Varnetot added, laughing:

"It is a fact that I made the fortune of that man!"

And M. Sejour, the veterinary, concluded gravely, carrying a glass of brandy to his lips:

"Say what you will, but with women like that, such things should not be."

FLORENTINE

WE were talking about girls, for what else is there to talk about among men, One of us said:

"Wait! A strange story occurs to me on this subject."

And he related it:

"One evening of last winter I was suddenly taken with one of those desolate lassitudes which are overwhelming in their attack upon soul and body from time to time. I was at home alone, and I knew well that if I remained there I should have a frightful fit of despondency, of the kind that leads to suicide when they return often.

"I put on my coat and went out without knowing at all what I was going to do. Having descended to the boulevard, I began to walk along past the cafe's nearly empty, for it was raining. One of those thin rains was falling that dampens the spirits as much as the clothes; not one of those good showers, striking one in a cascade and driving passers under the porte-cochers, out of breath, but a rain that unceasingly deposits upon you inperceptible droplets and covers your clothing with a glistening, penetrating moisture.

"What should I do? I went up and returned, seeking some place to pass a couple of hours and discovering for the first time that there was not a place of diversion in all Paris in the evening. Finally I decided to enter the Folies Bergeres, that theater so amusing to street girls.

"There were very few in the great hall. The long, semicircular promenade contained but a few individuals, of a race usually known by their walk, their clothing, the cut of their hair and beard, their hats and their complexion. It is not often that one sees among them a man who seems clean, perfectly clean, and whose clothing has altogether the same air. As for the girls, they are always the same, as you know, plain, weary, dropping, walking with that quick step and that air of imbecile disdain which they assume, I know not why.

"I said to myself that truly not one of these flagging creatures, greasy rather than fat, either bloated or very thin, with the paunch of a prelate and their long legs bowed, was worth the louis that they obtained with much difficulty after having demanded five.

"But suddenly I perceived one of them, a little one that appeared genteel, not at all young, but fresh, droll and provoking. I stopped her and, in beastly fashion, without thinking, set my price for the night. I did not wish to return home alone, all alone; I preferred rather the company and embrace of this worthless woman.

"And so I followed her. She lived in a big, big house in Martyr Street. The gas was already extinguished on the staircase. I mounted slowly, constantly lighting taper matches, striking the steps with my feet, stumbling and ill at ease, following a petticoat, the rustle of which I heard before me.

"She stopped at the fourth story and, having shut again the inside door, she asked:

" 'And you wish to remain until tomorrow?'

"' Yes. You know that was the agreement.'

" 'All right, my dear. I only wanted to know. Wait for me here a minute; I will return immediately.'

"And she left me in the darkness. I heard her close two doors, then it seemed to me she was speaking with somebody. I was surprised and disturbed. The idea of blackmail occurred to me. But I have fists and solid muscles. 'We shall see,' I thought..

"I listened with all attention, both of ear and mind. Someone was moving, walking about, but with great precaution. Then another door was opened, and it seemed to me that I still heard talking, but in a very low voice.

"She returned, bringing a lighted candle. 'You can enter now,' she said.

"She spoke familiarly, as a sign of possession. I entered,

and after having crossed a dining room, where it was evident nobody ever dined, I entered a chamber like that of all these girls, a furnished room with rep curtains and eider-down silk quilt with suspicious poppy-red sports.

"She continued: 'Put yourself at ease, my dear.'

"I inspected the apartment with an eye of suspicion. There seemed nothing disquieting, however. She undressed herself so quickly that she was in bed before I had my overcoat off. Then she began to laugh:

" 'Well, what is the matter with you? Are you changed into a pillar of salt? Come! Make haste!

"I imitated her and joined her. Five minutes later I had a foolish desire to dress again and go out. But the overwhelming lassitude which had seized me at my house returned to me, depriving me of all strenght to move, and I remained, in spite of the disgust which I had for this public bed. The sensual charm which I believed I saw down there under the lights of the theater had disappeared in my arms, and I had with me, flesh to flesh, only a vulgar girl, like all the rest, whose indifferent and complaisant kiss had an aftertaste of garlic.

"I began to talk to her:

" 'Have you been here long?' I said

" 'Six months the fifteenth of January.'

" 'Where were you before that?'

" 'I was in Clauzel Street. But the janitor made me so miserable that I left.'

"And she began to relate an interminable story of the *concierge* who had made some scandal about her.

"Suddenly I heard something moving near us. At first there was a sigh, then a light noise, but distinct, as if someone had fallen from a chair.

"I sat up quickly in bed and demanded: 'What was that noise?'

"She answered with assurance and composure: 'Don't disturb yourself, my dear' it is my neighbor. The partition is so thin that we hear all as if they were here. These are dirty boxes. They are made of pasteboard.'

"My indolence was so strong that I got down under the

clothes again. We continued our talk. Incited by the curiosity which drives all men to question these creatures upon their first adventure, to wish to raise the veil from their first fault in order to find in them some far-off trace of innocence, that we may find something to love, perhaps in the rapid recital evoked by their candor and the shame of long ago, I asked her about her first lover.

"I knew that she lied. What did it matter? Among all the lies I might discover, perhaps, some sincere or touching incident.

" 'Come,' I said, 'tell me who he was.'

" 'He was an oarsman.'

" 'Ah ! Tell me about it. Where were you?'

" 'I was at Argenteuil.'

" 'What were you doing there?'

" 'I was maid in a restaurant.'

" 'What restaurant.'

" 'At the Freshwater Sailors; do you know it?'

" 'Well, yes; Bonanfan's.'

" 'Yes, that's the one.'

" 'And how did he pay his court, this oarsman?'

" 'While I was making his bed. He forced me.'

"But suddenly I recalled the theory of a doctor of my acquaintance, an observing, philosophic doctor who, in his practice in a great hospital, had daily examples of these girls mothers and public girls and knew all the shame and misery of women, the poor women who become the hideous prey of the wandering male with money in his pocket.

" 'Invariably,' he told me, 'is a girl debauched by a man of her own class and station in life. I have made volumes of observations upon it. It is customary to accuse the rich of culling the flower of innocence from the children of the people. That is not true. The rich pay for the culled bouquet. They cull also, but at the second flowering; they never cut the first.'

"Then turning toward my companion, I began to laugh.

" 'You may as well know that I know all about your story. The oarsman was not the first, as you well know.'

" 'Oh yes, my dear, I swear it!'

"'You are lying.'

"'Oh no, I promise you I am not.'

" 'You lie. Come, tell me the truth.'

"She seemed to hesitate, astonished. I continued:

" 'I am a sorcerer, my good child, a hypnotist. If you do not tell me the truth I shall put you to sleep, and then I can find it out.'

"She was afarid, being stupid like her kind. She murmured:

" 'How did you ever guess it?'

"I replied: 'Come, speak.'

" 'Oh! The first time, that amounted to nothing. It was at a festival in the country. They called in a chef for the occasion, Monsieur Alexander. After he came he had it all his own way in the house. He ordered everybody, even to the master and mistress, as if he had been a king. He was a large, handsome man who would not stay in place before his stove. He was always crying out: "Here, some butter-some eggs-some Madeira!" and it was necessary to carry him everything on the run, or he would get angry and say things to you that would make you blush under the skirts.

" 'When the day was finished he would smoke his pipe before the door. And as I passed him with a pile of plates he said to me this: "Come, little goose, come down to the edge of the lake and show me the country." As for me, I went, like a fool, and scarcely had we arrived at the bank when he forced me so quickly that I did not even know that it was done. And then he went away by the nine o'clock train, and I never saw him again after that.'

"I asked :Is that all?'

"She stammered: 'Oh! I believe Florentine belongs to him.'

" 'Who is Florentine?'

" 'He is my little boy.'

" 'Ah! Very well. And you made the oarsman believe that he was the father, did you not?'

"'Yes.'

" 'He had money, this oarsman?'

" 'Yes; he lcft me income of three hundred francs for

Florentine's support.'

"I commenced to be amused. I continued:

" 'Very well, my girl, very well. You are all less sensual than one would believe. And how old is Florentine now?'

"She answered: 'Twelve years old. He will take his first communion in the spring.'

" 'That is good, and since that you have made a trade with your conscience.'

"She sighed resignedly: 'One must do what she can.'

"But a great noise in another part of the room made me leap out of bed with a bound; it was the noise of one falling, then rising and groping with his hands upon the wall. I had seized the candle and was looking about, frightened and furious. She got up also and tried to hold me back saying:

" 'It is nothing, my dear; I assure you it is nothing.'

"But I had discovered on which side of the wall this strange noise was. I went straight toward, a conceled door at the head of the bed and opened it suddenly-and perceived there a poor little boy, trembling and staring at me with frightened eyes, a pale, thin little boy beside a large chair filled with straw, from which he had falled.

"When he saw me he began to cry and, opening his arms to his mother:

" 'It was not my fault, Mamma; it was not my fault. I was asleep and I fell. You mustn't scold me, for it was not my fault.'

"I turned toward the woman and said:

" 'What does he mean?'

"She seemed confused and disheartene. But finally she said in a broken voice:

" 'What can you expect? I do not earn enough to put the child in school! I must take care of him somehow, and I cannot afford to hire another room. He sleeps with me when I have no one. When someone comes for an hour or two he can stay in the closet very well and keep quiet; he knows how. But when one remains all night, as you have, his muscles are fatigued from sleeping on the chair-and it is not the child's fault. I would like to see you-you-sleep all night on a chair. You would sing another song.'

"She was angry, wrought up, and was crying.

"The child wept too. A poor child pitful and timid, a good child of the closet, of the cold, dark closet, a child who came from time to time to get a little warmth in the bed a moment empty.

"I, too, had a desire to weep.

"And I returned home to my own bed."

THAT PIG OF A MORIN

"THERE MY FRINED," I said to Labarbe, "you have just repeated those five words. That pig of a Morin.' Why on earth do I never hear Morin's name mentioned without his being called a *pig* ?"

Labarbe, who is a Deputy, looked at me with eyes like an owl's, and said: "Do you mean to say that you do not know Morin's story, and yet come form La Rochelle?" I was obliged to declare that I did not know Morin's story, and then Labarbe rubbed his hands, and began his recital.

"You knew Morin, did you not, and you remember his large linen-draper's shop on the Quai de la Rochelle?"

"Yes, perfectly."

"All right, then. You must know that in 1862 or 63 Morin went to spend a fortnight in Paris for pleasure, or for his pleasures, but under the pretext of renewing his stock, and you also know what a fortnight in Paris means for a country shopkeeper; it makes his blood grow hot. The theater every evening, women's dresses rustling up against you, and continual excitement; one goes almost mad with it. One sees nothing but dancers in tights, actresses in very low dresses, round legs, fat shoulders, all nearly within reach of one's hands, without daring or being able to touch, and one scarcely ever tastes an inferior dish. And one leaves it, with heart still all in a flutter, and a mind still exhilarated by a sort of longing for kisses which tickle one's lips.

"Morin was in that state when he took his ticket for La Rochelle by the 8:40 night express. And he was walking up and down the waiting-room at the station, when he stopped suddenly in front of a young lady who was kissing an old one. She had her veil up, and Morin murmured with delight: 'By Jove, what a pretty woman !'

"When she had said 'Good-bye' to the old lady, she went into the waiting-room, and Morin followed her ; then, she went on to the platform and Morin still followed her; then she got into an empty carriage, and he again followed her. There were very few travelers by the express, the engine whistled, and the train started. They were alone. Morin devoured her with his eyes. She appeared to be about nineteen or twenty, and was fair, tall, and with demure looks. She wrapped a railway rug round her legs and stretched herself on the seat to sleep.

"Morin asked himself: 'I wonder who she is ?' And a thousand conjectures, a thousand projects went through his head. He said to himself : 'So many adventures are told as happening on railway journeys, that this may be one that is going to present itself to me. Who knows? A piece of good luck like that happens very quickly, and perhaps I need only be a little venturesome. Was it not Danton who said : "Audacity, more audacity, and always audacity"? If it was not Danton it was Mirabeau, but that does not matter. But then, I have no audacity, and that is the difficulty. Oh! If one only knew, if one could only read people's minds ! I will bet that every day one passes by magnificent opportunities without knowing it, though a gesture would be enough to let me know that she did not ask for anything better.'

"Then he imagined to himself combinations which led him to triumph. He pictured some chivalrous deed, or merely some slight service which he rendered her, a lively, gallant conversation ended in a declaration, which ended in-in what you thinks.

"But he could find no opening : had no pretext, and he waited for some fortunate circumstance, with his heart ravaged, and his mind topsy-turvy. The night passed, and the pretty girl still slept, while Morin was meditating his own fall. The day broke and soon the first ray of sunlight appeared in the sky. a long, clear ray which shone on the face of the sleeping girl, and woke her, so she sat up, looked at the country, then at Morin and smiled. She smiled like a happy woman, with an engaging and bright look, and Morin trembled. Certainly that smile was intended for him, it was a discreet invitation, the signal which he was waiting for. That smile meant to say : 'How stupid, what a ninny. what a dolt, what a donkey you are, to have sat there on your seat like a post all night.

" 'Just look at me, am I not charming ? And you have sat like that for the whole night, when you have been alone with a pretty woman, you great simpleton!'

"She was still smilling as she looked at him, she even began to laugh ;

and he lost his head trying to find something suitable to say, no matter what. But he could think of nothing, nothing, and then, seized with a coward's courage, he said to himself : 'So much the worse, I will risk everything,' and suddenly, without the slightest warning, he went toward her, his arms extended, his lips protruding and seizing her in his arms kissed her.

"She sprang up with a bound, crying out : 'Help! help!' and screaming with terror ; then she opened the carriage door, and waved her arm outside; then mad with terror she was trying to jump out, while Morin, who was almost distracted, and feeling sure that she would throw herself out, held her by her skirt and stammered : 'Oh! Madame! Oh! Madame!'

"They train slackened speed, and then stopped. Two guards rushed up at the young woman's frantic signals, and she threw herself into their arms, stammering : 'That man wanted-wanted-to-to-' And then she fainted.

"They were at Mauzé station, and the gendarme on duty arrested Morin. When the victim of his brutality had regained her consciousness, she made her charge against him, and the police drew it up. The poor lineu-draper did not reach home till night, with a prosecution hanging over him for an outrage on morals in a public place.

II

"At that time I was editor of the 'Fanal des Charentes' and I used to meet Morin every day at the Cafe du Commerce. The day after his adventure he came to see me, as he did not know what to do. I did not hide my opinion from him, but said to him : 'You are no better than a pig. No decent man behaves like that.'

"He cried. His wife had given him a beating, and he foresaw his trade ruined. his name dragged through the mire and dishonored, his friends outraged and taking no more notice of him. In the end he excited my pity, and I sent for my colleague Rivet, a bantering, but very sensible little man, to give us advice.

"He advised me to see the Public Prosecutor, who was a friend of mine. and so I sent Morin home, and went to call on the magistrate. He told me that the woman who had been insluted was a young lady, Mademoiselle Henriette Bonnel, who had just received her certificate as governess in Paris, and spent her holidays with her uncle and aunt, who were very respectable tradespeople in Mauzé, and what made Morin's case all the more serious was that the uncle had lodged a complaint. But the public official had consented to let the matter drop if this complaint were withdrawn, so that we must try and get him to do this.

"I went back to Morin's and found him in bed, ill with excitement and distress. His wife, a tall, raw-boned woman with a bread, was abusing him continually, and she showed me into the room, shouting at me : 'So you have come to see that pig of a Morin. Well, there he is, the darling!' And she planted herself in front of the bed, with her hands on her hips. I told him how matters stood, and he begged me to go and see her uncle and aunt. It was a delicate mission, but I undertook it, and the poor devil never ceased repeating: 'I assure you I did not even kiss her, no, not even that. I will take my oath to it!'

"I replied : 'It is all the same ; you are nothing but a pig.' And I took a thousand francs which he gave me, to employ them as I thought best, but as I did not care venturing to her uncle's house alone, I begged Rivet to go with me, which he agreed to do, on the condition that we went immediately, for he had some urgent business at La Rochelle that afternoon. So two hours later we rang at the door of a nice country-house. A pretty girl came and opened the door to us, who was assuredly the young lady in question, and I said to Rivet in a low voice : 'Confound it! I begin to understand Morin!'

"The uncle, Monsieur Tonnelet, subscribed to 'The Fanal',

and was a fervent political co-religionist of ours. He received us with open arms, and congratulated us and wished us joy ; he was delighted at having the two editors in his house, and Rivet whispered to me : 'I think we shall be able to arrange the matter of that pig of a Morin for him.'

"The niece had left the room, and I introduced the delicate subject. I waved the specter of scandal before his eyes ; I accentuated the inevitable depreciation which the young lady would suffer if such an affair got known, for nobody would believe in a simple kiss. The good man seemed undecided, but could not make up his mind about anything without his wife, who would not be in until late that evening. But suddenly he uttered an exclamation of triumph : 'Look here, I have an excellent idea. I will keep you here to dine and sleep, and when my wife comes home, I hope we shall be able to arrange matters.'

"Rivet resisted at first, but the wish to extricate that pig of a Morin decided him, and we accepted the invitation. So the uncle got up radiant, called his niece, and proposed that we should take a stroll in his grounds, saying : 'We will leave serious matters until the morning.' Rivet and he began to talk politics, while I soon found myself lagging a little behind with the girl, who was really charming! charming! and with the greatest precaution I began to speak to her about her adventure, and try to make her my ally. She did not, however, appear the least confused, and listened to me like a person who was enjoying the whole thing very much.

"I said to her : 'Just think. Mademoiselle, how unpleasant it will be for you. You will have to appear in court, to encounter malicious looks, to speak before everybody, and to recount that unfortunate occurrence in the railway-carriage, in public. Do you not think, between ourselves, that it would have been much better for you to have put that dirty scoundrel back into his place without calling for assistance, and merely to have changed your carriage?' She began to laugh, and replied : 'What you say is quite true! but what could I do ? I was frightened, and when one is frightened, one does not stop to reason with oneself. As soon as I realized the situation, I was very sorry that I had called out, but then it was too late. You must also remember that the idiot threw himself upon me like a madman, without saying a word and looking like a lunatic. I did not even know what he wanted of me.'

"She looked me, full in the face, without being nervous or intimidated, and I said to myself : 'She is a funny sort of girl, that : I can quite see how that pig Morin came to make a mistake,' and I went on, jokingly: 'Come Mademoiselle, confess that he was excusable, for after all, a man cannot find himself opposite such a pretty girl as you are, without feeling a legitimate desire to kiss her.'

"She laughed more than ever, and showed her teeth, and said : 'Between the desire and the act. Monsieur, there is room for respect' It was a funny expression to use, although it was not very clear, and I asked abruptly : 'Well now, supposing I were to kiss you now, what would you do ?' She stopped to look at me from head to foot, and then said calmly : 'Oh! you ? That is quite another matter.'

"I knew perfectly well, by Jove, that it was not the same thing at all, as everybody in the neighborhood called me 'Handsome Labarbe.' I was thirty years old in those days, but I asked her : 'And why, pray ?'

"She shrugged her shoulders, and replied : 'Well, because you are not so stupid as he is.' And then she added, looking at me slyly : 'Nor so ugly, either.'

"Before she could make a movement to avoid me, I had implanted a hearty kiss on her cheek. She sprang aside, but it was too late, and then she said:

'Well, you are not very bashful either! But don't do that sort of thing again.'

"'I put on a humble look and said in a low voice : 'Oh! Mademoselle, as for me, if I long for one thing more than another, it's to be summoned before a magistrate on the same charge as Morin.'

" 'Why ? ' She asked.

"Looking steadily at her, I replied : 'Because you are one of the most beautiful creatures living ; because it would be an honor and a glory for me to have offered you violence, and because people would have said, after seeing you :

"Well, Labarbe has richly deserved what he has got, but he is a lucky fellow, all the same." '

"She began to laugh heartily again, and said : 'How funny you are!' And she had not finished the word *funny,* before I had her in my arms and was kissing her ardently wherever I could find a place, on her forehead, on her eyes, on her lips occasionally, on her cheeks, in fact, all over her head, some part of which she was obliged to leave exposed, in spite of herself, in order to defend the others. At last she managed to release herself, blushing and angry. 'You are very unmannerly. Monsieur,' she said, 'and I am sorry I listened to you.'

"I took her hand in some confusion, and stammered out: "I beg your pardon, Mademoiselle. I have offended you ; I have acted like a brute ! Do not be angry with me for what I have done. If you knew-'

"I vainly sought for some excuse, and in a few moments she said : "There is nothing for me to know. Monsieur.' But I had found something to say, and I cried : 'Mademoiselle, I love you!'

"She was really surprised, and raised her eyes to look at me, and I went on : 'Yes, Mademoiselle, and pray listen to me. I do not know Morin, and I do not care anything about him. It does not matter to me the least if he is committed for trial and locked up meanwhile. I saw you here last year, and I was so taken with you, that the thought of you has never left me since, and it does not matter to me whether you believe me or not. I thought you adorable, and the remembrance of you took such a hold on me that I longed to see you again, and so I made use of that fool Morin as a pretext, and here I am. Circumstances have made me exceed the due limits of respect, and I can only beg you to pardon me.'

"She read the truth in my looks, and was ready to smile again ; then she murmured : 'You humbug!' But I raised my hand, and said in a sincere voice (and I really believe that I was sincere) : 'I swear to you that I am speaking the truth.' She replied quite simply : 'Really ?'

"We were alone, quite alone, as Rivet and her uncle had disappeared in a side walk, and I made her a real declaration of love, while I squeezed and kissed her hands, and she listened to it as to something new and agreeable, without exactly knowing how much of it she was to believe, while in the end I felt agitated, and at last really myself believed what I said. I was pale, anxious, and trembling, and I gently put my arm round her waist, and spoke to her softly, whispering into the little curls over her ears. She seemed dead, so absorbed in thought was she.

"Then her hand touched mine, and she pressed it, and I gently circled her waist with a trembling, and gradually a firmer, grasp. She did not move now, and I touched her cheeks with my lips, and suddenly, without seeking them mine met hers. It was a long, long kiss, and it would have lasted longer still, if I had not heard a *Hum ! Hum!* just behind me. She made her escape through the bushes, and I turning round saw Rivet coming toward me, and walking in the middle of the path. He said without even smiling: 'So that is the way in which you settle the affair of that pig Morin.'

"I replied conceitedly : 'One does what one can, my dear fellow. But what about the uncle ? How have you got on with him ? I will answer for the niece.'

" 'I have not been so fortunate with him,' he replied. Whereupon I took his arm, and we went indoors.

III

"Dinner made me lose my head altogether. I sat beside her, and my hand continually met hers under the table cloth, my foot touched hers, and our looks encountered each other.

"After dinner we took a walk by moonlight, and I whispered all the tender things I could think of to her. I held her close to me, kissed her every moment, moistening my lips against hers, while her uncle and Rivet were disputing as they walked in front of us. We went in, and soon a messenger brought a telegram from her aunt, saying that she would return by the first train the next morning, at seven o'clock.

" 'Very well, Henriette,' her uncle said, 'go and show the gentlemen their rooms.' She showed Rivet his first, and he whispered to me : "There was no danger of her taking us into yours first." Then she took me to my room, and as soon as she was alone with me, I took her in my arms again and tried to excite her senses and overcome her resistance, but when she felt that she was near succumbing, she escaped out of the room, and I got between the sheets, very much put out and excited and feeling rather foolish, for I knew that I should not sleep much. I was wondering how I could have committed such a mistake, when there was a gentle knock at my door, and on my asking who was there, a low voice replied: 'I'.

"I dressed myself quickly and opened the door, and she came in : 'I forgot to ask you what you take in the morning,' she said, 'chocolate, tea, or coffee?' I put my arms around her impetuously and said, devouring her with kisses:

'I will take – I will take– ' But she freed herself from my arms, blew out my candle, and disappeared, and left me alone in the dark, furious, trying to find some matches and not able to do so. At last I got some and I went into the passage, feeling half mad, with my candlestick in my hand.

"What was I going to do ? I did not stop to reason, I only wanted to find her, and I would. I went a few steps without reflecting, but then I suddenly thought to myself : 'Suppose I should go into the uncle's room, what should I say ? ' And I stood still, with my head a void, and my heart beating.

"But in a few moments, I thought of an answer : 'Of course, I shall say that I was looking for Rivet's room, to speak to him about an important matter,' and I began to inspect all the doors, trying to find hers, and at last I took hold of a handle at a venture, turned it and went in. There was Henriette, sitting on her bed and looking at me in tears. So I gently turned the key, and going up to her on tiptoe, I said : 'I forgot to ask you for something to read, Mademoiselle.' I will not tell you the book I read, but it is the most wonderful of romances, the most divine of poems. And when once I had turned the first page, she let me turn over as many leaves as I liked, and I got through so many chapters that our candles were quite burned out.

"Then, after thanking her, I was stealthily returning to my room, when a rough hand seized me, and a voice-it was Rivet's–whispered in my ear : 'So you have not yet quite settled that affair of Morin's ?'

"At seven o'clock the next morning, she herself brought me a cup of chocolate. I have never drunk anything like it, soft, velvety, perfumed, delicious. I could scarcely take away my lips from the cup, and she had hardly left the room when Rivet came in. He seemed nervous and irritable like a man who had not slept, and he said to me crossly: 'If you go on like this, you will end by spoiling the affair of that pig of a Morin!'

"At eight o'clock the aunt arrived. Our discussion was very short, for they withdrew their complaint, and I left five hundred francs for the poor of the town. They wanted to keep us for the day, and they arranged an excursion to go and see some ruins. Henriette made signs to me to stay, behind her uncle's back, and I accepted, but Rivet was determined to go, and though I took him aside, and begged and prayed him to do this for me he appeared quite exasperated and kept saying to me: 'I have had enough of that pig of a Morin's affair, do you hear ?'

"Of course I was obliged to go also, and it was one of the hardest moments of my life. I could have gone on arranging that business as long as I lived, and when we were in the railway carriage, after shaking hands with her in silence, I said to Rivet: 'You are a mere brute! And he replied: 'My dear fellow, you were beginning to excite me confoundedly.'

"On getting to the 'Fanal' office, I saw a crowd waiting for us, and as soon as they saw us, they all exclaimed: 'Well, have you settled the affair of that pig of a Morin?' All La Rochelle was excited about it, and Rivet, who had got over his ill humor on the journey, had great difficulty in keeping himself from laughing as he said : 'Yes, we have managed it, thanks to Labarbe.' And we went to Morin's.

"He was sitting in an easy-chair, with mustard plasters on his legs, and cold bandages on his head, nearly dead with misery. He was coughing with the short cough of a dying man, without anyone knowing how he had caught it, and his wife seemed like a tigress ready to eat him. As soon as he saw us he trembled violently as to make his hands and knees shake, so I said to him immediately: 'It is all settled, you dirty scamp, but don't do such a thing again.

"He got up choking, took my hands and kissed them as if they had belonged to a prince, cried, nearly fainted, embraced Rivet, and even kissed Madame Morin, who gave him such a push as to send him staggering back into his chair. But he never got over the blow ; his mind had been too much upset. In all the country round, moreover, he was called nothing but 'that pig of a Morin,' and the epithet went through him like a sword-thrust every time he heard it. When a street-boy called after him : 'Pig!' he turned his head instinctively. His friends also overwhelmed him with horrible jokes, and used to chaff him, whenever they were eathing ham, by saying : 'It's a bit of you!' He died two years later.

"As for myself, when I was a candidate for the Chamber of Deputies in 1875,1 called on the new notary of Foncerre, Monsieur Belloncle, to solicit his vote, and a tail, handsome, and evidently wealthy lady received me. 'You do not know me again ?' she said.

"I stammered out : 'But - no, Madame.'

" 'Henriette Bonnel ?'

" 'Ah!' And I felt myself turning pale, while she seemed perfectly at her ease, and looked at me with a smile.

"As soon as she had left me alone with her husband, he took both my hands, and squeezing them as if he meant to crush them, he said : 'I have been intending to go and see you for a long time, my dear sir, for my wife has very often talked to me about you. I know under what painful circumstances you made her acquaintance, and I know also how perfectly you behaved, how full of delicacy, tact, and devotion you showed yourself in the affair —' He hesitated, and then said in a lower tone, as if he had been saying something low and coarse : 'in the affair of that pig of a Morin.' "

AN ARTIFICE

THE old doctor and his young patient were talking by the side of the fire. There was nothing really the matter with her, except that she had one of those little feminine ailments from which pretty women frequently suffer-slight anemia, nervous attack and a suspicion of fatigue, probably of that fatigue from which newly married people often suffer at the end of the first month of their married life, when they have made a love match.

She was lying on the couch and talking. "No, Doctor," she said; "I shall never be able to understand a woman deceiving her husband. Even allowing that she does not love him, that she pays no heed to her vows and promises, how can she give herself to another man? How can she conceal the intrigue from other people's eyes? How can it be possible to love amid lies and treason?

The doctor smiled and replied: "It is perfectly easy, and I can assure you that a woman does not think of all those little subtle details when she has made up her mind to go astray. I even feel certain that no woman is ripe for true love until she has passed through all the promiscuousnes sand all the is ksomeness of married life, which, according to an illustrious man, is nothing but an exchange of ill-tempered words by day and perfunctory caresses at night. Nothing is more true, for no woman can love passionately until after she has married.

"As for dissimulation all women have plenty of it on hand on such occasions. The simplest of them are wonderful tacticians and extricate themselves from the greatest dilemmas in an extraordinary way"

The young woman, however, seemed incredulous. "No, Doctor," she said; "one never thinks until after it has happened of what one ought to have done in a dangerous affair, and women are certainly more liable than men to lose their heads on such occasions."

The doctor raised his hands. "After it has happened, you say! Now I will tell you something that happened to one of my female patients whom I always considered an immaculate woman.

"It happened in a provincial town. One night when I was sleeping profoundly, in that deep, first sleep from which it is so difficult to rouse yourself, it seemed to me in my dreams as if the bells in the town were sounding a fire alarm, and I woke up with a start. It was my own bell which was ringing wildly, and as my footman did not seem to be answering the door, I in turn pulled the bell at the head of my bed. Soon I heard banging and steps in the silent house, and then Jean came into my room and handed me a letter which said: 'Madame Leliévre begs Doctor Simeon to come to her immediately.'

"I thought for a few moments, and then I said to myself: 'A nervous attack, vapors, nonsense; I am too tired.' And so I replied: 'As Doctor Simeon is not at all well, he must beg Madame Leliévre to be kind enough to call in his colleague, Monsieur Bonnet.'

"I put the note into an envelope and went to sleep again, but about half an hour later the street bell rang again, and Jean came to me and said: There is somebody downstairs-I do not quite know whether it is a man or a woman, as the individual is so wrapped up-who wishes to speak to you immediately. He says it is a matter of life and death for two people.' Whereupon I sat up in bed and told him to show the person in.

"A kind of black phantom appeared who raised her veil as soon as Jean had left the room. It was Madame Bertha Leliéve, quite a young woman, who had been married for three years to a large shopkeeper in the town and was said to have been the prettiest girl in the neighborhood.

"She was terribly pale; her face was contracted like the faces of mad people are occasionally, and her hands trembled violently. Twice she tried to speak without being able to utter a sound, but at last she stammered out:

'Come-quick-quick, Doctor. Come-my-my lover has just died im my bedroom.' She stopped, half suffocated with emotion, and then went on: "My husband will-be coming home from the club very soon.

"I jumped out of bed without even considering that I was only in my nightshirt and dressed myself in a few moments. Then I said: 'Did you come a short time ago?'

" 'No, she said, standing like a statue petrified with horror. 'It was my servant -she knows.' And then after a short silence she went on: 'I was there-by his side.' And she uttered a sort of cry of horror, and after a fit of choking, which made her gasp, she wept violently, shaking with spasmodic sobs for a minute or two. Then her tears suddenly ceased, as if dried by an internal fire, and with an air of tragic calmness she said: 'Let us make haste.'

"I was ready, but I exclaimed: 'I quite forgot to order my carriage.'

" 'I have one,' she said: 'it is his, which was waiting for him!' She wrapped herself up so as to completely conceal her face, and we started.

"When she was by my side in the darkness of the carriage she suddenly seized my hand and, crushing it in her delicate fingers, she said with a shaking voice that proceeded from a distracted heart: 'Oh! If you only knew, if you only knew what

I am suffering! I loved him; I have loved him distractedly, like a madwoman, for the last six months.'

" 'Is anyone up in your house?' I asked.

" 'No, nobody except Rose, who knows everything.'

"We stopped at the door. Evidently everybody was asleep, and we went in without making any noise by means of her latchkey and walked upstairs on tiptoe. The frightened servant was sitting on the top of the stairs with a lighted candle by her side, as she was afraid to stop by the dead man. I went into the room, which was turned upside down, as if there had been a struggle in it. The bed, which was tumbled and open, seemed to be waiting for somebody; one of the sheets was thrown onto the floor, and wet napkins with which they had bathed the young man's temples were lying by the side of a wash hand basin and a glass, while a strong smell of vinegar pervaded the room.

"The dead man's body was lying at full length in the middle of the room, and I went up to it, looked at it and touched it. I opened the eyes and felt the hands, and then, turning to the two women who were shaking as if they were frozen, I said to them: 'Help me to lift him onto the bed.' When we had laid him gently onto it I listened to his heart, put a looking glass to his lips and then said: 'It is all over; let us make haste and dress him.' It was a terrible sight!

"I took his limbs one by one, as if they had belonged to some enormous doll, and held them out to the clothes which the women brought, and they put on his socks, drawers, trousers, waistcoat and lastly the coat, but it was a difficult matter to get the arms into the sleeves.

"When it came to buttoning his boots the two women kneeled down, while I held the light. As his feet were rather swollen it was very difficult, and as they could not find a buttonhook they had to use their hairpins. When the terrible toilet was over I looked at our work and said: 'You ought to arrange his hair a little.' The girl went and brought her mistress's large-toothed comb and brush, but as she was trembling and pulling out his long, tangled hair in doing it, Mme Leliévre took the comb out of her hand and arranged his hair as if she were caressing him. She parted it, brushed his beard, rolled his mustaches gently round her fingers, as she had no doubt been in the habit of doing in the familiarities of their intrigue.

"Suddenly, however, letting go of his hair, she took her dead lover's inert head in her hands and looked for a long time in despair at the dead face, which no longer could smile at her. Then, throwing herself onto him, she took him into her arms and kissed him ardently. Her kisses fell like blows onto his closed mouth and eyes, onto his forehead and temples, and then, putting her lips to his ear, as if he could still hear her and as if she were about to whisper something to him, to make their embraces still more ardent, she said several times in a heartrending voice: 'Adieu, my darling!'

"Just then the clock struck twelve, and I started up, 'Twelve o'clock! I exclaimed. That is the time when the club closes. Come, madame, we have not a moment to lose!'

"She started up, and I said: 'We must carry him into the drawing room.' When we had done this I placed him on a sofa and lit the chandeliers, and just then the front door was opened and shut noisily. The husband had come back, and I said:

'Rose, bring me the basin and the towels and make the room look tidy. Make haste, for heaven's sake! Monsieur Leliévre is coming in.'

"I heard his steps on the stairs and then his hands feeling along the walls. 'Come here, my dear fellow,' I said: 'we have had an accident.'

"And the astonished husband appeared in the door with a cigar in his mouth and said: 'What is the matter? What is the meaning of this?'

" 'My dear friend,' I said, going up to him, 'you find us in great embarrassment. I had remained late, chatting with your wife and our friend, who had brought me in his carriage, when he suddenly fainted, and in spite of all we have done he has remained unconscious for two hours. I did not like to call in strangers, and if you will now help me downstairs with him I shall be able to attend to him better at his own house.'

"The husband, who was surprised but quite unsuspicious, took off his hat. Then he took his rival, who would be quite inoffensive for the future, under the arms. I got between his two legs as if I had been a horse between the shafts, and we went downstairs while his wifc lighted us. When we got outside I held the body up so as to deceive the coachman and said:

'Come, my friend; it is nothing; you feel better already, I expect. Pluck up your courage and make an attempt. It will soon be over.' But as I felt that he was slipping out of my hands I gave him a slap on the shoulder which sent him forward and made him fall into the carriage; then I got in after him.

"Monsieur Leliévre, who was rather alarmed, said to me: 'Do you think it is anything serious?' To which I replied, 'No,' with a smile, as I looked at his wife, who had put her arm into that of her legitimate husband and was trying to see into the carriage.

"I shook hands with them and told my coachman to start, and during the whole drive the dead man kept falling against me. When we got to his house I said that he had become unconscious on the way home and helped to carry him upstairs, where I certified that he was dead and acted another comedy to his distracted family. At last I got back to bed, not without swearing at lovers."

The doctor ceased, though he was still smiling, and the young woman, who was in a very nervous state, said: "Why have you told me that terrible story?"

He gave her a gallant bow and replied:

"So that I may offer you my services if necessary."

THE MAD WOMAN

"I Can tell you a terrible story about the Franco-Prussian war," Monsieur d'Endolin said to some friends assembled in the smoking-room of Baron de Ravot's chateau. "You know my house in the Faubourg de Cormeil. I was living there when the Prussians came, and I had for a neighbor a kind of mad woman, who had lost her senses in consequence of a series of misfortunes. At the age of seven and twenty she had lost her father, her husband, and her newly born child, all in the space of a month.

"When death has once entered into a house, it almost invariably returns immediately, as if it knew the way, and the young woman, overwhelmed with grief, took to her bed and ws delirious for six weeks. Then a species of calm lassitude succeeded that violent crisis, and she remained motionless, eating next to nothing, and only moving her eyes. Every time they tried to make her get up, she screamed as if they were about to kill her, and so they ended by leaving her continually in bed, and only taking her out to wash her, to change her linen, and to turn her mattress.

"An old servant remained with her, to give her something to drink, or a little cold meat, from time to time. What passed in that despairing mind ? No one ever knew, for she did not speak at all now. Was she thinking of the dead? Was she dreaming sadly, without any precise recollection of anything that had happened? Or was her memory as stagnant as water without any current? But however this may have been for fifteen years she remained thus inert and secluded.

"The war broke out, and in the beginning of December the Germans came to Cormeil. I can remember it as if it were yesterday. It was freezing hard enough to split the stones, and I myself was lying back in an armchair, being unable to move on account of the gout, when I heard their heavy and regular tread, and could see them pass from my window.

"They defiled past interminably, with that peculiar motion of a puppet on wires, which belongs to them. Then the officers billeted their men on the inhabitants, and I had seventeen of them. My neighbor, the crazy woman, had a dozen, one of whom was the Commandant, a regular violent, surely swashbuckler.

"During the first few days, everything went on as usual. The officers next door had been told that the lady was ill, and they did not trouble themselves about that in the least, but soon that woman whom they never saw irritated them. They asked what her illness was, and were told that she had been in bed for fifteen years, in consequence of terrible grief. No doubt they did not believe it, and thought that the poor mad creature would not leave her bed out of pride, so that she might not come near the Prussians, or speak to them or even see them.

"The Commandant insisted upon her receiving him. He was shown into the room and said to her roughly: 'I must beg you to get up, Madame, and come downstairs so that we may all see you.' But she merely turned her vague eyes on him, without replying, and so he continued: 'I do not intend to tolerate any insolence, and if you do not get up of your own accord, I can easily find means to make you walk without any assistance.'

"But she did not give any signs of having heard him, and remained quite motionless. Then he got furious, taking that calm silence for a mark of supreme contempt; so he added: 'If you do not come downstairs to-morrow—' And then he left the room.

"The next day the terrified old servant wished to dress her, but the mad woman began to scream violently, and resisted with all her might. The officer ran upstairs quickly, and the servant threw herself at his feet and cried: 'She will not come down. Monsieur, she will not. Forgive her, for she is so unhappy.'

"The soldier was embarrassed, as in spite of his anger, he did not venture to order his soldiers to drag her out. But suddenly he began to laugh, and gave some orders in German, and soon a party of soldiers was seen coming out supporting a mattress as if they were carrying a wounded man. On the bed, which had been unmade, the mad woman, who was still silent, was lying quite quietly, for she was quite indifferent to anything that went on, as long as they let her lie. Behind her, a soldier was carrying a parcel of feminine attire, and the officer said, rubbing his hands : 'We will just see whether you cannot dress yourself alone, and take a little walk.'

"And then the procession went of in the direction of the forest of Imauville; in two hours the soldiers came back alone, and nothing more was seen of the mad woman. What had they done with her? Where had they taken her to? No one knew.

"The snow was falling day and night, and enveloped the plain and the woods in a shroud of frozen foam, and the wolves came and howled at our very doors.

"The thought of that poor lost woman haunted me, and I made several applications to the Prussian authorities in order to obtain some information, and was nearly shot for doing so. When spring returned, the army of occupation withdrew, but my neighbor's house remained closed, and the grass grew thick in the garden walks. The old servant had died during the winter, and nobody troubled any longer about the occurrence; I alone thought about it constantly. What had they done with the woman? Had she escaped through the forest? Had somebody found her, and taken her to a hospital, without being able to obtain any information from her? Nothing happened to relieve my doubts; but by degrees, time assuaged my fears.

"Well, in the following autumn the woodcock were very plentiful, and as my gout had left me for a time, I dragged myself as far as the forest. I had already killed four or five of the long-billed birds, when I knocked over one which fell into a ditch full of branches, and I was obliged to get into it, in order to pick it up, and I found that it had fallen close to a dead, human body. Immediately the recollection of the mad woman struck me like a blow in the chest. Many other people had perhaps died in the wood during that disastrous year, but though I do not know why, I was sure, sure, I tell you, that I should see the head of that wretched maniac.

"And suddenly I understood, I guessed everything. They had abandoned her on that mattress in the cold, deserted wood ; and, faithful to her fixed idea, she had allowed herself to perish under that thick and light counterpane of snow, without moving either arms or legs.

"Then the wolves had devoured her, and the birds had built their nests with the wool from her torn bed. and I took charge of her bones. I only pray that our sons may never see any wars again."

A PIECE OF STRING

A LONG all the roads around Goderville the peasants and their wives were coming toward the burgh because it was market day. The men were proceeding with slow steps, the whole body bent forward at each movement of their long twisted legs, deformed by their hard work, by the weight on the plow which, at the same time, raised the left shoulder and swerved the figure, by the reaping of the wheat which made the knees spread to make a firm "purchase," by all the slow and painful labors of the country. Their blouses, blue, "stiff-starched," shining as if varnished, ornamented with a little design in white at the neck and wrists, puffed about their bony bodies, seemed like ballons ready to carry them off. From each of them a head, two arms, and two feet protruded.

Some led a cow or a calf by a cord, and their wives, walking behind the animal, whipped its haunches with a leafy branch to hasten its progress. They carried large baskets on their arms from which, in some cases, chickens and, in others, ducks thrust out their heads. And they walked with a quicker, livelier step than their husbands. Their spare straight figures were wrapped in a scanty little shawl, pinned over their flat bosoms, and their heads were enveloped in a white cloth glued to the hair and surmounted by a cap.

Then a wagon passed at the jerky trot of a nag, shaking strangely, two men seated side by side and a woman in the bottom of the vehicle, the latter holding on to the sides to lessen the hard jolts.

In the public square of Goderville there was a crowd, a throng of human beings and animals mixed together. The horns of the cattle, the tall hats with long nap of the rich peasants, and the headgear of the peasant women rose above the surface of the assembly. And the clamorous, shrill, screaming voices made a continuous and savage din which sometimes was dominated by the robust lungs of some countryman's laugh, or the long lowing of a cow tied to the wall of a house.

All that smacked of the stable, the dairy and the dirt heap, hay and sweat, giving forth that unpleasant odor, human and animal, peculiar to the people of the field.

Maître Hauchecome, of Breaute, had just arrived at Goderville, and he was directing his steps toward the public square, when he perceived upon the ground a little piece of string, Maître Hauchecome, economical like a true Norman, thought that everything useful ought to be picked up, and be bent painfully, for he suffered from rheumatism. He took the bit of thin cord from the ground and began to roll it carefully when he noticed Maître Malandian, the harness-maker, on the threshold of his door, looking at him. They had heretofore had business together on the subject of a halter, and they were on bad terms, being both good haters. Maître Hauchecome was seized with a sort of shame to be seen thus by his enemy, picking a bit of string out of the dirt. He concealed his "find" quickly under his blouse, then in his trousers' pocket; then he pretended to be still looking on the ground for something which he did not find, and he went toward the market, his head forward, bent double by his pains.

He was soon lost in the noisy and slowly moving crowd, which was busy with interminable bargainings. The peasants milked, went and came, perplexed always in fear of being cheated, not daring to decide, watching the vender's eye, ever trying to find the trick in the man and the flaw in the beast.

The women, having placed their great baskets at their feet, had taken out the poultry which lay upon the ground, tied together by the feet, with terrified eyes and scarlet crests.

They heard offers, stated their prices with a dry air and impassive face, or perhaps, suddenly deciding on some proposed reduction, shouted to the customer who was slowly going away : "All right, Maître Authirne, I'll give it to you for that."

Then little by little the square was deserted, and the Angelus ringing at noon, those who had stayed too long, scattered to their shops.

At Jourdain's the great room was full of people eating, as the big court was full of vehicles of all kinds, carts, gigs, wagons, dump carts, yellow with dirt, mended and patched, raising their shafts to the sky like two arms, or perhaps with their shafts in the ground and their backs in the air.

Just opposite the diners seated at the table, the immense fireplace, filled with bright flames, cast a lively heat on the backs of the row on the right. Three spits were turning on which were chickens, pigeons, and legs of mutton;

and an appetizing odor or roast beef and gravy dripping over the nicely browned skin rose from the hearth, increased the jovialness, and made everybody's mouth water.

All the aristocracy of the plow ate there, at Maître Jourdain's, tavern keeper and horse dealer, a rascal who had money.

The dishes were passed and emptied, as were the jugs of yellow cider. Everyone told his affairs, his purchases, and sales. They discussed the crops. The weather was favorable for the green things but not for the wheat.

Suddenly the drum beat in the court, before the house. Everybody rose except a few indifferent persons, and ran to the door, or to the windows, their months still full and napkins in their hands.

After the public crier had ceased his drum-beating, he called out in a jerky voice, speaking his phrases irregularly;

"It is hereby made known to the inhabitants of Goderville, and in general to all persons present at the market, that there was lost this morning, on the road to Benzeville, between nine and ten o'clock, a black leather pocket book containing five hundred francs and some business papers. The finder is requested to return same with all haste to the mayor's office or to Maître Fortune Houlbreque of Manneville, there will be twenty francs reward."

Then the man went away. The heavy roll of the drum and the crier's voice were again heard at a distance.

Then they began to talk of this event, discussing the chances that Maître Houlbreque had of finding or not finding his pocket book.

And the the meal concluded. They were finishing their coffee when a chief of the gendarmes appeared upon the threshold.

He inquired :

"Is Maître Hauchecome, of Breaute, here?"

Maître Hauchecome, seated at the other end of the table replied :

"Here I am."

And the officer resumed:

"Maître Hauchecome, will you have the goodness to accompany me to the mayor's office? The mayor would like to talk to you."

The peasant, surprised and disturbed, swallowed at a draught his tiny glass of brandy, rose, and, even more bent than in the morning, for the first steps after each rest were especially difficult, set out, repeating : "Here I am, here I am."

The mayor was awaiting him, seated on an armchair. He was the notary of the vicinity, a stout, serious man, with pompous phrases.

"Maître Hauchecome," said he, "you were seen this morning to pick up, on the road to Benzevillle, the pocket book lost by Maître Houlbreque, of Manneville."

The countryman, astounded, looked at the mayor, already terrified, by this suspicion resting on him without his knowing why.

"Me? Me? Me pick up the pocket book?"

"Yes, you, yourself."

"Word of honor, I never heard of it."

"But you were seen"

"I was seen, me? Who says he saw me?."

"Monsieur Malandain, the harness-maker."

The old man remembered, understood, and flushed with anger.

"Ah, he saw me, the clodhopper, he saw me pick up this string, here, M'sieu' the Mayor." And rummaging in his pocket he drew out the little piece of string.

But the mayor, incredulous, shook his head.

"You will not make me believe, Maître Hauchecome, that Monsieur Malandain, who is a man worthy of credence, mistook this cord for a pocket book."

The peasant, furious, lifted his hand, spat at one side to attest his honor, repeating:

"It is nevertheless the truth of the good God, the sacred truth, M'sieu' the Mayor. I repeat it on my soul and my salvation."

The mayor resumed:

"After picking up the object, you stood like a stilt, looking a long while in the mud to see if any piece of money had fallen out."

The good old man choked with indignation and fear.

"How anyone can tell—how anyone can tell—such lies to take away an honest man's reputation! How can anyone—"

There was no use in his protesting, nobody believed him. He was confronted with Monsieur Malandain, who repeated and maintained his affirmation. They abused each other for an hour. At his own request Maître Hauchecome was searched, nothing was found on him.

Finally the mayor, very much perplexed, discharged him

with the warning that he would consult the public prosecutor and ask for further orders.

The news had spread. As he left the mayor's office, the old man was surrounded and questioned with a serious or bantering curiosity, in which there was no indignation. He began to tell the story of the string. No one believed him. They laughed at him.

He went along, stopping his friends, beginning endlessly his statements and his protestations, showing his pockets turned inside out, to prove that he had nothing.

They said:

"Old rascal, get out!"

And he grew angry, becoming exasperated, hot, and distressed at not being believed, not knowing what to do and always repeating himself.

Night came, He must depart. He started on his way with three neighbors to whom he pointed out the place where he had picked up the bit of string; and all along the road he spoke of his adventure.

In the evening he took a turn in the village of Breaute, in order to tell it to everybody. He only met with incredulity.

It made him ill at night.

The next day about one o'clock in the afternoon, Marius Paumelle, a hired man in the employ of Maître Breton, husbandman at Ymanville, returned the pocket book and its contents belonging to Maître Houlbreque of Manneville.

This man claimed to have found the object in the road; but not knowing how to read, he had carried it to the house and given it to his employer.

The news spread through the neighborhood. Maître Hauchecome was informed of it. He immediately went the circuit and began to recount his story completed by the happy climax. He was in triumph.

"What grieved me so much was not the thing itself, as the lying. There is nothing so shameful as to be placed under a cloud on account of a lie."

He talked of his adventure all day long, he told it on the highway to people who were passing by, in the wineshop to people who were drinking there, and to persons coming out of church the following Sunday. He stopped strangers to tell them about it. He was calm now, and yet something disturbed him without his knowing exactly what it was. People had the air of joking while they listened. They did not seem convinced. He seemed to feel that remarks were being made behind his back.

On Tuesday of the next week he went to the market at Goderville, urged soley by the necessity he felt of discussing the case.

Malandain, standing at his door, began to laugh on seeing him pass. Why?

He approached a farmer from Crequetot, who did not let him finish, and giving him a thump in the stomach said to his face:

"You big rascal."

Then he turned his back on him.

Maître Hauchecome was confused, why was he called a big rascal?

When he was seated at the table, in Jourdain's tavern he commenced to explain "the affair."

A horse dealer from Monvilliers called to him:

"Come, come, old sharper, that's an old trick; I know all about your piece of string!"

Hauchecome stammered:

"But since the pocket book was found."

But the other man replied:

"Shut up, papa, there is one that finds, and there is one that reports. At any rate you are mixed with it."

The peasant stood choking. He understood They accused him of having had the pocket book returned by a confederate, by an accomplice.

He tried to protest. All the table began to laugh.

He could not finish his dinner and went away, in the midst of jeers.

He went home ashamed and indignant, choking with anger and confusion, the more dejected that he was capable with his Norman cunning of doing what they had accused him of, and even boasting of it as of a good turn. His innocence to him, in a confused way, was impossible to prove, as his sharpness was known. And he was stricken to the heart by the injustice of the suspicion.

Then he began to recount the adventures again, prolonging his history every day, adding each time, new reasons, more energetic protestations, more solemn oaths which he imagined and prepared in his hours of solitude, his whole mind given up to the story of the string. He was believed so much the less as his defense was more complicated and his arguing more subtile.

"Those are lying excuses," they said behind his back.

He felt it, consumed his heart over it, and wore himself out with useless efforts. He wasted away before their very eyes.

The wags now made him tell about the string to amuse them, as they make a soldier who has been on a campaign tell about his battles. His mind, touched to the depth, began to weaken.

Toward the end of December he took to his bed.

He died in the first days of January, and in the delirium of his death struggles he kept claiming his innocence, reiterating:

"A piece of string, a piece of string,—look—here it is, M'sieu' the Mayor."

THE VENUS OF BRANIZA

SOME years ago there lived in Braniza a celebrated Talmudist, renowned no less on account of his beautiful wife than for his wisdom, his learning, and his fear of God. The Venus of Braniza deserved that name thoroughly; she deserved it for herself, on account of her singular beauty, and even more as the wife of a man deeply versed in the Talmud, for the wives of the Jewish philosophers are, as a rule, ugly or possess some bodily defect.

The Talmud explains this in the following manner: It is well known that marriages are made in heaven, and at the birth of a boy a divine voice calls out the name of his future wife, and *vice versa.* But just as a good father tries to get rid of his good wares out of doors, and only uses the damaged stuff at home for his children, so God bestows on the Talmudists those women whom other men would not care to have.

Well, God made an exception in the case of our Talmudist, and had bestowed a Venus on him, perhaps only in order to confirm the rule by means of this exception, and to make it appear less hard. This philosopher's wife was a woman who would have done honor to any king's throne, or to a pedestal in any sculpture gallery. Tall, and with a wonderfully voluptuous figure, she carried a strikingly beautiful head, surmounted by thick, black plaits, on her proud shoulders. Two large, dark eyes languished and glowed beneath long lashes, and her beautiful hands looked as if they were carved out of ivory.

This glorious woman, who seemed to have been designed by nature to rule, to see slaves at her feet, to provide occupation for the painter's brush, the sculptor's chisel, and the poet's pen, lived the life of a rare and beautiful flower shut up in a hothouse. She would sit the whole day long wrapped up in her costly furs looking down dreamily into the street.

She had no children; her husband, the philosopher, studied and prayed and studied again from early morning until late at night; his mistress was "the Veiled Beauty," as the Talmudists call the Kabbalah. She paid no attention to her house, for she was rich, and everything went of its own accord like a clock which has only to be wound up once a week; nobody came to see her, and she never went out of the house; she sat and dreamed and brooded and -yawned.

******

One day when a terrible storm of thunder and lightning had spent its fury over the town, and all windows had been opened in order to let the Messias in, the Jewish Venus was sitting as usual in her comfortable easy-chair, shivering in spite of her furs, and thinking. Suddenly she fixed her glowing eyes on her husband who was sitting before the Talmud, swaying his body backward and forward, and said suddenly:

"Just tell me, when will Messias, the son of David, come?"

"He will come," the philosopher replied, "when all the Jews have become either altogether virtuous or altogether vicious, says the Talmud."

"Do you believe that all the Jews will ever become virtuous?" the Venus continued.

"How am I to believe that?"

"So Messias will come when all the Jews have become vicious?"

The philosopher shrugged his shoulders, and lost himself again in the labyrinth of the Talmud, out of which, so it is said, only one man returned in perfect sanity. The beautiful woman at the window again looked dreamily out into the heavy rain, while her white fingers played unconsciously with the dark furs of her splendid robe.

* * * * * *

One day the Jewish philosopher had gone to a neighboring town, where an important question of ritual was to be decided. Thanks to his learning, the question was settled sooner than he had expected, and instead of returning the next morning, as he had intended, he came back the same evening with a friend who was no less learned than himself. He got out of the carriage at his friend's house and went home on foot. He was not a little surprised when he saw his windows brilliantly illuminated, and found an officer's servant comfortably smoking his pipe in front of his house.

"What are you doing here?" he asked in a friendly manner, but with some curiosity, nevertheless.

"I am on guard, lest the husband of the beautiful Jewess should come home unexpectedly."

"Indeed? Well, mind and keep a good lockout."

Saying this, the philosopher pretended to go away, but went into the house through the garden entrance at the back. When he got into the first room, he found a table laid for two, which had evidently only been left a short time previously. His wife was sitting as usual at her bedroom window wrapped in her furs, but her cheeks were suspiciously red, and her dark eyes had not their usual languishing look, but now rested on her husband with a gaze which expressed at the same time satisfaction and mockery. At that moment his foot struck against an object on the floor, which gave out a strange sound. He picked it up and examined it in the light. It was a pair of spurs.

"Who has been here with you? " asked the Talmudist.

The Jewish Venus shrugged her shoulders contemptu-ously, but did not reply.

"Shall I tell you? The Captain of Hussars has been with you."

"And why should he not have been here with me ?" she said, smoothing the fur on her jacket with her white hand.

"Woman! are you out of your mind?"

"I am in full possession of my senses," she replied, and a knowing smile hovered round her red voluptuous lips. "But must I not also do my part, in order that Messias may come and redeem us poor Jews?"

A NEW YEAR'S GIFT

JACQUES DE RANDAL, having dined at home alone, told his valet he might go and then sat down at a table to write his letters.

He finished out every year by writing and dreaming, making for himself a sort of review of things that had happened since last New Year's Day, things that were now all over and dead; and in proportion as the faces of his friends rose up before his eyes, he wrote them a few lines, a cordial "Good morning" on the first of January.

So he sat down, opened a drawer, took out of it a woman's photograph, gazed at it a few moments and kissed it. Then, having laid it beside a sheet of note paper, he began:

MY DEAR IRENE: *You must have by this time the little souvenir which I sent you. I have shut myself up this evening in order to tell you –*

The pen here ceased to move, Jacques rose up and began walking up and down the room.

For the last six months he had a mistress, not a mistress like the others, a woman with whom one engages in a passing intrigue, of the theatrical world or the demimonde, but a woman whom he loved and won. He was no longer a young man although still comparatively young, and he looked on life seriously in a positive and practical spirit.

Accordingly he drew up the balance sheet of his passion, as he drew up every year the balance sheet of friendships that were ended or freshly contracted, of circumstances and persons that had entered his life. His first ardour of love having grown calmer, he asked himself with the precision of a merchant making a calculation what was the state of his heart with regard to her, and he tried to form an idea of what it would be in the future. He found there a great and deep affection, made up of tenderness, gratitude and the thousand subtleties which give birth to long and powerful attachments.

A ring of the bell made him start. He hesitated. Should he open? But he deemed it was his duty to open on this New Year's night to the unknown who knocks while passing, no matter who it may be,

So he took a wax candle, passed through the antechamber, removed the bolts, turned the key, drew the door back and saw his mistress standing pale as a corpse, leaning against the wall.

He stammered: "What is the matter with you?"

She replied: "Are you alone?"

"Yes."

"Without servants?"

"Yes."

"You are not going out?"

"No."

She entered with the air of a woman who knew the house. As soon as she was in the drawing room she sank into the sofa and, covering her face with her hands, began to weep dreadfully.

He kneeled down at her feet, seized hold of her hands to remove them from her eyes, so that he might look at them, and exclaimed:

"Irene, Irene, what is the matter with you? I implore of you to tell me what is the matter with you."

Then in the midst of her sobs she murmured: "I can no longer live like this."

He did not understand.

"Like this? What do you mean?"

"Yes. I can no longer live like this. I have endured so much. He struck me this afternoon."

"Who—your husband?"

"Yes—my husband."

"Ha!"

He was astonished, having never suspected that her husband could be brutal. He was a man of the world, of the better class, a clubman, a lover of horses, a theatre-goer and an expert swordsman; he was known, talked about, appreciated everywhere, having very courteous manners but a very mediocre intellect, an absence of education and of the real culture needed in order to think like all well-bred people and, finally, a respect for all conventional prejudices,

He appeared to devote himself to his wife, as a man ought to do in the case of wealthy and well-bred people. He displayed enough anxiety about her wishes, her health, her dresses and, beyond that, left-her perfectly free.

Randal, having become Irene's friend, had a right to the affectionate hand, clasp which every husband endowed with good manners owes to his wife's intimate acquaintances. Then when Jacques, after having been for some time the friend, became the lover, his relations with the husband were more cordial.

Jacques had never dreamed that there were storms in this household, and he was scared at this unexpected revelation.

He asked:

"How did it happen? Tell me."

Thereupon she related a long history, the entire history of her life, since the day of her marriage—the first discussion arising out of a mere nothing, then accentuating itself in the estrangement which grows up each day between two opposite types of character.

Then came quarrels, a complete separation, not apparent, but real; next her husband showed himself aggressive, suspicious, violent. Now he was jealous, jealous of Jacques, and this day even, after a scene, he had struck her.

She added with decision: "I will not go back to him. Do with me what you like."

Jacques sat down opposite to her, their knees touching each other. He caught hold of her hands:

"My dear love, you are going to commit a gross, an irreparable, folly. If you want to quit your husband put wrongs on one side, so that your situation as a woman of the world may be saved."

She asked as she cast at him a restless glance:

"Then what do you advise me?"

"To go back home and to put up with your life there till the day when you can obtain either a separation or a divorce with the honours of war."

"Is not this thing which you advise me to do a little cowardly?"

"No, it is wise and reasonable. You have a high position, a reputation, to safeguard, friends to preserve and relations to deal with. You must not lose all these through a mere caprice."

She rose up and said with violence:

"Well, no! I cannot have any more of it! It is at an end! It is at an end!"

Then, placing her two hands on her lover's shoulders and looking at him straight in the face, she asked:

"Do you love me?"

"Yes."

"Really and truly?"

"Yes."

"Then keep me!"

He exclaimed:

"Keep you? In my own house? Here? Why, you are mad. It would mean losing you forever, losing you beyond hope of recall! You are mad!"

She replied slowly and seriously, like a woman who feels

the weight of her words:

"Listen, Jacques. He has forbidden me to see you again, and I will not play this comedy of coming secretly to your house. You must either lose me or take me."

"My dear Irene, in that case, obtain your divorce, and I will marry you."

"Yes, you will marry me in—two years at the soonest. Yours is a patient love."

"Look here! Reflect! If you remain here he'll come tomorrow to take you away, seeing that he is your husband, seeing that he has right and law on his side."

"I did not ask you to keep me in your own house, Jacques, but to take me anywhere you like. I thought you loved me enough to do that. I have made a mistake. Good-by!"

She turned round and went toward the door so quickly that he was only able to catch hold of her when she was outside the room.

"Listen, Irene."

She struggled and did not want to listen to him any longer, her eyes full of tears and with these words only on her lips.

"Leave me alone! Leave me alone! Leave me alone!"

He made her sit down by force and, falling once more on his knees at her feet, he now brought forward a number of arguments and counsels to make her understand the folly and terrible risk of her project. He omitted nothing which he deemed it necessary to say to convince her, finding in his very affection for her strong motives of persuasion.

As she remained silent and cold he begged of her, implored of her, to listen to him, to trust him, to follow his advice.

When he had finished speaking she only replied:

"Are you disposed to let me go away now? Take away your hands so that I may rise up."

"Look here, Irene."

"Will you let go?"

"Irene—is your resolution irrevocable?"

"Do let me go."

"Tell me only whether this resolution, this foolish resolution of yours, which you will bitterly regret, is irrevocable."

"Yes; let me go!"

"Then stay. You know well that you are at home here. We shall go away tomorrow morning."

She rose up, in spite of him, and said in a hard tone:

"No. It is too late. I do not want sacrifice. I want devotion."

"Stay! I have done what I ought to do; I have said what I ought to say. I have no further responsibility on your behalf. My conscience is at peace. Tell me what you want me to do and I will obey."

She resumed her seat, looked at him for a long time and then asked in a very calm voice:

"Explain, then."

"How is that? What do you wish me to explain?"

"Everything—everything that you have thought about before coming to this resolution. Then I will see what I ought to do."

"But I have thought about nothing at all. I ought to warn you that you are going to accomplish an act of folly. You persist; then I ask to share in this act of folly, and I even insist on it."

"It is not natural to change one's opinion so quickly."

"Listen, my dear love. It is not a question here of sacrifice or devotion. On the day when I realized that I loved you I said this to myself, which every lover ought to say to himself in the same case: 'The man who loves a woman, who makes an effort to win her, who gets her and who takes her, contracts, so far as he is himself and so far as she is concerned, a sacred engagement.' It is, mark you, a question of dealing with a woman like you and not with a woman of an impulsive and yielding disposition.

"Marriage, which has a great social value, a great legal value, possesses in my eyes only a very slight moral value, taking into account the conditions under which it generally takes place.

"Therefore, when a woman, united by this lawful bond but having no attachment to a husband whom she cannot love, a woman whose heart is free, meets a man for whom she cares and gives herself to him, when a man who has no other tie takes a woman in this way, I say that they pledge themselves toward each other by this mutual and free agreement much more than by the 'Yes' uttered in the presence of the mayor.

"I say that if they are both honourable persons their union must be more intimate, more real, more healthy, than if all the sacraments had consecrated it.

"This woman risks everything. And it is exactly because she knows it, because she gives everything, her heart, her body, her soul, her honour, her life, because she has foreseen all miseries, all dangers, all catastrophes, because she dares to do a bold act, an intrepid act, because she is prepared, determined to, brave everything—her husband, who might kill her, and society, which may cast her out. This is why she is heroic in her conjugal infidelity; this is why her lover in taking her must also have foreseen everything and preferred her to everything, whatever might happen. I have nothing more to say. I spoke in the beginning like a man of sense whose duty it was to warn you, and now there is left in me only one man—the man who loves you. Say then what I am to do!"

Radiant, she closed his mouth with her lips and said to him in a low tone:

"It is not true, darling! There is nothing the matter! My husband does not suspect anything. But I wanted to see, I wanted to know, what you would do. I wished for a New Year's gift—the gift of your heart—another gift besides the necklace you have just sent me. You have given it to me. Thanks! Thanks! God be thanked for the happiness you have given me!"

A QUEER NIGHT IN PARIS

MAÎTRE SAVAL, notary at Vernon, was passionately fond of music. Still young, though already bald, always carefully shaved, a little corpulent, as was fitting, wearing a gold pince-nez instead of old-fashioned spectacles, active, gallant and joyous, he passed in Vernon for an artist. He thrummed on the piano and played on the violin and gave musical evenings where interpretations were given of new operas.

He had even what is called a bit of a voice, nothing but a bit, a very little bit of a voice, but he managed it with so much taste that cries of "Bravo!" "Exquisite!" "Surprising!" "Adorable!" issued from every throat as soon as he had murmured the last note.

He was a subscriber to a music publisher in Paris who sent all new pieces to him. From time to time to the high society of the town he sent little notes something in this style:

"You are invited to be present on Monday evening at the house of M. Saval, notary, Vernon, at the first production of *Sais*"

A few officers, gifted with good voices, formed the chorus. Two or three of the vine dressers' families also sang. The notary filled the part of leader of the orchestra with so much skill that the bandmaster of the 190th Regiment of the line said one day at the Cafe de l'Europe:

"Oh, Monsieur Saval is a master. It is a great pity that he did not adopt the career of an artist."

When his name was mentioned in a drawing room there was always found somebody to declare: "He is not an amateur; he is an artist, a genuine artist." And two or three persons would repeat in a tone of profound conviction: "Oh yes, a genuine artist," laying particular stress on the word "genuine."

Every time that a new work was interpreted at a big Parisian theatre, M. Saval paid a visit to the capital. Last year, according to his custom, he went to hear *Henry VIII.* He then took the express which arrives in Paris at 4:30 P.M., intending to return by the 12:35 A.M. train so as not to have to sleep at a hotel. He had put on evening dress, a black coat and white tie, which he concealed under his overcoat with the collar turned up.

As soon as he had planted his foot on the Rue d'Amsterdam he felt in quite a jovial mood and said to himself:

"Decidedly the air of Paris does not resemble any other air. It has in it something indescribably stimulating, exciting, intoxicating, which fills you with a strange longing to gambol and to do many other things. As soon as I arrive here it seems to me, all of a sudden, that I have taken a bottle of champagne.

What a life one can lead in this city in the midst of artists! Happy are the elect, the great men who enjoy renown in such a city! What an existence is theirs!"

And he made plans; he would have liked to know some of those celebrated men, to talk about them in Vernon and to spend an evening with them from time to time in Paris.

But suddenly an idea struck him, He had heard allusions to little cafés in the outer boulevards at which well-known painters, men of letters and even musicians gathered, and he proceeded to go toward Montmartre at a slow pace.

He had two hours before him. He wanted to have a look round. He passed in front of taverns frequented by belated Bohemians, gazing at the different faces, seeking to discover the artists. Finally, he came to the sign of The Dead Rat and, allured by the name, he entered.

Five or six women, with their elbows resting on the marble tables, were talking in low tones about their love affairs, the quarrels of Lucie with Hortense and the scoundrelism of Octave. They were no longer young but were fat or thin, tired out, used up. You could see that they were almost bald, and they drank bocks like men.

M. Saval sat down at some distance from them and waited, for the hour for taking absinthe was at hand.

A tall young man soon came in and took at seat beside him. The landlady called him "Monsieur Romantin." The notary quivered. Was this the Romantin who had taken a medal at the last Salon?

The young man made a sign to the waiter:

"You will bring up my dinner at once and then carry to my new studio, 15 Boulevard de Clichy, thirty bottles of beer and the ham I ordered this morning. We are going to have a housewarming."

M. Saval immediately ordered dinner. Then he took off his overcoat so that his dress coat and his white tie could be seen. His neighbour did not seem to notice him. M. Saval glanced sideways at him, burning with the desire to speak to him.

Two young men entered in red velvet and peaked beards in the fashion of Henry III. They sat down opposite Romantin.

The first of the pair said:

"It is for this evening?"

Romantin pressed his hand.

"I believe you, old chap, and everyone will be there. I have Bonnat, Guillemet, Gervex, Beraud, Hébert, Duez, Clairin and Jean-Paul Laurens. It will be a glorious blowout! And women too! Wait till you see! Every actress without exception— of course, I mean, you know all those who have nothing to do this evening."

The landlord of the establishment came across.

"Do you often have this housewarming?"

The painter replied:

"Certainly—every three months, each quarter."

M. Saval could not restrain himself any longer and in a hesitating voice said: "I beg your pardon for intruding on you, monsieur, but I heard your name pronounced, and I would be very glad to know if you really are Monsieur Romantin whose work in the last Salon I have so much admired."

The painter answered:

"I am the person, monsieur."

The notary then paid the artist a very well-turned compliment, showing that he was a man of culture. The painter, gratified, thanked him politely in reply. Then they chatted. Romantin returned to the subject of his housewarming, going into details as to the magnificence of the forthcoming entertainment.

M. Saval questioned him as to all the men he was going to receive, adding:

"It would be an extraordinary piece of good fortune for a stranger to meet at one time so many celebrities assembled in the studio of an artist of your rank." Romantin, overcome, answered: "If it would be agreeable to you, come."

M. Saval accepted the invitation with enthusiasm, reflecting:

"I'll always have time enough to see *Henry VIII*.

Both of them had finished their meal. The notary insisted on paying the two bills, wishing to repay his neighbour's civilities. He also paid for the drinks of the young fellows in red velvet; then he left the establishment with the painter.

They stopped in front of a very long house, by no means high, the first story of which had the appearance of an interminable conservatory. Six studios stood in a row with their fronts facing the boulevards.

Romantin was the first to enter. Ascending the stairs, he opened a door and lighted a match and then a candle.

They found themselves in an immense apartment, the furniture of which consisted of three chairs, two easels and a few sketches lying on the floor along the walls. M. Saval remained standing at the door in a stupefied state of mind.

The painter remarked:

"Here you are! We've got to the spot, but everything has yet to be done."

Then, examining the high, bare apartment, whose ceiling was veiled in shadows, he said:

"We might make a great deal out of this studio."

He walked around it, surveying it with the utmost attention, then went on.

"I have a mistress who might easily give us a helping hand. Women are incomparable for hanging drapery. But I sent her to the country today in order to get her off my hands this evening. It is not that she bores me, but she is too much lacking in the ways of good society. It would be embarrassing to my guests."

He reflected for a few seconds and then added:

"She is a good girl but not easy to deal with. If she knew that I was holding a reception she would tear out my eyes."

M. Saval had not even moved; he did not understand.

The artist came over to him.

"Since I have invited you, you are going to give me some help."

The notary said emphatically:

"Make any use of me you please. I am at your disposal."

Romantin took off his jacket.

"Well, citizen, to work! We are first going to clean up."

He went to the back of the easel on which there was a canvas representing a cat and seized a very worn-out broom.

"I say! Just brush up while I look after the lighting."

M. Saval took the broom, inspected it and then began to sweep the floor very awkwardly, raising a whirlwind of dust.

Romantin, disgusted, stopped him: "Deuce take it! You don't know how to sweep the floor! Look at me!"

And he began to roll before him a heap of grayish sweepings, as if he had done nothing else all his life. Then he gave back the broom to the notary, who imitated him.

In five minutes such a cloud of dust filled the studio that Romantin asked:

"Where are you? I can't see you any longer."

M. Saval, who was coughing, came nearer to him. The painter said to him:

"How are you going to manage to get up a chandelier."

The other, stunned, asked:

"What chandelier?"

"Why, a chandelier to light—a chandelier with wax candles."

The notary did not understand.

He answered: "I don't know."

The painter began to jump about, cracking his fingers.

"Well, monseigneur, I have found out a way."

Then he went more calmly:

"Have you got five francs about you?"

M. Saval replied:

"Why, yes."

The artist said:

"Well, you'll go and buy for me five francs' worth of wax candles while I go and see the cooper."

And he pushed the notary in his evening coat into the street. At the end of five minutes they had returned, one of them with the wax candles and the other with the hoop of a cask. Then Romantin plunged his hand into a cupboard and drew forth twenty empty bottles, which he fixed in the form of a crown around the hoop. He then came down and went to borrow a ladder from the doorkeeper after having explained that he obtained the favours of the old woman by painting the portrait of her cat exhibited on the easel.

When he mounted the ladder he said to M. Saval:

"Are you active?"

The other, without understanding, answered:

"Why, yes."

"Well, you just climb up there and fasten this chandelier for me to the ring of the ceiling. Then you must put a wax candle in each bottle and light it. I tell you, I have a genius for lighting up. But off with your coat, damn it! You are just like a Jeames."

The door war opened violently. A woman appeared with her eyes flashing and remained standing on the threshold. Romantin gazed at her with a look of terror. She waited some seconds, crossed her arms over her breast and then in a shrill, vibrating, exasperated voice said:

"Ha, you villain, is this the way you leave me?"

Romantin made no reply. She went on:

"Ha, you scoundrel! You are again doing the swell, while you pack me off to the country. You'll soon see the way I'll settle your jollification. Yes, I'm going to receive your friends."

She grew warmer.

"I'm going to slap their faces with the bottles and the wax candles."

Romantin uttered one soft word:

"Mathilde."

But she did not pay any attention to him; she went on:

"Wait a little, my fine fellow! Wait a little!"

Romantin went over to her and tried to take her by the hands.

"Mathilde."

But she was now fairly under way, and on she went, emptying the vials of her wrath with strong words and reproaches. They flowed out of her mouth like a stream sweeping a heap of filth along with it. The words hurled out seemed struggling for exit. She stuttered, stammered, yelled, suddenly recovering her voice to cast forth an insult or a curse.

He seized her hands without her having even noticed it. She did not seem to see anything, so much occupied was she in holding forth and relieving her heart. And suddenly she began to weep. The tears flowed from her eyes without making her stem the tide of her complaints. But her words had taken a howling, shrieking tone; they were a continuous cry interrupted by sobbings. She commenced afresh twice or three times till she stopped, as if something were choking her, and at last she ceased with a regular flood of tears.

Then he clasped her in his arms and kissed her hair, himself affected.

"Mathilde, my little Mathilde, listen. You must be reasonable. You know, if I give a supper party to my friends it is to thank these gentlemen for the medal I got at the Salon. I cannot receive women. You ought to understand that. It is not the same with artists as with other people."

She stammered in the midst of her tears.

"Why didn't you tell me this?"

He replied:

"It was in order not to annoy you, not to give you pain. Listen, I'm going to see you home. You will be very sensible, very nice; you will remain quietly waiting for me in bed, and I'll come back as soon as it's over."

She murmured:

"Yes, but you will not begin over again?"

"No, I swear to you!"

He turned toward M. Saval, who had at last hooked on the chandelier.

"My dear friend, I am coming back in five minutes. If anyone arrives in my absence do the honours for me, will you not?"

And he carried off Mathilde, who kept drying her eyes with her handkerchief as she went along.

Left to himself, M. Saval succeeded in putting everything around him in order. Then he lighted the wax candles and waited.

He waited for a quarter of an hour, half an hour, an hour. Romantin did not return. Then suddenly there was a dreadful noise on the stairs, a song shouted out in chorus by twenty mouths and a regular march like that of a Prussian regiment. The whole house was shaken by the steady tramp of feet. The door flew open, and a motley throng appeared men and women in a row, holding one another arm in arm, in pairs, and kicking their heels on the floor in proper time-advancing into the studio like a snake uncoiling itself. They howled:

"Come, let us all be merry,
Pretty maids and soldiers gay!"

M. Saval, thunderstruck, remained standing in evening dress under the chandelier. The procession of revellers caught sight of him and uttered a shout:

"A Jeames! A Jeames!"

And they began whirling round him, surrounding him with a circle of vociferation. Then they took each other by the hand and went dancing about madly.

He attempted to explain:

"Messieurs – Messieurs – Mesdames – "

But they did not listen to him. They whirled about, they jumped, they brawled.

At last the dancing ceased. M. Saval uttered the word:

"Messieurs – "

A tall young fellow, fair-haired and bearded to the nose, interrupted him:

"What's your name, my friend?"

The notary, quite scared, said:

"I am Monsieur Saval."

A voice exclaimed:

"You mean Baptiste."

A woman said:

"Let the poor waiter alone! You'll end by making him get angry. He's paid to attend on us and not to be laughed at by us." -

Then M. Saval noticed that each guest had brought his own provisions. One held a bottle of wine, another a pie. This one had a loaf of bread, that one a ham.

The tall, fair young fellow placed in his hands an enormous sausage and gave him orders:

"Go and settle up the sideboard in the corner over there. You are to put the bottles at the left and the provisions at the right."

Saval, getting quite distracted, exclaimed:

"But, messieurs, I am a notary!"

There was a moment's silence and then a wild outburst of laughter. One suspicious gentleman asked:

"How are you here?"

He explained, telling about his project of going to the opera, his departure from Vernon, his arrival in Paris and the way in which he had spent the evening.

They sat around him to listen to him; they greeted him with words of applause and called him Scheherazade.

Romantin did not come back. Other guests arrived. M. Saval was presented to them so that he might begin his story over again. He declined; they forced him to relate it. They fixed him on one of three chairs between two women who kept constantly filling his glass. He drank; he laughed; he talked; he sang too. He tried to waltz with his chair and fell on the floor.

From that moment he forgot everything. It seemed to him, however, that they undressed him, put him to bed and that his stomach got sick.

When he awoke it was broad daylight, and he lay stretched with his feet against a cupboard in a strange bed.

An old woman with a broom in her hand was glaring angrily at him. At last she said:

"Clear out, you blackguard! Clear out! What right has anyone to get drunk like this?"

He sat up in his bed, feeling very ill at ease. He asked:

"Where am I?"

"Where are you, you dirty scamp? You are drunk. Take your rotten carcass out of here as quick as you can—and lose no time about it!"

He wanted to get up. He found that he was naked in the bed. His clothes had disappeared. He blurted out:

"Madame, I—"

Then he remembered. What was he to do? He asked:

"Did Monsieur Romantin come back?"

The doorkeeper shouted:

"Will you take your dirty carcass out of this so that he at any rate may not catch you here?"

M. Saval said in a state of confusion:

"I haven't got my clothes; they have been taken away from me."

He had to wait, to explain his situation, give notice to his friends and borrow some money to buy clothes. He did not leave Paris till evening.

And when people talk about music to him in his beautiful drawing room in Vernon, he declares with an air of authority that painting is a very inferior art.

THE HOLE

CUTS AND WOUNDS WHICH CAUSED DEATH

THAT was the heading of the charge which brought Leopold Renard, up holsterer, before the Assize Court.

Round him were the principal witnesses, Mme Flaméche, widow of the victim, Louis Ladureau, cabinetmaker, and Jean Durdent, plumber.

Near the criminal was his wife, dressed in black, a little ugly woman who looked like a monkey dressed as a lady.

This is how Renard described the drama:

"Good heavens, it is a misfortune of which I am the first and last victim and with which my will has nothing to do. The facts are their own commentary, Monsieur le President. I am an honest man, a hard-working man, an upholsterer in the same street for the last sixteen years, known, liked, respected and esteemed by all, as my neighbors have testified, even the porter, who is not *folâire* every day. I am fond of work, I am fond of saving, I like honest men and respectable pleasures. That is what has ruined me, so much the worse for me; but as my will had nothing to do with it, I continue to respect myself.

"Every Sunday for the last five years my wife and I have spent the day at Passy. We get fresh air, not to say that we are fond of fishing - as fond of it as we are of small onions. Mélie inspired me with that passion, the jade; she is more enthusiastic than I am the scold, and all the mischief in this business is her fault, as you will see immediately.

"I am strong and mild-tempered, without a pennyworth of malice in me. But she, oh la la! She looks insignificant, she is short and thin, but she does more mischief then a weasel. I do not deny that she has some good qualities; she has some, and those very important to a man in business. But her character! Just ask about it in the neighborhood; even the porter's wife, who has just sent me about my business-she will tell you something about it.

"Every day she used to find fault with my mild temper: 'I would not put up with this! I would not put up with that.' If I had listened to her. Monsieur le President, I should have had at least three bouts of fisticuffs a month."

Mme Renard interrupted him: "And for good reasons too; they laugh best who laugh last."

He turned toward her frankly. "Oh! very well, I can blame you, since you were the cause of it."

Then, facing the president again, he said:

"I will continue. We used to go to Passy every Saturday evening, so as to be able to begin fishing at daybreak the next morning. It is a habit which has become second nature with us, as the saying is. Three years ago this summer I discovered a place, oh! such a spot! There, in the shade, were eight feet of water at least and perhaps ten, a hole with a *retour* under the bank, a regular retreat for fish and a paradise for any fisherman. I might look upon that hole as my property, Monsieur le President, as I was its Christopher Columbus. Everybody in the neighborhood knew it, without making any opposition. They used to say: 'That is Renard's Place'; and nobody would have gone to it, not even Monsieur Plumsay, who is renowned, be it said without any offense, for appropriating other people's places.

"Well, I went as usual to that place, of which I felt as certain as if I had owned it. I had scarcely got there on Saturday when I got into Delila, with my wife. Delila is my Norwegian boat which I had built by Fourmaise and which is light and safe. Well, as I said, we got into the boat and we were going to bait, and for baiting there is nobody to be compared with me, and they all know it. You want to know with what I bait? I cannot answer that question; it has nothing to do with the accident; I cannot answer, that is my secret. There are more than three hundred people who have asked me; I have been offered glasses of brandy and liquors, fried fish, matelots,' to make me tell! But just go and try whether the chub will come. Ah! they have patted my stomach to get at my secret, my recipe. Only my wife knows, and she will not tell it any more than I shall! Is not that so, Melie?

The president of the court interrupted him:

"Just get to the facts as soon as you can."

The accused continued: "I am getting to them; I am getting to them. Well, on Saturday, July eighth, we left by the five-twenty-five train, and before dinner we went to ground bait as usual. The weather promised to keep fine, and I said to Melie: 'All right for tomorrow!' And she replied: 'It looks like it.' We never talk more than that together.

"And then we returned to dinner. I was happy and thirsty, and that was the cause of everything. I said to Melie: 'Look here, Mélie, it is fine weather, so suppose I drink a bottle of *Casque a meche*. 'That is a little white wine which we have christened so because if you drink too much of it it prevents you from sleeping and is the opposite of a nightcap. Do you understand me?

"She replied: 'you can do as you please, but you will be ill again and will not be able to get up tomorrow.' That was true, sensible, prudent and clearsighted, I must confess. Nevertheless, I could not withstand it, and I drank my bottle. It all comes from that.

"Well, I could not sleep. By Jove! It kept me awake till two o'clock in the morning, and then I went to sleep so soundly that I should not have heard the angel shouting at the Last Judgement.

"In short, my wife woke me at six o'clock and I jumped

out of bed, hastily put on my trousers and jersey, washed my face and jumped on board Delila. But it was too late, for when I arrived at my hole it was already taken. Such a thing had never happened to me in three years, and it made me feel as if I were being robbed under my own eyes. I said to myself, 'Confound it all! Confound it!' And then my wife began to nag at me. 'Eh! What about your *Casque a meche!* Get along, you drunkard! Are you satisfied, you great fool? I could say nothing, because it was all quite true, and so I landed all the same near the spot and tried to profit by what was left. Perhaps, after all, the fellow might catch nothing and go away.

"He was a little thin man in white linen coat and waistcoat and with a large straw hat, and his wife, a fat woman who was doing embroidery, was behind him.

"When she saw us take up our position close to their place she murmured: 'I suppose there are no other places on the river!' And my wife, who was furious, replied: 'People who know how to behave make inquiries about the habits of the neighborhood before occupying reserved spots.'

"As I did not want a fuss I said to her: 'Hold your tongue, Melie. Let them go on, let them go on; we shall see.'

"Well, we had fastened Delila under the willow trees and had landed and were fishing side by side Mélie and I, close to the two others; but here, monsieur, I must enter into details.

"We had only been there about five minutes when our male neighbor's float began to go down two or three times, and then he pulled out a chub as thick as my thigh, rather less, perhaps, but nearly as big! My heart beat and the perspiration stood on my forehead, and Mélie said to me: 'Well, you sot, did you see that?

"Just then Monsieur Bru, the grocer of Poissy, who was fond of gudgeon fishing, passed in a boat and called out to me: 'So somebody has taken your usual place, Monsieur Renard?, And I replied: 'Yes, Monsieur Bru, there are some people in this world who do not know the usages of common politeness.'

"The little man in linen pretended not to hear, nor his fat lump of a wife, either.

Here the president interrupted him a second time: "Take care, you are insulting the widow, Madame Flaméche, who is present."

Renard made his excuses: "I beg your pardon, I beg your pardon; my anger carried me away.... Well, not a quarter of an hour had passed when the little man caught another chub and another almost immediately and another five minutes later.

"The tears were in my eyes, and then I knew that Madame Renard was boiling with rage, for she kept on nagging at me: 'Oh, how horrid! Don't you see that he is robbing you of your fish? Do you think that you will catch anything? Not even a frog, nothing whatever. Why, my hands are burning just to think of it.'

"But I said to myself: 'Let us wait until twelve o'clock. Then this poaching fellow will go to lunch, and I shall get my place again.' As for me , Monsieur le President, I lunch on the spot every Sunday; we bring our provisions in Delila. But there! At twelve o'clock the wretch produced a fowl out of a newspaper, and while he was eating, actually he caught another chub!

"Mélie and I had a morsel also, just a mouthful, a mere nothing, for our heart was not in it.

"Then I took up my newspaper, to aid my digestion. Every Sunday I read the *Gil Blas* in the shade like that, by the side of the water. It is columbine's day, you know. Columbine who writes the articles in the *Gil Blas.* I generally put Madame Renard into a passion by pretending to know this Columbine. It is not true, for I do not know her and have never seen her, but that does not matter; she writes very well, and then she says things straight out for a woman. She suits me, and there are not many of her sort.

"Well, I began to taste my wife, but she got angry immediately and very angry, and so I held my tongue. At that moment our two witnesses, who are present here. Monsieur Ladureau and Monsieur Durdent, appeared on the other side of the river. We knew each other by sight. The little man began to fish again, and he caught so many that I trembled with vexation, and his wife said: 'It is an uncommonly good spot, and we will come here always. Desire.' As for me, a cold shiver ran down my back, and Madame Renard kept repeating: 'You are not a man; you have the blood of a chicken in your veins'; and suddenly I said to her:

'Look here, I would rather go away, or I shall only be doing something foolish.'

"And she whispered to me as if she had put a red-hot iron under my nose:' You are not a man. Now you are going to run away and surrender your place! Off you go, Bazaine!'

"Well, I felt that, but yet I did not move while the other fellow pulled out a bream. Oh! I never saw such a large one before, never! And then my wife began to talk aloud, as if she were thinking, and you can see her trickery. She said: That is what one might call stolen fish, seeing that we baited the place ourselves. At any rate they ought to give us back the money we have spent on bait.'

"Then the fat woman in the cotton dress said in turn: 'Do you mean to call us thieves, madame?' And they began to explain, and then they came to words. Oh Lord! those creatures know some good ones. They shouted so loud that our two witnesses, who were on the other bank, began to call out by way of a joke: 'Less noise over there; you will prevent your husbands from fishing.'

"The fact is that neither of us moved any more than if we had been two tree stumps. We remained there, with out noses over the water, as if we had heard nothing; but, by jove, we heard all the same. 'You are a mere liar.'

" 'You are nothing better than a streetwalker.'

" 'You are only a trollop.'

" 'You are a regular strumpet.'

" And so on and so on; a sailor could not have said more.

"Suddenly I heard a noise behind me and turned round. It was the other one, the fat woman, who had fallen on to my wife with her parasol. *Whack! whack!* Mélie got two of them, but she was furious, and she hits hard when she is in a rage, so she caught the fat woman by the hair and then, *thump, thump.* Slaps in the face rained down like ripe plums. I should have let them go on-women among themselves, men among themselves-it does not do to mix the blows, but the little man in the linen jacket jumped up like a devil and was going to rush at my wife. Ah! no, no, not that, my friend! I caught the gentleman with the end of my fist, *crash, crash,* one on the nose, the other in the stomach. He threw up his arms and legs and fell on his back into the river, just into the hole.

"I should have fished him out most certainly. Monsieur le President, if I had had the time. But unfortunately the fat woman got the better of it, and she was drubbing Mélie terribly. I know that I ought not to have assisted her while the man was drinking his fill, but I never thought that he would drown and said to myself:' Bah, it will cool him.'

"I therefore ran up to the women to separate them, and all I received was scratches and bites. Good lord, what creatures! Well, it took me five minutes, and perhaps ten, to separate those two viragoes. When I turned arond there was nothing to be seen, and the water was as smooth as a lake. The others yonder kept shouting: 'Fish him out!' It was all very well to say that, but I cannot swim and still less dive!

"At last the man from the dam came and two gentlemen with boat hooks, but it had taken over a quarter of an hour. He was found at the bottom of the hole in eight feet of water, as I have said, but he was dead, the poor little man in his linen suit! There are the facts, such as I have sworn to. I am innocent, on my honor." The witnesses having deposed to the same effect, the accused was acquitted.

A COUNTRY EXCURSION

FOR five months they had been talking of going to lunch at some country restaurant in the neighborhood of Paris, on Madame Dufour's birthday, and as they were looking forward very impatiently to the outing, they had risen very early that morning. Monsieur Dufour had borrowed the milkman's tilted cart, and drove himself. It was a very neat, two-wheeled conveyance, with a hood, and in it Madame Dufour, resplendent in a wonderful, sherry-colored silk dress, sat by the side of her husband.

The old grandmother and the daughter were accommodated with two chairs, and a yellow-haired youth, of whom, however, nothing was to be seen except his head, lay at the bottom of the trap.

When they got to the bridge of Neuilly, Monsieur Dufour said: "Here we are in the country at last!" At that warning his wife grew sentimental about the beauties of nature. When they got to the crossroads at Courbevoie, they were seized with admiration for the tremendous view down there: on the right was the spire of Argenteuil church, above it rose the hills of Sannois and the mill of Orgemont, while on the left, the aqueduct of Marly stood out against the clear morning sky. In the distance they could see the terrace of Saint-Germain, and opposite to them, at the end of a low chain of hills, the new fort of Cormeilles. Afar—a very long way off, beyond the plains and villages— one could see the somber green of the forests.

The sun was beginning to shine in their faces, the dust got into their eyes, and on either side of the road there stretched an interminable tract of bare, ugly country, which smelled unpleasantly. You would have thought that it had been ravaged by a pestilence which had even attacked the buildings, for skeletons of dilapidated and deserted houses, or small cottages left in an unfinished state, as if the contractors had not been paid, reared their four roofless walls on each side.

Here and there tall factory-chimneys rose up from the baren soil, the only vegetation on that putrid land, where the spring breezes wafted an odor of petroleum and soot, mingled with another smell that was even still less agreeable. At last however, they crossed the Seine a second time. It was delightful on the bridge; the river sparkled in the sun, and they had a feeling of quiet satisfaction and enjoyment in drinking in purer air, not impregnated by the black smoke of factories, nor by the miasma from the deposits of night-soil. A man whom they met told them that the name of the place was Bézons; so Monsieur Dufour pulled up, and read the attractive announcement outside an eating-house :

"Restaurant Poulin, stews and fried fish, private rooms, arbors, and swings."

"Well! Madame Dufour, will this suit you? Will you make up your mind at last?"

She read the announcement in her turn, and then looked at the house for a time.

It was a white country inn, built by the roadside, and through the open door she could see the bright zinc of the counter, at which two workmen out for the day were sitting. At last she made up her mind, and said:

"Yes, this will do; and, besides, there is a veiw."

So they drove into a large yard studded with trees, behind the inn, which was only separated from the river by the towing-path, and got out. The husband sprang out first, and held out his arms for his wife. As the step was very high, Madame Dufour, in order to reach him, had to show the lower part of her limbs, whose former slenderness had disappeared in fat. Monsieur Dufour, who was already getting excited by the country air, pinched her calf, and then, taking her in his arms, set her on to the ground, as if she had been some enormous bundle. She shook the dust out of the silk dress, and then looked round, to see in what sort of a place she was.

She was a stout woman, of about thirty-six, full-blown and delightful to look at. She could hardly breathe, as she was laced to tightly, which forced the heaving mass of her superabundant bosom up to her double chin. Next, the girl put her hand on to her father's shoulder, and jumped lightly down. The youth with the yellow hair had got down by stepping on the wheel, and he helped Monsieur Dufour to get the grandmother out. Then they unharnessed the horse, which they tied up to a tree, and the carriage fell back, with both shafts in the air. The man and boy took off their coats, washed their hands in a pail of water, and then joined the ladies, who had already taken possession of the swings.

Mademoiselle Dufour was trying to swing herself standing up, but she could not succeed in getting a start. She was a pretty girl of about eighteen; one of those women who suddenly excite your desire when you meet them in the street, and who leave you with a vague feeling of uneasiness and of excited senses. She was tall, had a small waist and large hips, with a dark skin, very large eyes, and very black hair. Her dress clearly marked the outlines of her firm, full figure, which was accentuated by the motion of her hips as she tried to swing herself higher. Her arms were stretched over her head to hold the rope, so that her bosom rose at every movement she made. Her hat, which a gust of wind had blown off, was hanging behind her, and as the swing gradually rose higher and higher, she showed her delicate limbs up to the knees each time, and the wind from the perfumed petticoats, more heady than the fumes of wine, blew into the faces of her father and friend, who were looking at her in admiration.

Sitting in the other swing, Madame Dufour kept saying in a monotonous voice:

"Cyprian, come and swing me; do come and swing me, Cyprian!" At last he complied, and turning up his shirt-sleeves, as if he intended to work very hard, with much difficulty he set his wife in motion. She clutched the two ropes, and held her legs out straight, so as not to touch the ground. She enjoyed feeling giddy from the motion of the swing, and her whole figure shook like a jelly on a dish, but as she went higher and higher, she grew too giddy and got frightened. Every time she was coming back, she uttered a shriek, which made all the little urchins come round, and, down below, beneath the garden hedge, she vaguely saw a row of mischievous heads, making various grimaces as they laughed.

When a servant girl came out, they ordered lunch. "Some fried fish, a stewed rabbit, salad, and dessert," Madame Dufour said, with an important air.

"Bring two quarts of beer and a bottle of claret," her husband said. "We will have lunch on the grass," the girl added. The grandmother, who had an affection for cats, had been petting one that belonged to the house, and had been bestowing the most affectionate words on it, for the last ten minutes. The animal, no doubt secretly pleased by her attentions, kept close to the good woman, but just out of reach of her hand, and quietly walked round the trees, against which she rubbed herself, with her tail up, purring with pleasure.

"Hallo!" exclaimed the youth with the yellow hair, who was ferreting about, "here are two swell boats!" They all went to look at them, and saw two beautiful skiffs in a wooden boathouse, which were as beautifully finished as if they had been objects of luxury. They were moored side by side, like two tall, slender girls, in their narow shining length, and aroused in one a wish to float in them on warm summer mornings and evenings, along flower-covered banks of the river, where the trees dip their branches into the water, where the rushes are continually rustling in the breeze, and where the swift kingfishers dart about like flashes of blue lightning.

The whole family looked at them with great respect.

"They are indeed two swell boats," Monsieur Dufour repeated gravely, and he examined them closely, commenting on them like a connoisseur. He had been in the habit of rowing in his younger days, he said, and when he had that in his hands—and he went through the action of pulling the oars—he did not care a fig for anybody. He had beaten more than one Englislunan formerly at the Joinville regattas. He grew quite excited at last, and offered to make a bet that in a boat like that he could row six miles an hour, without exerting himself.

"Lunch is ready," said the waitress, appearing at the entrance to the boathouse. They all hurried off, but two young men were already lunching at the best place, which Madame Dufour had chosen in her mind as her seat. No doubt they were the owners of the skiffs, for they were dressed in boating costume. They were stretched out, almost lying of chairs, and were sunburned, and had on flannel trousers and thin cotton jerseys, with short sleeves, which showed their bare arms, which were strong as blacksmiths'. They were two strong young fellows, who thought a great deal of their vigor, and who showed in all their movements that elasticity and grace of limb which can only be acquired by exercise, and which is so different from the awkwardness with which the same continual work stamps the mechanic.

They exchanged a rapid smile when they saw the mother, and then a look on seeing the daughter.

"Let us give up our place," one of them said ; "it will make us acquainted with them."

The other got up immediately, and holding his black and red boating-cap in his hand, he politely offered the ladies the only shady place in the garden. With many excuses they accepted, and so that it might be more rural, they sat on the grass, without either tables or chairs.

The two young men took their plates, knives, forks, etc., to a table a little way off, and began to eat again. Their bare arms, which they showed continually, rather embarrassed the young girl, who even pretended to turn her head aside, and not to see them. But Madame Dufour, who was rather bolder, tempted by feminine curiosity, looked at them every moment, and no doubt compared them with the secret unsightliness of her husband. She had squatted herself on the ground with her legs tucked under her, after the manner of tailors, and kept wriggling about continually, under the pretext that ants were crawling about her somewhere. Monsieur Dufour, whom the politeness of the strangers had put into rather a bad temper, was trying to find a comfortable position, which he did not, however, succeed in doing, while the youth with the yellow hair was eating as silently as an ogre.

"It is lovely weather, Monsieur," the stout lady said to one of the boating-men. She wished to be friendly, because they had given up their place.

"It is, indeed, Madame," he replied ; "do you often go into the country?"

"Oh! Only once or twice a year, to get a little fresh air; and you. Monsieur?"

"I come and sleep here every night."

"Oh! That must be very nice?"

"Certainly it is, Madame." And he gave them such a practical account of his daily life, that in the hearts of these shopkeepers, who were deprived of the meadows, and who longed for country walks, it roused that innate love of nature which they all felt so strongly the whole year round, behind the counter in their shop.

The girl raised her eyes and looked at the oarsman with emotion, and Monsieur Dufour spoke for the first time.

"It is indeed a happy life," he said. And then he added: "A little more rabbit, my dear?"

"No, thank you," she replied, and turning to the young men again, and pointing to their arms, asked: "Do you never feel cold like that?"

They both laughed, and amazed the family by telling of the enormous fatigue they could endure, of bathing while in a state of tremendous perspiration, of rowing in the fog at night, and they struck their chests violently, to show how they sounded.

"Ah! You look very strong," the husband said, and he did not talk any more of the time when he used to beat the English. The girl was looking at them askance now, and the young fellow with the yellow hair, as he had swallowed some wine the wrong way, and was coughing violently, bespattered Madame Dufour's sherry-colored silk dress. Madame got angry, and sent for some water to wash the spots.

Meanwhile it had grown unbearably hot, the sparkling river looked like a blaze of fire and the fumes of the wine were getting into their heads. Monsieur Dufour, who had a violent hiccough, had unbuttoned his waistcoat and the top of his trousers, while his wife, who felt choking, was gradually unfastening her dress. The youth was shaking his yellow wig in a happy frame of mind, and kept helping himself to wine, and as the old grandmother felt drunk, she endeavored to be very stiff and dignified. As for the girl, she showed nothing except a peculiar brightness in her eyes, while the brown skin on the cheeks became more rosy.

The coffee finished them off; they spoke of singing, and each of them sang, or repeated a couplet, which the others repeated enthusiastically. Then they got up with some difficulty, and while the two women, who were rather dizzy, were getting some fresh air, the two males, who were altogether drunk, were performing gymnastic tricks. Heavy, limp, and with scarlet faces, they hung awkwardly on to the iron rings, without being able to raise themselves, while their shirts were continually threatening to part company with their trousers, and to flap in the wind like flags.

Meanwhile, the two boating-men had got their skiffs into the water. They came back, and politely asked the ladies whether they would like a row.

"Would you like one, Monsieur Dufour ?" his wife exclaimed. "Please come!"

He merely gave her a drunken look, without understanding what she said. Then one of the rowers came up, with two fishing-rods in his hand; and the hope of catching a gudgeon, that great aim of the Parisian shopkeeper, made Dufour's dull eyes gleam. He politely allowed them to do whatever they liked, while he sat in the shade, under the bridge, with his feet dangling over the river, by the side of the young man with the yellow hair, who was sleeping soundly close to him.

One of the boating-men made a martyr of himself, and took the mother.

"Let us go to the little wood on the Ile aux Anglais!" he called out, as he rowed off. The other skiff went slower, for the rower was looking at his companion so intently, that he thought of nothing else. His emotion paralyzed his strength, while the girl, who was sitting on the steerer's, seat, gave herself up to the enjoyment of being on the water. She felt disinclined to think, felt a lassitude in her limbs, a complete self-relaxation, as if she were intoxicated. She had become very flushed, and breathed pantingly. The effect of the wine, increased by the extreme heat, made all the trees on the bank seem to bow, as she passed. A vague wish for enjoyment, a fermentation of her blood seemed to pervade her whole body, and she was also a little agitated by this *téte-â-téte* on the water, in a place which seemed depopulated by the heat, with this young man, who thought her so pretty, whose looks seemed to caress her skin, and whose eyes were as penetrating and exciting as the sun's rays.

Their inability to speak increased their emotion, and they looked about them. At last he made an effort and asked her name.

"Henriette," she said.

"Why! My name is Henri," he replied. The sound of their voices calmed them, and they looked at the banks. The other skiff had gone ahead of them, and seemed to be waiting for them. The rower called out :

"We will meet you in the wood; we are going as far as Robinson's,* because Madame Dufour is thirsty." Then he bent over his oars again and rowed off so quickly that he was soon out of sight.

Meanwhile, a continual roar, which they had heard for some time, came nearer; and the river itself seemed to shiver, as if the dull noise were rising form its depths.

"What is that noise ?" she asked. It was the noise of the weir, which cut the river in two, at the island. He was explaining it to her, when above the noise of the waterfall they heard the song of a bird, which seemed a long way of.

"Listen!" he said ; "the nightingales are singing during the day, so the females must be sitting."

A nightingale! She had never heard one before, and the idea of listening to one roused visions of poetic tenderness in her heart. A nightingale! That is to say, the invisible witness of the lover's interview which Juliette invoked on her balcony *; that celestial music which is attuned to human kisses; that eternal inspirer of all those languorous romances which open idealized visions to the poor, tender, little hearts of sensitive girls!

She wanted to hear a nightingle.

"We must not make a noise," her companion said, "and then we can go into the wood, and sit down close to it."

The skiff seemed to glide. They saw the trees on the island, the banks of which were so low that they could look into the depths of the thickets. They stopped, he made the boat fast, Henriette took hold of Henri's arm, and they went beneath the trees.

"Stoop," he said, so she bent down, and they went into an inextricable thicket of creepers, leaves, and reed grass, which formed an impenetrable retreat, and which the young man laughingly called "his private room."

Just above their heads, perched in one of the trees which hid them, the bird was still singing. He uttered shakes and *roulades,* and then long vibrating sounds that filled the air and seemed to lose themselves in the distance, across the level country, through that burning silence which hung low upon the whole country round. They did not speak for fear of frightening the bird away. They were sitting close together, and slowly Henri's arm stole round the girl's waist and squeezed it gently. She took that daring hand, but without anger, and kept removing it whenever he put it round her; not, however, feeling at all embarrassed by this caress, just as if it had been somthing quite natural which she was resisting just as naturally.

She was listening to the bird in ecstasy. She felt an infinite longing for happiness, for some sudden demonstration of tenderness, for a revelation of divine poesy. She felt such a softening at her heart, and such relaxation of her nerves, that she began to cry, without knowing why. The young man was now straining her close to him, and she did not remove his arm; she did not think of it. Suddenly the nightingale stopped, and voice called out in the distance:

"Henriette!"

"Do not reply", he said in a low voice, "you will drive the bird away."

But she had no idea of doing so, and they remained in the same position for some time. Madame Dufour had sat down somewhere or other, for from time to time they heard the stout lady break out into little bursts of laughter.

The girl was still crying; she was filled with strange sensations. Henri's head was on her shoulder, and suddenly he kissed her on the lips. She was surprised and angry, and, to avoid him, she stood up.

They were both very pale when they quitted their grassy retreat. The blue sky looked dull to them, the ardent sun was clouded over to their eyes, they perceived not the solitude and the silence. They walked quickly side by side, without speaking or touching each other, appearing to be irreconcilable en emies, as if disgust had sprung up between them, and hatred between their souls. From time to time Henriette called out : "Mamma!"

By and by they heard a noise in the thicket, and Madame Dufour appeared, looking rather confused, and her companion's face was wrinkled with smiles that he could not check.

Madame Dufour took his arm, and they returned to the boats. Henri went on first, still without speaking, by the girl's side, and at last they got back to Bézons. Monsieur Dufour, who had sobered up, was waiting for them very impatiently, while the youth with the yellow hair was having a mouthful of something to eat before leaving the inn. The carriage was in the yard, with the horse in, and the grandmother, who had already got in, was frightened at the thought of being overtaken by night, before they got back to Paris, the outskirts not being safe.

The young men shook hands with them, and the Dufour family drove off.

"Good-bye, until we meet again!" the oarsmen cried, and the answers they got were a sigh and a tear.

******

Two months later, as Henri was going along the Rue des Martyrs, he saw "Dufour, Ironmonger," over a door. So he went in, and saw the stout lady sitting at the counter. They recognized each other immediately, and after an interchange of polite greetings, he inquired after them all.

"And how in Mademoiselle Henriette?" he inquired, specially.

"Very well, thank you; she is married."

"Ah! Mastering his feelings, he added: "To whom was she married?"

"To that young man who went with us, you know; he has joined us in business."

"I remember him, perfectly."

He was going out, feeling unhappy, though scarcely knowing why, when Madame called him back.

"And how is your friend ?" she asked, rather shyly.

"He is very well, thank you".

A MEETING

IT was all an accident, a pure accident. Tired of standing, Baron d'Etraille went— as all the princess's rooms were open on that particular evening—into an empty bedroom, which appeared almost dark after coming out of the brilliantly lighted drawing rooms.

He looked round for a chair in which to have a doze, as he was sure his wife would not go away before daylight: As soon as he got inside the door he saw the big bed with its azure-and-gold hangings in the middle of the great room, looking like a catafalque in which love was buried, for the princess was no longer young. Behind it a large bright spot looked like a lake seen at a distance from a window. It was a big looking glass which, discreetly covered with dark drapery very rarely let down, seemed to look at the bed, which was its accomplice. One might almost fancy that it felt regrets and that one was going to see in it charming shapes of nude women and the gentle movement of arms about to embrace them.

The baron stood still for a moment, smiling and rather moved, on the threshold of this chamber dedicated to love. But suddenly something appeared in the looking glass, as if the phantoms which he had evoked had come up before him. A man and a woman who had been sitting on a low couch hidden in the shade had risen, and the polished surface, reflecting their figures, showed that they were kissing each other before separating.

The baron recognized his wife and the Marquis de Cervigné. He turned and went away, like a man fully master of himself, and waited till it was day before taking away the baroness. But he had no longer any thoughts of sleeping.

As soon as they were alone he said:

"Madame, I saw you just now in the Princess de Raynes's room. I need say no more, for I am not fond either of reproaches, acts of violence or of ridicule. As I wish to avoid all such things, we shall separate without any scandal. Our lawyers will settle your position according to my orders. You will be free to live as you please when you are no longer under my roof, but as you will continue to bear my name, I must warn you that should any scandal arise I shall show myself inflexible.

She tried to speak, but he stopped her, bowed and left the room.

He was more astonished and sad than unhappy. He had loved her dearly during the first period of their married life, but his ardour had cooled, and now he often had a caprice, either in a theatre or in society, though he always preserved a certain liking for the baroness.

She was very young, hardly four and twenty, small, slight—too slight—and very fair. She was a true Parisian doll: clever, spoiled, elegant, coquettish, witty, with more charm than real beauty. He used to say familiarly to his brother when speaking of her:

"My wife is charming, attractive, but—there is nothing to lay hold of. She is like a glass of champagne that is all froth—

when you have got to the wine it is very good, but there is too little of it unfortunately."

He walked up and down the room in great agitation, thinking of a thousand things. At one moment he felt in a great rage and felt inclined to give the marquis a good thrashing, to horsewhip him publicly in the club. But he thought that would not do; it would not be the thing; *he* would be laughed at and not the other, and he felt that his anger proceeded more from wounded vanity than from a broken heart. So he went to bed but could not get to sleep.

A few days afterward it was known in Paris that the Baron and Baroness d'Etraille had agreed to an amicable separation on account of incompatibility of temper. Nobody suspected anything; nobody laughed, and nobody was astonished.

The baron, however, to avoid meeting her, travelled for a year; then he spent the summer at the seaside and the autumn in shooting, returning to Paris for the winter. He did not meet his wife once.

He did not even know what people said about her. At any rate, she took care to save appearances, and that was all he asked for.

He got dreadfully bored, travelled again, restored his old castle of Villebosc, which took him two years; then for over a year he received relays of friends there, till at last, tired of all these commonplace, so-called pleasures, he returned to his mansion in the Rue de Lills, just six years after their separation.

He was then forty-five, with a good crop of gray hair, rather stout and with that melancholy look of people who have been handsome, sought after, much liked and are deteriorating daily.

A month after his return to Paris he took cold on coming out of his club and had a bad cough, so his medical man ordered him to Nice for the rest of the winter.

He started by the express on Monday evening. He was late, got to the station only a very short time before the departure the train and had barely time to get into a carriage, with only one other occupant, who was sitting in a comer so wrapped in furs and cloaks that he could not even make out whether it was a man or a woman, as nothing of the figure could be seen. When he perceived that he could not find out he put on his travelling cap, rolled himself up in his rugs and stretched himself out comfortably to sleep.

He did not wake up till the day was breaking and looked immediately at his fellow traveller. He had not stirred all night and seemed still to be sound asleep.

Baron d'Etraille made use of the opportunity to brush his hair and his beard and to try and freshen himself up a little generally, for a night's travelling changes one's looks very much when one has attained a certain age.

A great poet has said:

When we are young our mornings are triumphant!

Then we wake up with a cool skin, a bright eye and glossy hair. When one grows old one wakes up in a different state. Dull eyes, red, swollen cheeks, dry lips, the hair and beard all disarranged, impart an old, fatigued, worn-out look to the face.

The baron opened his travelling dressing case, made himself as tidy as he could and then waited.

The engine whistled and the train stopped, and his neighbour moved. No doubt he was awake. They started off again, and then an oblique ray of the sun shone into the carriage, just onto the sleeper, who moved again, shook himself and then calmly showed his face.

It was a young, fair, pretty, stout woman, and the baron looked at her in amazement. He did not know what to believe. He could have sworn that it was his wife—but wonderfully changed for the better: stouter—why, she had grown as stout as he was, only it suited her much better than it did him.

She looked at him quietly, did not seem to recognize him and then slowly laid aside her wraps. She had that calm assurance of a woman who is sure of herself, the insolent audacity of a first awaking, knowing and feeling that she was in her full beauty and freshness.

The baron really lost his head. Was it his wife or somebody else who was as like her as any sister could be? As he had not seen her for six years he might be mistaken.

She yawned, and he knew her by the gesture. She turned and looked at him again, calmly, indifferently, as if she scarcely saw him, and then looked out at the country again.

He was upset and dreadfully perplexed and waited, looking at her sideways, steadfastly.

Yes; it was certainly his wife. How could he possibly have doubted? There could certainly not be two noses like that, and a thousand recollections flashed through him, slight details of her body, a beauty spot on one of her limbs and another on her back. How often he had kissed them! He felt the old feeling of the intoxication of love stealing over him, and he called to mind the sweet odour of her skin, her smile when she put her arms onto his shoulders, the soft intonations of her voice, all her graceful, coaxing ways.

But how she had changed and improved! It was she and yet not she. He thought her riper, more developed, more of a woman, more seductive, more desirable, adorably desirable.

And this strange, unknown woman, whom he had accidentally met in a railway carriage belonged to him; he had only to say to her:

"I insist upon it."

He had formerly slept in her arms, existed only in her love, and now he had found her again certainly, but so changed that he scarcely knew her. It was another and yet she at the same time. It was another who had been born, formed and grown since he had left her. It was she, indeed; she whom he had possessed but who was now altered, with a more assured smile and greater self-possession. There were two women in one, mingling a great deal of what was new and unknown with many sweet recollections of the past. There was something singular, disturbing, exciting about it—a kind of mystery of love in which there floated a delicious confusion. It was his wife in a new body and in a new flesh which his lips had never pressed.

And he remembered that in six or seven years everything changes in us; only outlines can be recognized, and sometimes even they disappear.

The blood, the hair, the skin, all change and are reconstituted, and when people have not seen each other for a long time they find when they meet another totally different being, although it be the same and bear the same name.

And the heart also can change. Ideas may be modified and renewed, so that in forty years of life we may, by gradual and constant transformations, become four or five totally new and different beings.

He dwelt on this thought till it troubled him; it had first taken possession of him when he surprised her in the princess's room. He was not the least angry; it was not the same woman that he was looking at—that thin, excitable doll of those days.

What was he to do? How should he address her? And what could he say to her? Had she recognized him?

The train stopped again. He got up, bowed and said: "Bertha, do you want anything I can bring you?"

She looked at him from head to foot and answered, without showing the slightest surprise or confusion or anger, but with the most perfect indifference

"I do not want anything—thank you."

He got out and walked up and down the platform in order to think and, as it were, to recover his senses after a fall. What should he do now? If he got into another carriage it would look as if he were running away. Should he be polite or importunate? That would look as if he were asking for forgiveness. Should he speak as if he were her master? He would look like a fool, and besides, he really had no right to do so.

He got in again and took his place.

During his absence she had hastily arranged her dress and hair and was now lying stretched out on the seat, radiant, but without showing any emotion.

He turned to her and said: "My dear Bertha, since this singular chance has brought us together after a separation of six years—a quite friendly separation are we to continue to look upon each other as irreconcilable enemies? We are shut up together, tête-à-tête, which is so much the better or so much the worse. I am not going to get into another carriage, so don't you think it is preferable to talk as friends till the end of our journey?"

She answered quite calmly again: "Just as you please." Then

he suddenly stopped, really not knowing what to say, but as he had plenty of assurance he sat down on the middle seat and said:

"Well, I see I must pay my court to you; so much the better. It is, however, really a pleasure, for you are charming. You cannot imagine how you have improved in the last six years. I do not know any woman who could give me that delightful sensation which I experienced just now when you emerged from your wraps. I should really have thought such a change impossible."

Without moving her head or looking at him she said: "I cannot say the same with regard to you; you have certainly deteriorated a great deal."

He got red and confused, and then with a smile of resignation he said:

"You are rather hard."

"Why?" was her reply. "I am only stating facts. I don't suppose you intend to offer me your love? It must, therefore, be a matter of perfect indifference to you what I think about you. But I see it is a painful subject, so let us talk of something else. What have you been doing since I last saw you?" He felt rather out of countenance and stammered:

"I have travelled, shot and grown old, as you see. And you?" She said quite calmly: "I have taken care of, appearances as you ordered me."

He was very nearly saying something brutal, but he checked himself and kissed his wife's hand.

"And I thank you," he said.

She was surprised. He was indeed strong and always master of himself. He went on: "As you have acceded to my first request, shall we now talk without any bitterness?"

She made a little movement of surprise.

"Bitterness! I don't feel any; you are a complete stranger to me. I am only trying to keep up a difficult conversation."

He was still looking at her, carried away in spite of her harshness, and he felt seized with a brutal desire, the desire of the master.

Perceiving that she had hurt his feelings, she said:

"How old are you now? I thought you were younger than you look."

He grew pale.

"I am forty-five," and then he added: "I forgot to ask after Princess de Raynes Are you still intimate with her?"

She looked at him as if she hated him:

"Yes, certainly I am. She is very well, thank you."

They remained sitting side by side, agitated and irritated. Suddenly he said:

"My dear Bertha, I have changed my mind. You are my wife, and I expect you to come with me today. You have, I think, improved both morally and physically, and I am going to take you back again. I am your husband, and it is my right to do so."

She was stupefied and looked at him, trying to divine his thoughts, but his face was resolute and impenetrable.

I am very sorry," she said, "but I have made other engagements."

"So much the worse for you," was his reply. "The law gives me the power, and I mean to use it."

They were getting to Marseilles, and the train whistled and slackened speed. The baroness got up, carefully rolled up her wraps, and then turning to her husband, she said:

"My dear Raymond, do not make a bad use of the tête-à-tête which I had carefully prepared. I wished to take precautions, according to your advice, so that I might have nothing to fear from you or from other people, whatever might happen. You are going to Nice, are you not?"

"I shall go wherever you go."

"Not at all; just listen to me, and I am sure that you will leave me in peace. In a few moments, when we get to the station, you will see the Princess de Raynes and Countess Hermit waiting for me with their husbands. I wished them to see us and to know that we spent the night together in the railway carriage. Don't be alarmed; they will tell it everywhere as a most surprising fact.

"I told you just now that I had carefully followed your advice and saved appearances. Anything else does not matter, does it? Well, in order to do so, I wished to be seen with you. You told me carefully to avoid any scandal, and I am avoiding it, for I am afraid—I am afraid—"

She waited till the train had quite stopped, and as her friends ran up to open the carriage door, she said:

"I am afraid that I am *enceinte.*"

The princess stretched out her arms to embrace her, and the baroness said, pointing to the baron, who was dumb with astonishment and trying to get at the truth:

"You do not recognize Raymond? He has certainly changed a good deal and he agreed to come with me so that 1 might not travel alone. We take little trips like this occasionally, like good friends who cannot live together. We are going to separate here; he has had enough of me already."

She put out her hand, which he took mechanically, and then she jumped out onto the platform among her friends who were waiting for her.

The baron hastily shut the carriage door, for he was too much disturbed to say a word or come to any determination. He heard his wife's voice and their merry laughter as they went away.

He never saw her again, nor did he ever discover whether she had told him a lie or was speaking the truth.

A FAMILY

I WAS going to see my friend Simon Radevin once more, for I had not seen him for fifteen years. Formerly he was my most intimate friend, and I used to spend long, quite and happy evenings with him. He was one of those men to whom one tells the most intimate affairs of the heart and in whom one finds, when quietly talking, rare, clever, ingenious and refined thoughts-thoughts which stimulate and capture the mind.

For years we had scarcely been separeted: we had lived, traveled, thought and dreamed together, had liked the same things with the same liking, admired the same books, comprehended the same works, shivered with the same sensations and very often laughed at the same individuals, whom we understood completely by merely exchanging a glance.

Then he married-quite unexpectedly married a little girl from the-provinces, who had come to Paris in search of a husband. How ever could that little, thin, insipidly fair girl, with her weak hands, her light, vacant eyes and her clear, silly voice, who was exactly like a hundred thousand marriageable dolls, have picked up that intelligent, clever young fellow? Can anyone understand these things? No doubt he had hoped for happiness, simple, quiet and long-enduring happiness, in the arms of a good, tender and faithful woman; he had seen all that in the transparent looks of that schoolgirl with light hair.

He had not dreamed of the fact than an active, living and vibrating man grows tired as soon as he had comprehended the stupid reality of a commonplace life, unless, indeed, he becomes so brutalized as to be callous to externals.

What would he be like when I met him again? Still lively, witty, lighthearted and enthusiastic, or in a state of mental torpor through provincial life? A man can change a great deal in the course of fifteen years!

The train stopped at a small station, and as I got out of the carriage a stout, a very stout man with red cheeks and a big stomach rushed up to me with open arms, exclaiming: "George!"

I embraced him, but I had not recognized him, and then I said in astonishment:

"By Jove! You have not grown thin!"

And he replied with a laugh: "What did you expect? Good living, a good table and good nights! Eating and sleeping, that is my existence!"

I looked at him closely, trying to find the features I held so dear in that broad face. His eyes alone had not altered, but I no longer saw the same look in them, and I said to myself: "If looks be the reflection of the mind, the thoughts in that head are not what they used to he-those thoughts which I knew so well."

Yet his eyes were bright, full of pleasure and friendship, but they had not that clear, intelligent expression which tells better than do words the value of the mind. Suddenly he said to me:

"Here are my two eldest children." A girl of fourteen, who was almost a woman, and a boy of thirteen, in the dress of a pupil from a lycée, came forward in a hesitating and awkward manner, and I said in a low voice: "Are they yours?"

"Of course they are," he replied, laughing.

"How many have you?"

"Five! there are three more indoors."

He said that in a proud, self-satisfied, almost triumphant manner, and I felt profound pity, mingled with a feeling of vague contempt, for this vainglorious and simple reproducer of his species who spent his nights in his country house in uxorious pleasures.

I got into a carriage, which he drove himself, and we set off through the town, a dull, sleepy, gloomy town where nothing was moving in the streets save a few dogs and two or three maidservants. Here and there a shopkeeper standing at his door took off his hat, and Simon retured the salute and told me the man's name-no doubt to show me that he knew all the inhabitants personally. The thought struck me that he was thinking of becoming an candidate for the Chamber of Deputies, that dream of all who have buried themselves in the provinces.

We were soon out of the town; the carriage turned into a garden which had some pretensions to a park and stopped in front of a turreted house which tried to pass for a choteau.

"That is my den," Simon said, so that he might be complimented on it, and I replied that it was delightful.

A lady appeared on the steps, dressed up for a visitor, her hair done for a visitor and with phrases ready prepared for a visitor. She was no longer the light-haired insipid girl I had seen in church fifteen years previously, but a stout lady in curls and flounces, one of those ladies of uncertain age, without intellect, without any of those things which constitute a woman. In short she was a mother, a stout, commonplace mother, a human layer and brood mare, a machine of flesh which procreates, without mental care save for her children and her housekeeping book.

She welcomed me, and I went into the hall where three

children, ranged according to their height, were ranked for review like firemen before a mayor. "Ah! ah! so there are the others?" said I. And Simon, who was radiant with pleasure, named them: "Jean, Sophie and Gontran."

The door of the drawing room was open. I went in, and in the depths of an easy chair I saw something trembling, a man, an old, paralyzed man. Mme Radevin came forward and said: "This is my grandfather, monsieur; he is eighty-seven." And then she shouted into the shaking old man's ears: "This is a friend of Simon's, grandpapa."

The old gentleman tried to say "Good day" to me, and he muttered: "Oua, oua, oua," and waved his hand.

I took a seat, saying: "You are very kind, monsieur."

Simon had just come in, and he said with a laugh: "So! You have made Grandpapa's acquaintance. He is priceless, is that old man. He is the delight of the children, and he is so greedy that he almost kills himself at every meal. You have no idea what he would eat if he were allowed to do as he pleased. But you will see, you will see. He looks all the sweets over is if they were so many girls. You have never seen anything funnier; you will see it presently."

I was then shown to my room to change my dress for dinner, and hearing a great clatter behind me on the stairs, I turned round and saw that all the children were following me behind their father- to do me honor, no doubt.

My windows looked out onto a plain, a bare, interminable plain, an ocean of grass, of wheat and of oats without a clump of trees or any rising ground, a striking and melancholy picture of the life which they must be leading in that house.

A bell rang; it was for dinner, and so I went downstairs. Mme Radevin took my arm in a ceremonious manner, and we went into the dining room. A footman wheeled in the old man's armchair, who gave a greedy and curious look at the dessert as with difficulty he turned his shaking head from one dish to the other.

Simon rubbed his hands, saying: "You will be amused." All the children understood that I was going to be indulged with the sight of their greedy grandfather and they began to laugh accordingly, while their mother merely smiled and shrugged her shoulders. Simon, making a speaking trumpet of his hands, shouted at the old man: "This evening there is sweet rice cream," and the wrinkled face of the grandfather brightened; he trembled violently all over, showing that he had understood and was very pleased. The dinner began.

"Just look!" Simon whispered. The grandfather did not like the soup and refused to eat it, but he was made to, on account of his health. The foot man forced the spoon into his mouth, while the old man blew energetically, so as not to swallow the soup, which their father, who was also amused, said: "Isn't the old man funny?"

During the whole meal they were all taken up solely with him. With his eyes he devoured the dishes which were put on the table and with trembling hands tried to seize them and pull them to him. They put them almost within his reach to see his useless efforts, his trembling clutches at them, the piteous appeal of his whole nature, of his eyes, of his mouth and of his nose as he smelled them. He slobbered onto his table napkin with eagerness while uttering inarticulate grunts, and the whole family was highly amused at this horrible and grotesque scene.

Then they put a tiny morsel onto his plate, which he ate with feverish gluttony in order to get something more as soon as possible. When the rice cream was brought in he nearly had a fit and groaned with greediness. Gontran called out to him: "You have eaten too much already; you will have no more." And they pretended not to give him any. Then he began to cry- cry and tremble more violently than ever, while all the children laughed. At lalst, however, they gave him his helping, a very small piece. As he ate the first mouthful of the pudding he made a comical and greedy noise in his throat and a movement with his neck like ducks do when they swallow too large a morsel, and then, when he had done, he began to stamp his feet so as to get more.

I was seized with pity for this pitiable and ridiculous Tantalus and interposed on his behalf. "Please, will you not give him a little more rice?"

But Simon replied: "Oh no, my dear fellow; if he were to eat too much, it might harm him at his age."

I held my tongue and thought over these words. Oh, ethics! Oh, logic! Oh, wisdom! At his age! So they deprived him of his only remaining pleasure out of regard for his health! His health! What would he do with it, inert and trembling wreck that he was? They were taking care of his life, so they said. His life? How many days? Ten, twenty, fifty or a hundred? Why? For his own sake? Or to preserve, for some time longer, the spectacle of his impotent greediness in the family?

There was nothing left for him to do in this life, nothing whatever. He had one single wish left, one sole pleasure; why not grant him that last solace constantly, until he died?

After playing cards for a long time I went up to my room and to bed; I was low-spirited and sad, sad! I sat at my window, but I heard nothing but the beautiful warbling of a bird in a tree, somewhere in the distance. No doubt the bird was singing thus in a low voice during the night to lull his mate, who was sleeping on her eggs.

And I thought of my poor friend's five children and to myself pictured him snoring hy the side of his ugly wife.

UGLY

CERTAINLY at this blessed epoch of the equalilty of mediocrity, of rectangular abomination, as Edgar Allan Poe says—at this delightful period when everybody dreams of resembling everybody else, so that it has become impossible to tell the president of the Republic from a waiter—in these days which are the forerunners of that promising, blissful day when everything in this world will be of a dull, neutral uniformity, certainly at such an epoch one has the right, or rather it is one's duty, to be ugly.

Lebeau, however, assuredly exercised that right with the most cruel vigor. He fulfilled that duty with the fiercest heroism, and to make matters worse the mysterious irony of fate had caused him to be born with the name of Lebeau, while an ingenious godfather, the unconscious accomplice of the pranks of destiny, had given him the Christian name of Antinous.

Even among our contemporaries, who were already on the highroad to the coming ideal of universal hideousness, Antinous Lebeau was remarkable for his ugliness; and one might have said that he positively threw zeal, too much zeal, into the matter, though he was not hideous like Mirabeau, who made people exclaim, "Oh! the beautiful monster!"

Alas! No. He was without any beauty of ugliness. He was ugly, that was all, nothing more nor less; in short, he was uglily ugly. He was not humpbacked nor knock-kneed nor potbellied; his legs were not like a pair of tongs, and his arms were neither too long nor too short, and yet there was an utter lack of uniformity about him, not only in painters' eyes but also in everybody's, for nobody could meet him in the street without turning to look after him and thinking: "Good heavens! what an object.

His hair was of no particular color, a light chestnut mixed with yellow. There was not much of it; still he was not absolutely bald but just bald enough to allow his butter-colored pate to show. Butter-colored? Hardly! The color of margarine would be more applicable, and such pale margarine!

His face was also like margarine, but of adulterated margarine, certainly. His cranium, the color of unadulterated margarine, looked almost like butter in comparison.

There was very little to say about his mouth! Less than little; the sum total was—nothing. It was a chimerical mouth.

But take it that I have said nothing about him, and let us replace this vain description by the useful formula: "Impossible to describe." But you must not forget that Antinous Lebeau was ugly, that the fact impressed everybody as soon as they saw him and that nobody remembered ever having seen an uglier person; and let us add, as the climax of his misfortune, that he thought so himself.

From this you will see that he was not a fool and not ill-natured either, but of course he was unhappy. An unhappy man thinks only of his wretchedness, and people take his nightcap for a fool's cap; while, on the other hand, goodness is only esteemed when it it cheerful. Consequently Antinous Lebeau passed for a fool and an ill-tempered fool; he was not even pitied because he was so ugly.

He had only one pleasure in life, and that was to go and roam about the darkest streets on dark nights and to hear the streetwalkers say:

"Come home with me, you handsome dark man!

It was, alas! a furtive pleasure, and he knew that it was not true. For occasionally, when the woman was old or drunk and he profited by the invitation, as soon as the candle was lighted in the garret they no longer murmured the fallacious "handsome dark man." When they saw him the old women grew still older and the drunken women got sober. And more than one, although hardened against disgust and ready for all risks, said to him, in spite of liberal payment:

"My little man. I must say you are most confoundedly ugly".

At last, however, he renounced even that lamentable pleasure when he heard the still more lamentable words which a wretched woman could not help uttering when he went home with her:

"Well, I must have been very hungry!"

Alas! It was he who was hungry, unhappy man; hungry for something that should resemble love, were it ever so little; he longed not to live like a pariah any more, not to be exiled and proscribed by his ugliness. And the ugliest, the most repugnant woman would have appeared beautiful to him if she would only not think him ugly or, at any rate, not tell him so and not let him see that she felt horror at him on that account.

The consequence was that when he one day met a poor blear-eyed creature, with her face covered with scabs and bearing evident signs of alcoholism, with a driveling mouth and ragged and filthy petticoats, to whom he gave liberal alms for which she kissed his hand, he took her home with him, had her cleansed, dressed and taken care of, made her his servant and then his house-keeper. Next he raised her to the rank of his mistress, and finally, of course, he married her.

She was almost as ugly as he was! Almost, but certainly not quite; for she was hideous, and her hideousness had its charm and its beauty, no doubt; that something by which a woman can attract a man. And she had proved that by deceiving him, and she let him see it better still by seducing another man.

That other man was actually uglier than he was.

He was certainly uglier, a collection of every physical and moral ugliness, a companion of beggars whom she had picked up among her former vagrant associates, a jailbird, a dealer in little girls, a vagabond covered with filth, with legs like a toad's, with a mouth like a lamprey's and a death's head in which the nose had been replaced by two holes.

"And you have wronged me with a wretch like that," the poor cuckold said. "And in my own house! And in such a manner that I might catch you in the very act! And why, why, you wretch? Why, seeing that he is uglier than I am?"

"Oh no!" she exclaimed. "You may say what you like, that I am a dirty slut and a strumpet, but do not say that he is uglier than you are."

And the unhappy man stood there, vanquished and overcome by her last words, which she uttered without understanding all the horror which he would feel at them.

"Because, you see, he has his own particular ugliness, while you are merely ugly like everybody else is."

VIRTUE

EVERY FRIDAY, regularly, about eleven o'clock in the morning, he came into the courtyard, put down his soft hat at his feet, struck a few chords on his guitar and began a ballad in a full, rich voice. And soon at every window in the four sides of that dull, barracklike building appeared some girls, one in an elegant dressing gown, another in a little jacket, most of them with their bosoms and arms bare, all of them just out of bed with their hair hastily twisted up, their eyes blinking in the sudden blaze of sunlight, their complexions dull and their eyes still heavy with sleep.

They swayed in time to his slow melody and gave

themselves up to the enjoyment of it. Pennies and even silver poured into the handsome singer's hat, and more than one of them would have liked to follow the penny which she threw to him and go with this singer who had the voice of a siren. For he seemed to say to all these amorous girls: "Come, come to my retreat, for there you will find a place of crystal and gold, wreaths which are always fresh and happiness and love which never die."

That was what they seemed to hear, these unhappy girls, when they heard him sing the old legends which in childhood they had believed. That was what they understood by the simple words of the ballad—that and noting else. How could anyone doubt it, seeing the fresh roses on their cheeks and the tender lights which flickered like mystic fires in their eyes, now for the moment once more the eyes of innocent young girls? But, alas, of young girls who had grown up too quickly, who were too precocious and who had too soon become what they were, poor vendors of love, always in search of that love for which they were paid.

That was why when he had finished his second ballad, and sometimes sooner, concupiscent looks appeared in their eyes. The boatman of their dreams, the water sprite of the fairy tales, vanished in the midst of childish recollections, and the singer reassumed his real shape, that of a wandering minstrel and strolling player whom they wished to requite with love. And the coppers and small silver were showered on him again, with engaging smiles, with the leers of amorous women, even with a *"Pst, Pst,"* which soon transformed the barrack like courtyard into an enormous cageful of twittering birds. Several of them could not restrain themselves but ejaculated, their eyes filled with desire: "How handsome—good heavens, *how* handsome he is!"

He was really handsome—nobody could deny it—even too handsome, with that regular beauty which almost palls on you. He had large, gentle, almond-shaped eyes, a Grecian nose, a bow-shaped mouth, hidden by a heavy mustache, and long, black curly hair; in short, a head fit to be put into a hairdresser's window or, better still, perhaps, onto the front page of the ballads he was singing. What made him still handsomer was that his self-conceit wore a clock of sovereign indifference, for not only was he blind to the ogling and deaf to the *"Pst, Pst,"* but when he had finished he shrugged his shoulders, winked mischievously and curled his lips contemptuously, as if to say: "The stove is not being heated for you, my little kittens!"

You would have thought that he wished to show his contempt, make himself commonplace in the eyes of these amorous girls and to dampen their ardor, for he cleared his throat ostentatiously and offensively, far more than was necessary, after singing, as if he would have liked to spit at them. But even this did not make him unpoetical in their eyes, and most of them, absolutely mad over him, went so far as to say that he did it "like a swell!"

The girl who in her enthusiasm has been the first to utter an exclamation of intense passion, after tossing him small silver, had thrown him a twenty-franc gold piece and made up her mind to have an answer. This morning, instead of a *"Pst, Pst,"* she spoke out boldly despite the presence and silence of the others.

At first they were dumfounded at her audacity, and then all their cheeks flushed with jealousy, and the flame of desire shot from their eyes. Then from every window there came a perfect torrent of:

"Yes, come up, come up." "Don't go there! Come here." Meanwhile there was a shower of halfpence, of francs, of gold coins, of cigars and oranges, while lace pocket handkerchiefs, silk neckties and scarfs fluttered in the air and fell round the singer like a flight of many-colored butterflies.

The minstrel picked up the spoils calmly, almost carelessly, stuffed the money into his pocket, made a bundle of the furbelows, which he tied up as if they has been soiled linen, and then, rising up, he put his felt hat on his head and said:

"Thank you, ladies, but indeed I cannot."

They thought that he was embarrassed by so many simultaneous demands, and one of them said: "Let him choose."

"Yes, yes, that is it!" they exclaimed in unison.

But he repeated: "I tell you I cannot."

They put his refusal down to his gallantry, and several of them exclaimed, almost with tears of emotion: "He is all heart!"

And the same voice that had spoken before (it was the one who wished to settle the matter amicably) said: "We must draw lots."

"Yes, yes, we will," they all cried. And again there was a deeper silence than before, for it was caused by anxiety, their hearts beating almost audibly.

The singer profited by it to say slowly: "I cannot allow that either; I neither desire all of you at once nor one after the other—at any time! I tell you once for all."

"Why? Why?" Now they were almost screaming, angry and sorry at the same time. Their cheeks had turned from scarlet to livid; their eyes flashed fire, and some shook their fists menacingly.

"Silence!" cried the girl who had spoken first. "Be quiet, you pack of hussies! Let him explain himself and tell us why!"

"Yes, yes, be quiet! Make him explain himself, in God's name!"

Then in the expectant silence that ensued the singer said, opening his arms wide with a gesture of despairing inability to do what they wanted:

"Why do you want me? It is very flattering, but I cannot gratify you, for I have two girls of my own at home".

THE INN

LIKE all the little wooden inns in the higher Alps, tiny *auberges* situated in the bare and rocky gorges which intersect the white summits of the mountains, the inn of Schwarenbach is a refuge for travelers who are crossing the Gemmi.

It is open six months in the year and is inhabited by the family of Jean Hauser. As soon as the snow begins to fall and fills the valley so as to make the road down to Loeche impassable, the father, with mother, daughter and the three sons, depart, leaving the house in charge of the old guide, Gaspard Hari, with the young guide, Ulrich Kunsi, and Sam the great mountain dog.

The two men and the dog remain till spring in their snowy prison, with nothing before their eyes except immense, white slopes of the Balmhorn, surrounded by light, glistening summits and shut up, blocked up and buried by the snow which rises around them, enveloping and almost burying the little house up to the eaves.

It was the day on which the Hauser family were going to return to Loeche, as winter was approaching and the descent was becoming dangerous. Three mules started first, laden with baggage and led by the three sons. Then the mother, Jeanne Hauser, and her daughter Louise mounted a fourth mule and set off in their turn. The father follwed them, accompanied by the two men in charge, who were to escort the family as far as the brow of the descent. First of all they skirted the small lake, now frozen over, at the foot of the mass of rocks which stretched in front of the inn; then they followed the valley which was dominated on all sides by snow-covered peaks.

A ray of sunlight glinted into that little white, glistening, frozen desert, illuminating it with a cold and dazzling flame. No living thing appeared among this ocean of hills; there was no stir in that immeasurable solitude, no noise disturbed the profound silence.

By degrees the young guide, Ulrich Kunsi, a tall, long-legged Swiss, left Daddy Hauser and old Gaspard benind in order to catch up with the mule which carried the two women. The younger one looked at him as he approached, as if she would call him with her sad eyes. She was a young, lighthaired peasant girl, whose milk-white cheeks and pale hair seemed to have lost their color by long dwelling amid the ice. When Ulrich had caught up with the animal which carried the women he put his hand on the crupper and relaxed his speed. Mother Hauser began to talk to him and enumerated with minutest detail all that he would have to attend to during the winter. It was the first winter he would spend up there, while old Hari had already spent fourteen winters amid the snow at the inn of Schwarenbach.

Ulrich Kunsi listened without appearing to understand and looked incessantly at the girl. From time to time he replied: "Yes, Madame Hauser," but his thoughts seemed far away, and his calm features remained unmoved.

They reached Lake Daube, whose broad, frozen surface reached to the bottom of the valley. On the right the Daubenhorn showed its black mass, rising up in a peak above the enormous moraines of the Lommëon glacier which soared above the Wildstrubel. As they approached the neck of the Gemmi, where the descent to Loëche begins, the immense horizon of the Alps of the Valais. from which the broad, deep valley of the Rhone separated them, came in view.

In the distance there was a group of white, unequal, flat or pointed mountain summits which glistened in the sun: the Mischabel with its twin peaks, the huge group of the Weisshorn, the heavy Brunegghorn, the lofty and formidable pyramid of Mont Cervin, slayer of men, and the Dent Blanche, that terrible conquette.

Then beneath them, as at the bottom of a terrible abyss, they saw Loeche, its houses looking like grains of sand which had been thrown into that enormous crevice which finishes and closes the Gemmi and which opens down below on to the Rhone.

The mule stopped at the edge of the path which turns and twists continually, zigzaging fantastically and strangely along the steep side of the mountain as far as the almost invisible little village at its feet. The women jumped into the snow and the two old men joined them.

"Well," Father Hauser said, "good-by and keep up your spirits till next year, my friends," and old Hari replied: "Till next year."

They embraced each other, and then Mme Hauser in her turn offered her cheek, and the girl did the same. When Ulrich Kunsi's turn came he whispered in Louise's ear:

"Do not forget those up yonder," and she replied: "No," in such a low voice that he guessed what she had said without hearing it.

"Well, adieu," Jean Hauser repeated, "and don't fall in." Then, going before the two women he commenced the descent, and soon all three disappeared at the first turn in the road, while the two men returned to the inn at Schwarenbach.

They walked solwly side by side without speaking. The parting was over, and they would be alone together for four or five months. Then Gaspard Hari began to relate his life last winter. He had remained with Michael Canol, who was too old now to stand it, for an accident might happen during that long solitude. They had not been dull, however; the only thing was to be resigned to it from the first, and in the end one would find plenty of distraction, games and other means of whiling away the time.

Ulrich Kunsi listened to him with his eyes on the ground, for in thought he was with those who were descending to the village. They soon came in sight of the inn which was scarcely visible, so small did it look, a mere black speck at the foot of that enormous billow of snow. When they opened the door Sam, the great curly dog, began to romp round them.

"Come, my boy," old Gaspard said, "we have no women now, so we must get our own dinner ready. Go and peel the potatoes." And they both sat down on wooden stools and began to put the bread into the soup.

The next morning seemed very long to Kunsi. Old Hari smoked and smoked beside the hearth, while the young man looked out of the window at the snowcovered mountain opposite the house. In the afternoon he went out and, going over the previous day's ground again, he looked for the traces of the mule that had carried the two women; then when he had reached the neck of the Gemmi he laid himself down of his stomach and looked at Loëche.

The village, in its rocky pit, was not yet buried under the snow, although the white masses came quite close to it, balked, however, of their prey by the pine woods which protected the hamlet. From his vantage point the low houses looked like paving stones in a large meadow. Hauser's little daughter was three now in one of those gray-colored houses. In which? Ulrich Kunsi was too far away to be able to make them out separately. How he would have liked to go down while he was yet able!

But the sun had disappeared behind the lofty crest of the Wildstrubel, and the young man returned to the chalet. Daddy Hari was smoking and, when he saw his mate come in, proposed a game of cards to him. They sat down opposite each other for a long time and played the simple game called brisque; then they had supper and went to bed.

The following days were like the first, bright and cold,

without any more snow. Old Gaspard spent his afternoons in watching the eagles and other rare birds which ventured on to those frozen heights, while Ulrich journeyed regularly to the neck of the Gemmi to look at the village. In the evening they played at cards, dice or dominoes and lost and won trilling sums, just to create an interest in the game.

One morning Hari, who was up first, called his compainon. A moving cloud of white spray, deep and light, was falling on them noiselessly and burying them by degrees under a dark, thick coverlet of foam. This lasted four days and four nights. It was necessary to free the door and the windows, to dig out a passage and to cut steps to get over this frozen powder which a twelve-hour frost had made as hard as the granite of the moraines.

They lived like prisoners, not venturing outside their abode. They had divided their duties nad performed them regularly. Ulrich Kunsi undertook the scouring, washing and everything that belonged to cleanliness. He also chopped up the wood, while Gaspard Hari did the cooking and attended to the fire. Their regular and monotonous work was relieved by long games at cards or dice, but they never quarreled and were always calm and placid. They were never even impatient or ill humored, nor did they ever use hard words for they had laid in a stock of patience for this wintering on the top of the mountain.

Sometimes old Gaspard took his rifle and went after chamois and occasionally killed one. Then there was a feast in the inn at Schwarenbach, and they reveled in fresh meat. One morning he went out as usual. The thermometer outside marked eighteen degrees of frost, and as the sun had not yet risen, the. hunter hoped to surprise the animals at the aproaches to the Wildstrubel. Ulrich, being alone, remained in bed until ten o'clock. He was of a sleepy nature but would not have dared to give way like that to his inclination in the presence of the old guide, who was ever an early riser. He breakfasted leisurely with Sam, who also spent his days and nights in sleeping in front of the fire; then he felt low-spirited and even frightened at the solitude and was seized by a longing for his daily game of cards, as one is by the domination of an invincible habit. So he went out to meet his companion who was to return at four o'clock.

The snow had leveled the whole deep valley, filled up the crevasses, obliterated all signs of the two lakes and covered the rocks, so that between the high summits there was nothing but an immense white, regular, dazzling and frozen surface. For three weeks Ulrich had not been to the edge of the precipice from which he had looked down onto the village, and he wanted to go there before climbing the slopes which led to the Wildstrubel. Loëche was now covered by the snow, and the houses could scarcely be distinguished, hidden as they were by that white cloak.

Turning to the right, Ulrich reached the Lommëon glacier. He strode along with a mountaineer's long swinging pace, striking the snow, which was as hard as a rock, with his iron-shod stick and with piercing eyes looking for the little black, moving speak in the distance on that enormous white expanse.

When he reached the end of the glacier he stopped, and asked himself whether the old man had taken that road, and then he began to walk along the moraines with rapid and uneasy steps. The day was declining; the snow was assuming a rosy tint, and a dry, frozen wind blew in rough gusts over its crystal surface. Ulrich uttered a long, shrill, vibrating call. His voice sped through the deathlike silence in which the mountains were sleeping; it reached into the distance over the profound and motionless waves of glacial foam, like the cry of a bird over the waves of the sea; then it died away, and nothing answered him.

He started off again. The sun had sunk behind the mountaintops which still were purpled with the reflection from the heavens, but the depths of the valley were becoming gray, and suddenly the young man felt frightened. It seemed to him as if the silence, the cold, the solitude, the wintry death of these mountains. were taking possession of him, were stopping and freezing his blood, making his limbs grow stiff and turning him into a motionless and frozen object, and he began to run rapidly toward the dwelling. The old man, he thought, would have returned during his absence. He had probably taken another road and would, no doubt, be sitting before the fire with a dead chamois at his feet.

He soon came in sight of the inn, but no smoke rose from it. Ulrich ran faster. Opening the door, he met Sam who ran up to him to greet him, but Gaspard Hari had not returned. Kunsi, in his alarm, turned round suddenly, as if he had expected to find his comrade hidden in a corner. Then he relighted the fire and made the soup, hoping every moment to see the old man come in. From time to time he went out to see if Gaspard were not in sight. It was night now, that wan night of the mountain, a livid night, with the crescent moon, yellow and dim, Just disappearing behind the mountaintops and shining faintly on the edge of the horizon.

Then the young man went in and sat down to warm his hands and feet, while he pictured to himself every possible sort of accident. Gaspard might have broken a leg, have fallen into a crevasse, have taken a false step and dislocated his ankle. Perhaps he was lying on the snow, overcome and stiff with the cold. in agony of mind, lost and perhaps shouting for help, calling with all his might in the silence of the night.

But where? The mountain was so vast, so rugged so dangerous in places. especially at that time of the year, that it would have required ten or twenty guides walking for a week in all directions to find a man in that immense space Ulrich Kunsi, however, made up his mind to set out with Sam if Gaspard did not return by one in the morning, and he made his preparations.

He put provisions for two days into a bag, took his steel climbing irons, tied a long. thin, strong rope round his waist and looked to see that his ironshod stick and his ax, which served to cut steps in the ice, were in order. Then he waited. The fire was burning on the hearth; the great dog was snoring in front of it, and the clock was ticking in its case of resounding wood, as regularly as a heart beating.

He waited, his ears on the alert for distant sounds, and shivered when the wind blew against the roof and the walls. It struck twelve, and he trembled. Then as he felt frightened and shivery, he put some water on the fire so that he might have hot coffee before starting. When the clock struck one he got up. woke Sam. opened the door and went off in the direction of the Wildstrubel. For five hours he ascended, scaling the rocks by means of his climbing irons, cutting into the ice, advancing continually and occasionally hauling up the dog, who remained below at the foot of some slope that was too steep for him, by means of the rope. About six o'clock he reached one of the summits to which old Gaspard often came after chamois, and he waited till it should be daylight.

The sky was growing pale overhead, and suddenly a strange light, springing. nobody could tell whence, suddenly illuminated the immense ocean of pale mountain peaks which stretched for many leagues around him. It seemed as if this vague brightness arose from the snow itself in order to spread itself into space. By degrees the highest and most(distant summits assumed a delicate. fleshlike rose color, and the red sun appeared behind the ponderous giants of the Bernese Alps.

Ulrich Kunsi set off again, walking like a hunter, stooping and looking for any traces and saying to his dog: "Seek old fellow seek!"

He was descending the mountain now, scanning the depths closely and from time to time shouting, uttering a loud, prolonged, familiar cry which soon died away in that silent vastness. Then he put his ear to the ground to listen. He thought he could distinguish a voice, and so he began to run and shout again But he heard nothing more and sat down, worn out and in despair. Toward midday he breakfasted and gave Sam, who was as tired as himself, something to eat also; then he recommenced his search.

When evening came he was still walking having traveled more than thirty miles over the mountains. As he was too far away to return home and too tired to drag himself along any farther, he dug a hole in the snow and crouched in it with his dog under a blanket which he had brought with him. The man and the dog lay side by side. warming themselves one against the other, but frozen to the marrow nevertheless. Ulrich scarcely slept, his mind haunted by visions and his limbs shaking with cold.

Day was breaking when he got up. His legs were as stiff as iron bars, and his spirits so low that he almost fell with excitement whenever he thought he heard a noise.

Suddenly he imagined that he also was going to die of cold in the midst of this vast solitude. The terror of such a death roused his energies and gave him renewed vigor. He was descending toward the inn, falling down and getting up again, and followed at a distance by Sam. who was limping on three legs. They did not reach Schwarenbach until four o'clock in the afternoon. The house was empty and the young man made a fire, had something to eat and went to sleep, so worn out that he did not think of anything more.

He slept for a long time, for a very long time, the unconquerable sleep of exhaustion. But suddenly a voice, a cry, a name: "Ulrich," aroused him from his profound slumber and made him sit up in bed. Had he been dreaming? Was it one of those strange appeals which cross the dreams of disquieted minds? No, he heard it still, that reverberating cry which had entered at his ears and remained in his brain, thrilling him to the tips of his sinewy fingers. Certainly somebody had cried out and called: "Ulrich!" There was somebody there near the house, there could be no doubt of that. and he opened the door and shouted: "Is it you, Gaspard?" with all the strength of his lungs. But there was no reply, no murmur. no groan, nothing. It was quite dark, and the snow looked wan.

The wind had risen that icy wind which cracks the rocks and leaves nothing alive on those deserted heights. It came in sudden gusts, more parching and more deadly than the burning wind of the desert and again Ulrich shouted:

"Gaspard! Gaspard! Gaspard!" Then he waited again. Everything was silent on the mountain! Then he shook with terror, and with a bound he was inside the inn. He shut and bolted the door and then fell into a chair, trembling all over, for he felt certain that his comrade had called him at the moment of dissolution.

He was certain of that, as certain as one is of conscious life or of taste when eating. Old Gaspard Hari had been dying for two days and three nights somewhere, in some hole in one of those deep, untrodden ravines whose whiteness is more sinister than subterranean darkness. He had been dying for two days and three nights and he had just then died, thinking of his comrade. His soul, almost before it was released, had taken its flight to the inn where Ulrich was sleeping, and it had called him by that terrible and mysterious power which the spirits of the dead possess. That voiceless soul had cried to the worn-out soul of the sleeper; it had uttered its last farewell, or its reproach, or its curse on the man who had not searched carefully enough.

And Ulrich felt that it was there, quite close to him, behind the wall, behind the door which he had just fastened. It was wandering about like a night bird which skims a lighted window with his wings, and the terrified young man was ready to scream with horror. He wanted to run away but did not dare go out; he did not dare and would never dare in the future, for that phantom would remain there day and night round the inn, as long as the old man's body was not recovered and deposited in the consecrated earth of a churchyard.

Daylight came, and Kunsi recovered some of his courage with the return of the bright sun. He prepared his meal, gave his dog some food and then remained motionless on a chair tortured at heart as he thought of the old man lying on the snow. Then as soon as night once more covered the mountains, new terrors assailed him. He now walked up and down the dark kitchen which was scarcely lighted by the flame of one candle. He walked from one end of it to the other with great strides, listening, listening to hear the terrible cry of the preceding night again break the dreary silence outside. He felt himself a lone, unhappy man, as no man had ever been alone before! Alone in this immense desert of snow, alone five thousand feet above the inhabited earth, above human habitations above that stirring, noisy, palpitating life, alone under an icy sky! A mad longing impelled him to run away, no matter where, to get down to Loëche by flinging himself over the precipice, but he did not even dare to open the door, as he felt sure that the other, the *dead,* man would bar his road, so that he might not be obliged to remain up there alone.

Toward midnight, tired with walking, worn out by grief and fear, he fell into a doze in his chair, for he was afraid of his bed, as one is of a haunted spot. But suddenly the strident cry of the preceding evening pierced his ears, so shrill that Ulrich stretched out his arms to repulse the ghost, and he fell onto his back with his chair.

Sam. who was awakened by the noise began to howl as frightened dogs do and trotted all about the house, trying to find out where the danger came from. When he got to the door he sniffed beneath it, smelling vigorously, with his coat bristling and his tail stiff while he growled angrily. Kunsi, who was terrified, jumped up and, holding his chair by one leg, cried: "Don't come in; don't come in, or I shall kill you." And the dog, excited by this threat, barked angrily at that invisible enemy who defied his master's voice. By degrees, however, he quieted down, came back and stretched himself in front of the fire. But he was uneasy and kept his head up and growled between his teeth.

Ulrich, in turn, recovered his senses, but as he felt faint with terror, he went and got a bottle of brandy out of the sideboard and drank off several glasses, one after another, at a gulp. His ideas became vague, his courage revived, and a feverish glow ran through his veins.

He ate scarcely anything the next day and limited himself to alcohol; so he lived for several days, like a drunken brute. As soon as he thought of Gaspard Hari he began to drink again and went on drinking until he fell onto the floor, overcome by intoxication. And there he remained on his face, dead drunk, his limbs benumbed, and snoring with his face to the ground. But scarcely had he digested the maddening and burning liquor than the same cry, "Ulrich," woke him like a bullet piercing his brain, and he got up, still staggering, stretching out his hands to save himself from falling and calling to Sam to help him. And the dog, who appeared to be going mad like his master, rushed to the door, scratched it with his claws and gnawed it with his long white teeth, while the young man, his neck thrown back and his head in the air, drank the brandy in gulps, as if it were cold water, so that it might by and by send his thoughts, his frantic terror and his memory to sleep again.

In three weeks he had consumed all his stock of ardent spirits. But his continual drunkenness only lulled his terror, which awoke more furiously than ever as soon as it was impossible for him to calm it by drinking. His fixed idea which had been intensified by a month of drunkenness and which was continually increasing in his absolute solitude penetrated him like a gimlet. He now walked about his house like a wild beast in its cage, putting his ear to the door to listen if the other were there and defying him through the wall. Then as soon as he dozed, overcome by fatigue, he heard the voice which made him leap to his feet.

At last one night, as cowards do when driven to extremity, he sprang to the door and opened it to see who was calling him and to force him to keep quiet. But such a gust of cold wind blew into his face that it chilled him to the bone. He closed and bolted the door again immediately without noticing that Sam had rushed out. Then as he was shivering with cold, he threw some wood on the fire and sat down in front of it to warm himself. But suddenly he started, for somebody was scratching at the wall and crying. In desperation he called out: "Go away!" but was answered by another long, sorrowful wail.

Then all his remaining senses forsook him from sheer fright. He repeated:

"Go away!" and turned round to find some comer in which to hide, while the other person went round the house still crying and rubbing against the wall. Ulrich went to the oak sidedboard which was full of plates and dishes and of provisions and, lifting it up with superhuman strength, he dragged it to the door so as to form a barricade. Then piling up all the rest of the furniture, the mattresses, paillasses, and chairs, he stopped up the windows as men do when assailed by an enemy.

But the person outside now uttered long, plaintive, mournful groans, to which the young man replied by similar groans, and thus days and nights passed without their ceasing to howl at each other. The one was continually walking round the house and scraped the walls with his nails so vigorously that it seemed as if he wished to destroy them, while the other, inside, followed all his movements, stooping down and holding his ear to the walls and replying to all his appeals with terrible cries. One evening, however, Ulrich heard nothing more, and he sat down, so overcome by fatigue that he went to sleep immediately and awoke in the morning without a thought, without any recollection of what had happened, just as if his head had been emptied during his heavy sleep. But he felt hungry, and he ate.

The winter was over, and the Gemmi pass was practicable again, so the Hauser family started off to return to their inn. As soon as they had reached the top of the ascent the women mounted their mule and spoke about the two men whom they would meet again shortly. They were, indeed, rather surprised that neither of them had come down a few days before, as soon as the road became passable, in order to tell them all about their long winter sojourn. At last, however, they saw the inn, still covered with snow, like a quilt. The door and the windows were closed, but a little smoke was coming out of the chimney, which reassured old Hauser; on going up to the door, however, he saw the skeleton of an animal which had been torn to pieces by the eagles, a large skeleton lying on its side.

They all looked closely at it, and the mother said: "That must be Sam." Then she shouted: "Hi! Gaspard!" A cry from the interior of the house answered her, so sharp a cry that one might have thought some animal uttered it. Old Hauser repeated: "Hi! Gaspard!" and they heard another cry, similar to the first.

Then the three men, the father and the two sons, tried to open the door, but it resisted their efforts. From the empty cow stall they took a beam to serve as a bittering-ram and hurled it against the door with all their might. The wood gave way, and the boards flew into splinters; then the house was shaken by a loud voice, and inside, behind the sideboard which was overturned, they saw a man standing upright, his hair falling onto his shoulders and a beard descending to his breast, with shining eyes and nothing but rags to cover him. They did not recognize him, but Louise Hauser exclaimed: "It is Ulrich, Mother." And her mother declared that it was Ulrich, although his hair was white.

He allowed them to go up to him and to touch him, but he did not reply to any of their questions, and they were obliged to take him to Loéche, where the doctors found that he was mad. Nobody ever knew what had become of his companion.

Little Louise Hauser nearly died that summer of decline, which the medical men attributed to the cold air of the mountains.

THE THIEF

"CERTAINLY," exclaimed Dr Sorbier, who, while appearing to be thinking of something else, had been listening quietly to those surprising accounts of burglaries and of daring acts which might have been borrowed from the trial of Cartouche. "Certainly I do not know any viler fault or any meaner action than to attack a girl's innocence, to corrupt her, to profit by a moment of unconscious weakness and of madness, when her heart is beating like that a frightened fawn, when her body, which has been unpolluted up till then, is palpitating with desire and her pure lips seek those of her seducer—when her whole being is feverish and vanquished and she abandons herself without thinking of the irremediable strain, or of her fall or of the painful awakening on the morrow.

"The man who has brought this about slowly, viciously, and none can tell with what science of evil, and who, in such a case, has not steadiness and self restraint enough to quench that flame by some icy words, who has not sense enough for two, who cannot recover his self-possession and master the runaway brute within him, who loses his head on the edge of the precipice over which the girl is going to fall, is as contemptible as any man who breaks open a lock, or as any rascal on the lookout for a house left defenceless and without protection, or as any adventurer looking for some easy and profitable stroke of business or as that thief whose various exploits you have just related to us.

"I, for my part, utterly refuse to absolve him even when extenuating circumstances plead in his favour, even when he is carrying on a dangerous flirtation in which a man tries in vain to keep his balance and not to exceed the limits of the game any more than at lawn tennis, even when the parts are reversed and a man's adversary is some precocious, curious, seductive girl who shows you immediately that she has nothing to learn and nothing to experience, except the last chapter of love—one of those girls from whom may fate always preserve our sons and whom a psychological novel writer has christened 'demivirgins.'

"It is of course difficult and painful for that coarse and unfathomable vanity which is characteristic of every man and which might be called malism not to stir such a charming fire, to act the Joseph and the fool, to turn away his eyes and, as it were, to put wax into his ears, as did the companions of Ulysses when attracted by the divine, seductive songs of the sirens. It is hard not to touch that pretty table, covered with a perfectly new cloth, at which you are invited to take a seat before anyone else in such a suggestive voice and are requested to quench your thirst and to taste that new wine whose fresh and strange flavour you will never forget. But who would hesitate to exercise such self-restraint if, when he rapidly examines his conscience in one of those instinctive moments of reason in which a man thinks clearly and recovers his head, if he were to measure the gravity of the fault, think of the error, think of its consequences, of the reprisals, of the uneasiness which he would always feel in the future and which would destroy the repose and the happiness of his life?

"You may guess that behind all these moral reflections, such as a gray beard like myself may indulge in, there is a story hidden and, sad as it is, I am sure it will interest you on account of the strange heroism that it shows."

He was silent for a few moments, as if to classify his recollections, and with elbows resting on the arms of his easy chair and eyes looking into space, he continued in the slow voice of a hospital professor who is explaining a case to his class of students at a bedside:

"He was one of those men who, as our grandfathers used to say, never met with a cruel woman, the type of an adventurous knight who was always foraging, who had something of the scamp about him but who despised danger and was bold even to rashness. He was ardent in the pursuit of pleasure, had an irresistible charm about him and was one of those men in whom we excuse the greatest excesses as the most natural things in the world. He had run through all his money through gambling and with pretty girls and so became, as it were, a soldier of fortune, who amused himself whenever and however he could, and was at that time quartered at Versailles.

I knew him to the very depths of his childish heart, which was only too easily penetrated and sounded. I loved him like some old bachelor uncle loves a nephew who plays him tricks but who knows how to make him indulgent and how to wheedle him. He had made me his confidant far more than his adviser, kept me informed of his slightest tricks, though he always pretended to be speaking about one of his friends and not about himself, and I must confess that his youthful impetuosity, his careless gaiety and his amorous ardour sometimes distracted my thoughts and made me envy the handsome, vigorous young fellow who was so happy, in being alive. I had not the courage to check him, to show him his right road and to call out to him: 'Take care!' as children do at blind man's buff.

"And one day, after one of those interminable cotillions, where the couples do not leave each other for hours but have a loose rein and can disappear together without anybody noticing it, the poor fellow at last discovered what love was, that real love which takes up its abode in the very centre of the heart and in the brain and is proud of being there, which rules like a sovereign and a tyrannous master. He grew desperately enamoured of a pretty but badly brought-up girl, who was as disquieting and as wayward as she was pretty.

"She loved him, however, or rather she idolized him despotically, madly, with all her enraptured soul and all her excited person. Left to do as she pleased by imprudent and frivolous parents, suffering from neurosis, in consequence of the unwholesome friendships contracted at the convent school, instructed by what she saw and heard and knew was going on around her, in spite of her deceitful and artificial conduct, knowing that neither her father nor her mother, who were very proud of their race as well as avaricious, would ever agree to let her marry the man whom she had taken a liking to—that handsome fellow who had little besides visionary ideas and debts and who belonged to the middle classes—she laid aside all scruples, thought of nothing but of belonging to him altogether, of taking him for her lover and of triumphing over his desperate resistance as an honourable man.

"By degrees the unfortunate man's strength gave way; his heart grew softened; his nerves became excited, and he allowed himself to be carried away by the current which buffeted him, surrounded him and left him on the shore like a waif and a stray.

"They wrote letters full of temptation and of madness to each other, and not a day passed without their meeting, either accidentally, as it seemed, or at parties and balls. She had given him her lips in long, ardent caresses, and she had sealed their compact of mutual passion with kisses of desire and of hope. And at last she brought him to her room, almost in spite of himself."

The doctor stopped, and his eyes suddenly filled with tears

as these former troubles came back to his mind. Then in a hoarse voice he went on, full of the horror of what he was going to relate:

"Each night for months he scaled the garden wall and, holding his breath and listening for the slightest noise, like a burglar who is going to break into a house, he entered by the servants' door, which she had left open, went barefoot down a long passage and up the broad staircase, which creaked occasionally, to the second story, where his mistress's room was, and stopped there nearly the whole night.

"One night, when it was darker than usual and he was hurrying lest he should be later than the time agreed on, the officer knocked up against a piece of furniture in the anteroom and upset it. It so happened that the girl's mother had not gone to sleep yet, either because she had a sick headache or else because she had sat up late over some novel. Frightened at the unusual noise which disturbed the silence of the house, she jumped out of bed, opened the door, saw someone indistinctly running away and keeping close to the wall and, immediately thinking that there were burglars in the house, she aroused her husband and the servants by her frantic screams. The unfortunate man knew what he was about and, seeing his dilemma, he determined to be taken for a common thief rather than dishonour his adored mistress and betray the secret of their guilty love. So he ran into the drawing room, felt on the tables and whatnots, filled his pockets at random with valuable knickknacks and then cowered down behind the grand piano, which barred up a corner of a large room.

"The servants, who had run in with lighted candles, found him and, overwhelming him with abuse, seized him by the collar and dragged him, panting and half dead with shame and terror, to the nearest police station. He defended himself with intentional awkwardness when he was brought up for trial, kept up his part with the most perfect self-possession and without any signs of the despair and anguish that he felt in his heart. Condemned and degraded and made to suffer martyrdom in his honour as a man and as a soldier, he did not protest but went to prison as one of those criminals whom society destroys like noxious vermin.

"He died there of misery and of bitterness of spirit, with the name of the fair-haired idol for whom he had sacrificed himself on his lips, as if it had been an ecstatic prayer. He entrusted his will to the priest who administered extreme unction to him and requested him to give it to me. In it, without mentioning anybody and without in the least lifting the veil, he at last explained the enigma and cleared himself of those accusations, the terrible burden of which he had borne until his last breath.

"I have always thought myself, though I do not know why, that the girl married and had several charming children, whom she brought up with austere strictness and in the serious piety of former days!"

IN THE WOOD

THE mayor was just going to sit down to breakfast, when he was told that the rural policeman was waiting for him at the *mairie* with two prisoners. He went there immediately and found old Hochedur standing up and watching a middle-class couple of mature years with stern looks.

The man, a fat old fellow with a red nose and white hair, seemed utterly dejected, while the woman, a little roundabout, stout creature with shining cheeks, looked at the agent who had arrested them with defiant eyes. "What is it? What is it, Hochedur?"

The rural policeman made his deposition. He had gone out that morning at his usual time in order to partol his beat from the forest of Champioux as fas as the boundaries of Argenteuil. He had not noticed anything unusual in the country except that it was a fine day and that the wheat was doing well, when the son of old Bredel, who was going over his vines a second time, called out to him;

"Here, Daddy Hochedur, go and have a look into the skirts of the wood, in the first thicket, and you will catch a pair of pigeons there who must be a hundred and thirty years old between them!"

He went in the direction that had been indicated to him

and had gone into the thicket. There he heard words and gasps which made him suspect a flagrant breach of morality. Advancing, therefore, on his hands and knees as if to surprise a poacher, he had arrested this couple at the very moment when they were going to abandon themselves to their natural instincts.

The mayor looked at the culprits in astonishment, for the man was certainly sixty and the woman fifty-five at least. So he began to question them, beginning with the man, who replied in such a weak voice that he could scarcely be heard.

"What is your name?"

"Nicholas Beaurain."

"Your occupation?"

"Haberdasher in the Rue des Martyrs, in Paris."

"What were you doing in the wood?"

The haberdasher remained silent, with his eyes on his fat stomach and his hands resting on his thighs, and the mayor continued:

"Do you deny what the officer of the municipal authorities states?"

"No, monsieur."

"So you confess it?"

"Yes, monsieur."

"What have you to say in your defense?"

"Nothing, monsieur."

"Where did you meet the partner in your misdemeanor?"

"She is my wife, monsieur."

"Your wife?"

"Yes, monsieru."

"Then-then-you do not love together in Paris?"

"I beg your pardon, monsieur, but we are living together!"

"But in that case you must be mad, altoghther mad, my dear sir, to get caught like that in the conutry at ten o'clock in the morning."

The haberdasher seemed ready to cry with shame, and he murmured: "It was she who enticed me! I told her it was stupid, but when a woman has got a thing into her head, you know, you cannot get it out."

The mayor, who liked open speaking, smiled and replied:

"In your case the contrary ought to have happened. You would not be here if she had had the idea only in her head."

Then M. Beaurain was seized with rage and, turning to his wife, he said: "Do you see to what you have brought us with your poetry? And now we shall have to go before the courts at out age for a breach of morals! And we shall have to shut up the shop, sell our good will and go to some other neighborhood! That's what it has come to!"

Mme Beaurain got up and, without looking at her husband, explained herself without any embarrassment, without useless modesty and almost without hesitation.

"Of course, monsieur, I know that we have made ourselves ridiculous. Will you allow me to plead my case like an advocate, or rather like a poor woman? And I hope that you will be kind enough to send us home and to spare us the disgrace of a prosecution.

"Years ago, when I was young, I made Monsieur Beaurain's acquaintance on Sunday in this neighborhood. He was employed in a draper's shop, and I was a saleswoman in a ready-made clothing establishment. I remember it as if it were yesterday. I used to come and spend Sundays here occasionally with a friend of mine. Rose Levéque, with whom I lived in the Rue Pigalle, and Rose had a sweetheart, while I had not. He used to bring us here, and one Saturday he told me, laughing, that he should bring a friend with him the next day. I quite understood what he meant, but I replied that it would be no good, for I was virtuous, monsieur.

"The next day we met Monsieur Beaurain at the railway station. In those days he was good looking, but I had made up my mind not to yield to him, and I did not yield. Well, we arrived at Bezons. It was a lovely day, the sort of day that tickles your heart. When it is fine even now, just as it used to be formerly, I grow quite foolish, and when I am in the country I utterly lose my head. The verdure, the swallows flying so swiftly, the smell of the grass, the scanet poppies, the daisies, all that makes me quite excited! It is like champagne when one is not used to it!

"Well, it was lovely weather, warm and bright, and it seemed to penetrate into your body by your eyes when you looked and by your mouth when you breathed. Rose and Simon hugged and kissed each other every minute, and that gave me something to look at! Monsieur Beaurain and I walked behind them without speaking much, for when people do not know each other well they cannot find much to talk about. He looked timid, and I liked to see his embarrassment. At last we got to the little wood; it was cool as in a bath there, and we all four sat down. Rose and her lover joked me because I looked rather stern, but you will understand that I could not be otherwise. And then they began to kiss and hug again without putting any more restraint upon themselves than if we had not been there. Then they whispered together and got up and went off among the trees without saying a word. You may fancy how I felt alone with this young fellow whom I saw for the first time. I felt so confused at seeing them go that it gave me courage and I began to talk. I asked him what his business was, and he said he was a linen draper's assistant, as I told you just now. We talked for a few minutes, and that made him bold, and he wanted to take liberties with me, but I told him sharply to keep his own place. Is not that true, Monsieur Beaurain?"

M. Beaurain, who was looking at his feet in confusion, did not reply, and she continued: "Then he saw that I was virtuous and he bagen to make love to me nicely, like an honorable man, and from that time he came every Sunday, for he was very much in love with me. I was very fond of him also, very fond of him! He was a good-looking fellow formerly, and in short he married me the next September, and we started business in the Rue des Martyrs.

"It was a hard struggle for some years, monsieur. Business did not prosper, and we could not afford many country excursions, and then we became unaccustomed to them. One has other things in one's head and thinks more of the cashbox than of pertty speeches when one is in business. We were growing old by degrees without perceiving it, like quiet people who do not think much about love. But one does not regret anything as long as one does not notice what one has lost.

"And after that, monsieur, business went better, and we became tranquil as to the future! Then, you see, I do not exactly know what passed within me -no, I really do not know-but I began to dream like a little boarding-school girl. The sight of the little carts full of flowers which are peddled about the streets made me cry; the smell of violets sought me out in my easy chair, behind my cashbox, and made my heart beat! Then I used to get up and go onto the doorstep to look at the blue sky between the roofs. When one looks at the sky from a street it seems like a river flowing over Paris, winding as it goes, and the swallows pass to and fro in it like fish. These sort of things are very stupid at my age! But what can one do, monsieur, when one has worked all one's life? A moment comes in which one perceives that one could have done something else, and then one regrets. Oh! yes! One feels great regret! Just think that for twenty years I might have gone and had kisses in the wood, like other women. I used to think how delightful it would be to lie under the trees loving someone! And I thought of it every day and every night! I dreamed of the moonlight on the water, until I felt inclined to drown myself.

"I did not venture to speak to Monsieur Beaurain about this at first. I knew that he would make fun of me and send me back to sell my needles and cotton. And then, to speak the truth, Monsieur Beaurain never said much to me, but when I looked in the glass I also understood quite well that I also no longer appealed to anyone!

"Well, I made up my mind. and I proposed an excursion into the country to him to the place where we had first become acquainted. He agreed without any distrust, and we arrived here this morning about nine o'clock.

"I felt quite young again when I got among the corn, for a woman's heart never grows old! And really I no longer saw my husband as he is at present, but just like he was formerly! That I will swear to you, monsieur. As true as I am standing here, I was intoxicated. I began to kiss him, and he was more surprised than if I had tried to murder him. He kept saying to me: 'Why, you must be mad this morning! What is the matter with you?' I did not listen to him; I only listened to my own heart, and I made him come into the wood with me. There is the story. I have spoken the truth, Monsieur le Maire, the whole truth."

The mayor was a sensible man. He rose from his chair, smiled and said: "Go in peace, madame, and sin no more-under the trees.

AN ADVENTURE

"COME! COME!" said Pierre Dufaille, shrugging his shoulders. "Do you know what you are talking about when you say that there are no more adventures? Say that there are no more adventurous men and you will be right! Yes, nobody takes a chance in these days, for as soon as there is any slight mystery or a spice of danger they draw back. If, however, a man is willing to go into anything blindly and to run the risk of anything that may happen he can still meet with adventures. Even I, who never look for them, met with one in my life, and a very startling one. Let me tell you of it.

"I was staying in Florence and was living very quietly. All I indulged in, in the way of, adventures, was to listen occasionally to the immoral proposals with which every stranger is beset at night on the Piazza della Signora by some worthy Pandarus or other with a head like that of a venerable priest. These excellent fellows generally introduce you to their families, where debauchery is carried on in a very simple and almost patriarchal fashion and where one does not run the slightest risk.

"One day as I was admiring Benvenuto Cellini's wonderful Perseus in front of the Loggia dei Lanzi, I suddenly felt my sleeve pulled somewhat roughly. On turning round I found myself face to face with a woman of about fifty who said to me with a strong German accent: You are French, monsieur, are you not?'

" 'Certainly I am,' I replied.

" 'And would you like to go home with a very pretty woman?"

" 'Most certainly I should,' I replied with a laugh.

"Nothing could have been runnier than the looks and serious air of the procuress, save the strangeness of the proposal, made in broad daylight and in very bad French. It was even worse when she added: 'Do you know everything they do in Paris?'

" 'What do you mean, my good woman?' I asked her, rather startled. "What is done in Paris that is not done everywhere else?'

"However, when she explained her meaning I replied that I certainly did not, and as I was not quite so immodest as the lady, I blushed a little. But not for long, for almost immediately afterward I grew pale when she said: 'I want to assure myself of it personally.' And she said this in the same phlegmatic manner, which did not seem so funny to me now but, on the contrary, rather frightened me.

"What?' I said. 'Personally! You? Explain yourself

"If I had been rather surprised before, I was now altogether astonished at her explanation. It was indeed an adventure—almost like a romance. I could scarcely believe my ears, but this is what she told me.

"She was the confidential attendant on a lady moving in high society, who wished to be initiated into the most secret refinements of Parisian high life, and had done me the honour of choosing me for her companion. But then this preliminary test!

" 'By Jove!' I said to myself. 'This old German hag is not so stupid as she looks!' And I laughed in my sleeve as I listened inattentively to what she was saying to persuade me.

" 'My mistress is the prettiest woman you can dream of, a real beauty, springtime! A flower!'

" 'You must excuse me, but if your mistress is really like springtime and a flower, you (pray excuse me for being so blunt) are not exactly that, and perhaps I should not exactly be in a mood to humour you, my dear lady, in the same way that I might her.'

"She jumped back, astonished in turn. 'Why, I only want to satisfy myself with my own eyes, not by injuring you.' And she finished her explanation, which had been incomplete before. All she had to do was to go with me to Mother Patata's well-known establishment and there to be present while I conversed with one of its fair and frail inhabitants.

" 'Oh!' I said to myself. 'I was mistaken in her tastes. She is of course an old, shrivelled-up woman, as I guessed, but she is a specialist. This is interesting;

upon my word! I never met with such a one before!'

"Here, gentlemen, I must beg you to allow me to hide my face for a moment. What I said was evidently not strictly correct, and I am rather ashamed of it; my excuse must be that I was young, that Patata's was a celebrated place of which I had heard wonderful things said but the entry to which was barred me on account of my small means. Five napoleons was the price! Fancy! I could not treat myself to it, and so I accepted the good lady's offer. I do not say that it was not disagreeable, but what was I to do? And then the old woman was a German, and so her five napoleons were a slight return for our five milliards, which we paid them as our war indemnity.

"Well, Patata's boarder was charming; the old woman was not too troublesome, and your humble servant did his best to sustain the ancient glory of Frenchmen.

"Let me drink my disgrace to the dregs! On the next day but one after, I was waiting at the statue of Perseus. It was shameful, I confess, but I enjoyed the partial restitution of the five milliards, and it is surprising how a Frenchman loses his dignity when he is travelling.

"The good lady made her appearance at the appointed time. It was quite dark and I followed her without a word, for, after all, I was not very proud of the part I was playing. But if you only knew how fair that little girl at Patata's was. As I went along I thought only of her and did not pay any attention to where we were going. I was only roused from my reverie by hearing the old woman say: 'Here we are. Try and be as entertaining as you were the day before yesterday.'

"We were not outside Patata's house but in a narrow street running by the side of a palace with high walls, and in front of us was a small door which the old woman opened gently.

"For a moment I felt inclined to draw back. Apparently the old hag was also ardent on her own account! She had me in a trap! No doubt she wanted in her turn to make use of my small talents! But, no! That was impossible!

" 'Go in! Go in!' she said. 'What are you afraid of? My mistress is so pretty, so pretty, much prettier than the little girl of the other day.'

"So it was really true, this story out of *The Arabian Nights?* Why not? And after all, what was I risking? The good woman would certainly nor injure me, and so I went in, though somewhat nervously.

"My friend, what an hour I spent there! Paradise! It would be useless, impossible to describe it to you. Apartments fit for a princess, and one of those princesses out of fairy tales, a fairy herself. An exquisite German woman, exquisite as German women can be when they try. An Undine of Heinrich Heine's, with hair like the Virgin Mary's, innocent blue eyes and a skin like strawberries and cream.

"Suddenly, however, my Undine got up, and her face convulsed with fury and pride. Then she rushed behind some hangings, where she began to give vent to a flood of German words which I did not understand, while I remained standing, dumfounded. But just then the old woman came in and said, shaking with fear: 'Quick, quick; dress yourself and go if you do not wish to be killed.'

"I asked no questions, for what was the good of trying to understand? Besides, the old woman, who grew more and more terrified, could not find any French words and chattered wildly. I jumped up and got into my shoes and overcoat and ran down the stairs and into the street.

"Ten minutes later I recovered my breath and my senses without knowing what streets I had been through or where I had come from, and I stole furtively into my hotel, as if I had been a malefactor.

"In the cafés the next morning nothing was talked of except a crime that had been committed during the night. A German baron had killed his wife with a revolver but had been liberated on bail, as he had appealed to his counsel to whom he had given the following explanation, to the truth of which the lady companion of the baroness had certified.

"She had been married to her husband almost by force; she detested him and had some particular reasons (which were not specified) for her hatred of him. In order to have her revenge on him she had him seized, bound and gagged by four hired ruffians, who had been caught and who had confessed everything. Thus, reduced to immobility and unable to help himself, the baron had been obliged to witness a degrading scene in which his wife caressed a Frenchman and thus outraged conjugal fidelity and German honour at the same time. As soon as he was set at liberty the baron had punished his faithless wife and was now seeking her accomplice."

"And what did you do?" someone asked Pierre Dufaille.

"The only thing I could do, by George!" he replied. "I put myself at the poor devil's disposal; it was his right, and so we fought a duel. Alas! It was with swords, and he ran me right through the body. That was also his right, but he exceeded his right when he called me her *ponce*. Then I gave him his change, and as I fell I called out with all the strength that remained to me: 'A Frenchman! A Frenchman! Long live France!"

A BAD ERROR

I MADE Mme Jadelle's acquaintance in Paris this winter. She pleased me infinitely at once. You know her as well as I—no—pardon me—nearly as well as I. You know that she is poetic and fantastic at one and the same time. You know she is free in her manner and of impressionable heart, impulsive, courageous, venturesome, audacious-above all, prejudiced and yet, in spite of that, sentimental, delicate, easily hurt, tender and modest.

She was a widow, and I adore widows, from sheer laziness. I was on the lookout for a wife, and I paid her my court. I knew her, and more than that, she pleased me. The moment came when I believed it would do to risk my proposal. I was in love with her and in danger of becoming too much so. When one marries he should not love his wife too much, or he is likely to make himself foolish; his vision is distorted, and he becomes silly and brutal at the same time. A man must assert himself. If he loses his head at first he risks being a nobody a year later.

So one day I presented myself at her house with light gloves on and I said to her: "Madame, I have the honour of loving you, and I have come to ask you if there is any hope of my pleasing you enough to warrant your placing your happiness in my care and taking my name."

She answered quietly: "What a question, sir! I am absolutely ignorant of whether you will please me sooner or later or whether you will not, but I ask nothing better than to make a trial of it. As a man, I do not find you bad. It remains to be seen how you are at heart and in character and habits. For the most part marriages are tempestuous or criminal because people are not careful enough in yoking themselves together. Sometimes a mere nothing is sufficient, a mania or tenacious opinion upon some moral or religious point, no matter what, a gesture which displeases or some little fault or disagreeable quality, to turn an affianced couple, however tender and affectionate, into a pair of irreconcilable enemies, incensed with, but chained to, each other until death. I will not marry, sir, without knowing the depths and corners and recesses of the soul of the man with whom I am to share my existence. I wish to study him at leisure, at least for some months.

"Here is what I propose. You will come and pass the summer in my house at De Lauville, my country place, and we shall see then if we are fitted to live side by side—I see you laugh! You have a bad thought. Oh, sir, if I were not sure of myself I would never make this proposition. 1 have for love, what you call love, you men, such a scorn, such a disgust, that a fall is impossible for me. Well, do you accept?"

I kissed her hand.

"When shall we start, madame?"

"The tenth of May."

"It is agreed."

A month later I was installed at her house. She was truly a singular woman. From morning until evening she was studying me. As she was fond of horses, we passed each day in riding through the wood, talking about everything, but she was always trying to probe my innermost thoughts, to which end she observed my slightest movement.

As for me, I became foolishly in love and did not trouble myself about the fitness of our characters. But I soon perceived that even my sleep was put under inspection. Someone slept in a little room adjoining mine, entering very late and with infinite precaution. This espionage for every instant finally made me impatient. I wished to hasten the conclusion and one evening thought of a way of bringing it about. She had received me in such a way that I had abstained from any new essay, but a violent desire invaded me to make her pay in some fashion for this restricted regime to which I had submitted, and I thought I knew a way.

You know Cesarine, her chambermaid, a pretty girl from Granville, where all the women are pretty, and as blond as her mistress was brunette? Well, one afternoon I drew the little soubrette into my room and, putting a hundred francs in her hand, I said to her:

"My dear child, I do not wish you to do anything villainous, but I desire the same privilege toward your mistress that she takes toward me." The little maid laughed with a sly look as I continued:

"I am watched day and night, I know. I am watched as I eat, drink, dress myself, shave and put on my socks, and I know it."

The little girl stammered: "Yes sir." Then she was silent. I continued:

"You sleep in the room next to mine to see if I snore or if I dream aloud; you cannot deny it!"

"Yes sir." Then she was silent again.

I became excited. "Oh well, my girl," I said, "you understand that it is not fair for everything to be known about me, while I know nothing of the person who is to be my wife. I love her with all my soul. She has the face, the heart and mind that I have dreamed of. and I am the happiest of men on this account; nevertheless, there are some things I would like to know better."

Cesarine decided to put my bank note in her pocket. I understood that the bargain was concluded.

"Listen, my girl," I said. "We men—we care much for certain—certain details—physical details, which do not hinder a woman from being charming but which can change her price in our eyes. I do not ask you to say anything bad of your mistress or even to disclose to me her defects, if she has any. Only answer me frankly four of five questions, which I am going to put to you. You know Madame Jadelle as well as you do yourself, since you dress and undress her every day. Now then, tell me this: Is she as plump as she has the appearance of being?"

The little maid did not answer.

I continued: "You cannot, my child, be ignorant of the fact that women put cotton padding, you know, where—where—where they nourish their infants and also where they sit. Tell me, does she use padding?"

Cesarine lowered her eyes. Finally she said timidly: "Ask whatever you want to, sir, I will answer all at one time."

"Well, my girl, there are some women whose knees meet, so much so that they touch with each step that they take, and there are others who have them far apart, which makes their limbs like the arches of a bridle, so that one might view the landscape between them. This is the prettier of the two fashions. Tell me how are your mistress's limbs?"

Still the maid said nothing.

I continued: "There are some who have necks so beautiful that they form a great fold underneath. And there are some that have large arms with a thin figure. There are some that are very large before and nothing at all behind, and there are some large behind and nothing at all in front. All this is very pretty, very pretty, but I wish to know just how your mistress is made. Tell me frankly, and I will give you much more money."

Cesarine looked at me out of the comer of her eye and, laughing with all her heart, answered: "Sir, aside from being dark. Mistress is made exactly like me."

Then she fled.

I had been made sport of. This was the time I found myself ridiculous, and I resolved to avenge myself at least upon this impertinent maid.

An hour later I entered the little room with precaution, where she listened to my sleeping, and unscrewed the bolts.

Toward midnight she arrived at her post of observation. I followed her immediately. On perceiving me she was going to cry out, but I put my hand over her mouth and, without too great effort, I convinced myself that if she had not lied Mme jadelle was very well made.

I even put much zest into this authentication which, though pushed a little far, did not seem to displease Cesarine. She was, in very fact, a ravishing specimen of the Norman peasant race, strong and fine at the same time. She was wanting perhaps in certain delicate attentions that Henry VI would have scorned, but I revealed them to her quickly, and as I adore perfumes, I gave her a box the next evening with a flask of lavender water.

We were soon more closely bound to each other than I could have believed, almost friends. She became an exquisite mistress, naturally *spirituelle* and broken to pleasure. She had been a courtesan of great merit in Paris.

The delights which she brought me enabled me to await Mme Jadelle's conclusion of proof without impatience. I became an incomparable character, supple, docile and complacent. My fiançee found me delightful beyond a doubt, and I judged from certain signs that I was soon to be accepted. 1 was certainly the happiest man in the world, awaiting tranquilly the legal kiss of the woman I loved, in the arms of a young and beautiful girl for whom I had much fondness.

It is here, madame, that I must ask your forbearance a little; I have arrived at a delicate point.

One evening as we were returning from a horseback ride, Mme Jadelle complained sharply that her grooms had not taken certain measures prescribed by her for the horse she rode. She repeated many times: "Let them take care, I have a way of surprising them."

I passed a calm night in my bed. I awoke early, full of ardour and energy. Then I dressed myself.

I was in the habit of going up on the tower of the house each morning to smoke a cigarette. This was reached by a limestone staircase lighted by a large window at the top of the first story.

I advanced without noise, my feet encased in morocco slippers with wadded soles, and was climbing the first steps when I perceived Cesarine bending out the window, looking down below.

Not that I saw Cesarine entirely, but only a part of Cesarine, and that the lower part. I loved this part just as much; of Mme Jadelle I would have preferred, perhaps, the upper. She was thus so charming, so round, this part which offered itself to me, and only slightly clothed in a white skirt.

I approached so softly that the girl heard nothing. I put myself on my knees; with infinite precaution I took hold of the two sides of the skirt and, quickly, I raised it. I recognized there the full, fresh, plump, sweet ischial tuberosities of my mistress and threw there—your pardon, madame—I threw there a tender kiss, a kiss of a lover who dares anything.

I was surprised. It was verbena! But I had no time for reflection. I received a sudden blow, or rather a push in the face which seemed to break my nose. I uttered a cry that made my hair rise. The person had turned around—it was Mme Jadelle!

She was fighting the air with her hands, like a woman who had lost consciousness. She gasped for some seconds, made a gesture of using a norsewhip and then fled.

Ten minutes later Cesarine, stupefied, brought me in a letter. I read:

Mme Jadelle hopes that M. de Brives will immediately rid her of his presence.

I departed. Well, I am not yet consoled. 1 have attempted every means and all explanations to obtain a pardon for my misunderstanding, but all proceedings have been nipped in the bud.

Since that moment, you see, I have in my—in my heart a scent of verbena which gives me an immoderate desire to smell the perfume again.

A POOR GIRL

YES, the memory of that evening can never be effaced. For half an hour I had the sinister sensation of invincible fatality; I had the same shivers that one has in descending the shaft of a mine. I touched the black depths of human misery; I seemed to comprehend fully how impossible an honest life is under some conditions.

It was just past midnight. I was going from the vaudeville to Drouot Street, following a crowd on the boulevard, all carrying umbrellas. A deluge of water poured rather than fell, veiling the gas jets and giving the street a sad appearance. The sidewalk glittered, more sticky than wet. The mass of people pressed on, seeing nothing.

Girls, with skirts raised, showed their ankles, allowing a white stocking to peep out in the dim nocturnal light, and waited in shadowed doorways. Some called to and some, bolder, jostled the passers, pronouncing in their ears two obscene, stupid words. They would follow a man some seconds and push against him, breathing in his face their putrid breath. Then, seeing their beguilements useless, they would leave him with an abrupt, discontented motion and start on again, swinging their hips.

I went along, spoken to by all, taken by the sleeve, harassed and moved with disgust. Suddenly I saw three of them running as if frightened, talking to each other in rapid fashion. Others also began to run, to flee, holding their robes with both hands in order to run more quickly. That day a blow had been given to the network of prostitution.

All at once I felt an arm under mine, while a terrified voice murmured in my ear: "Save me, sir, save me; do not leave me."

I looked at the girl. She was not twenty years old, yet faded already. I said to her: "Remain with me." And she murmured: "Oh, thank you!"

We arrived at the line of agents. She disclosed herself in order to let me pass. I met her farther on in Drouot Street.

My companion asked: "Will you come home with me?"

"No."

"Why not? You have rendered me a service that I shall not forget."

I answered, so not to embarrass her: "Because I am married."

"What difference does that make?"

"You see, my child, that is sufficient. I have helped you out of your difficulty, leave me quietly now."

The street was deserted and dark, truly unpleasant. And this woman, who held me by the arm, rendered more frightful still the sensation of sadness which enveloped me. She wished to embrace me. I recoiled with horror. And in a hard voice she said: "Once, for peace, won't you?"

And she made a movement of rage, then abruptly began to sob. I stood lost in wonder, not quite comprehending. Finally I said:

"Tell me, what is the matter with you?"

She murmured through her tears: "If you only knew it, it is not gay, this isn't."

"What is not gay?"

"This kind of life."

"Why have you chosen it then?"

"It was not my fault."

"Whose fault was it?"

"I know whose, I do."

A kind of interest in this abandoned creature took me and I said:

"Tell me your story."

And she told it to me.

"I was sixteen years old and in service at Yvetot at the house of Monsieur Lerable, a grain dealer. My parents were dead. I had no one. I saw, of course, that my master looked at me in a queer way and that he pinched my cheeks, and I had not long to ask myself what he meant. I knew things, certainly. In the country, one is sharpened. But Monsieur Lerable was, old and devout, going to Mass every Sunday. I somehow never believed him capable! But the day came when he wished to take me in my kitchen. I resisted him, but it was done.

"There was opposite us a grocer, Monsieur Dunstan, who had a very pleasant boy in his shop, so much so that I allowed myself to be cajoled by him. That happens to everybody, does it not? I would leave the door open evenings that he might come in.

"But one night Monsieur Lerable heard some noise. He went up and found Antoine and tried to kill him. It was a battle with chairs, jugs of water and everything. As for me, I found my courage and fled into the street. That was how I starred out.

"I was afraid, afraid of the world. But I dressed myself

under a doorway and began to walk straight on. I believed of a truth that someone had been killed and that the policemen were after me already. I reached the highway to Rouen. I told myself that at Rouen I should be concealed well enough.

"It was so dark I could not see the ditches, and I heard the dogs barking on the farms. Do you know all the things one hears at night? There are birds that cry like a man being murdered, beasts that yap and beasts that whistle, and many other things that I do not understand. I was all goose flesh. Each step I made the sign of the cross. One cannot imagine how the heart can be helped by that. When the day appeared the idea of the policemen always took me by force, and I ran all that I could. Then I tried to calm myself.

"I felt hungry, all the same, in spite of my fear, but I had not anything, not one sou, for I had forgotten my money, all that I had on earth, which was eighteen francs. So I was obliged to walk with an empty stomach.

"It was hot. The sun burned. Midday was past, and I kept going on. Suddenly I heard some horses behind me. I turned to look. The mounted policemen! My blood gave a leap; I thought I should fall, but I went on. They would catch me. They were looking at me now. Then one of them, the elder, said:

" 'Good day, mademoiselle.'

" 'Good day, sir.'

" 'Where are you going to?'

" 'I am going to Rouen in service at a place that has been offered me.'

" 'Walking, like this?'

" 'Yes, walking.'

"My heart beat, sir, so that I could say no more. I kept thinking to myself: 'Now they will take me.' And I had such a desire to run that my legs danced. But they would have caught me immediately, you see.

"The old one began: 'We can journey together as far as Barantin, mademoiselle, since we are taking the same route.'

"With pleasure, sir,' I said.

"And we chatted a little. I made myself as pleasant as I

could, you see, so much so that they believed what was not so. Then as we passed into a wood the old one said: 'Would you like to stop and rest a little on this moss?'

"And I, without thinking, said. 'As you wish, sir.'

"Then he dismounted and gave his horse to the other, and we two went away in the wood. There was nothing to be said. What could you have done in my place? He took what he wished and then said to me: 'It won't do to forget the comrade.'

"He returned to the horses, and the other rejoined me. I was so much ashamed that I could have wept, sir. But I dared not resist, you understand. Then we went on our way. I could speak no more; I had too much grief in my heart. And then I could no longer walk, I was so hungry. But in the village they gave me a glass of wine, which gave me new force for some time. And then they took to the trot so as not to go through Barantin in my company. And I seated myself by a ditch and wept until I had no more tears.

"I walked then for three hours more before reaching Rouen. It was seven o'clock in the evening when I arrived there. At first all the lights dazzled me. And then I did not know where I could sit down to rest. On the way there were the ditches and the grass where I could even tie down and sleep. But in the city, nothing.

"My limbs refused to hold my body, and I felt as if I were going to fall. And then it began to rain, a little fine rain, like this evening, which goes through you without your knowing it. I have no luck when it rains. I commenced to walk the streets. I looked at all the houses, saying to myself: 'There are beds and bread in there, but I cannot find as much as a crust or a bed of straw.'

"I went through some streets where women were speaking to men along the way. In such cases, sir, one must do what one can. I took my place with the others, inviting everybody. But no one answered me. I wished I was dead. This must have been near midnight. I no longer knew what I did. Finally a man listened to me. He asked me: 'Where do you live?' Some kind of ruse was necessary, and I answered: 'I cannot take you to my house for I live with Mamma. But are there not some houses where we could go?'

"He answered: 'It is not often that I spend twenty sous

for a room.' Then he added: 'Come along. I know a quiet spot where we shall not be interrupted.'

"He made me pass over a bridge then led me to the end of the town, into a meadow near the river. I could do nothing but follow him. He made me sit down and then began to ask why we had come there. As he was long in his affair, I found myself so worn out with fatigue that I fell asleep. He went away without giving me anything. I could not see a single step. Since that day I have had troubles that I can never be cured of, because I slept all that night in the wet.

"I was awakened by two officers who took me to the station house and then to prison, where I stayed eight days, while they tried to find out who I was and where I had come from. I would not tell for fear of the consequences. They found out, however, and released me after a verdict of innocence.

"Then it was necessary for me to make my living. I tried to find a place, but I could not because I had come out of prison. Then I recalled the old judge who had a turn to his eye, while he was judging me, like that of Father Lerable of Yvetot. And I went to find him. I was not deceived. He gave me a hundred sous when I left him, saying: 'You shall have as much every time, but don't come too often, not more than twice a week.' I understood that well because of his age. But it gave me a reflection. I said to myself: 'Young people make merry and amuse themselves, but they are never fat, while with the old it is the other way.' And since then I can always tell them, these old apes with their eyes in a groove and a little ghost of a head.

"Do you know what I did, sir? I dressed up like a country girl who had come to market and I walked the streets for my living. Oh! I could pinch their at the first blow. I would say to myself: 'Here is one who will bite.' He would approach. And then commence:

" 'Good day, mademoiselle.'

" 'Good day, sir.'

" 'Where are you going, like this?'

" 'I am returning home to Master's.'

" 'Do they live far, your people?'

" 'Rather far, but not so very.'

"Then he would not know what to say, and I would make my step a little slower to allow him to explain. Then he would give me some compliments in a low voice and then ask me to go home with him. I would refuse at first, you understand, and then yield. I had two or three of that son each morning, and all my afternoons free. That was the good time of my life. I was not made of spleen.

"But it seems one can never be quiet for a long time. It was my misfortune to make the acquaintance of a rich man of the world, an old president, who was all of seventy-five years old. One evening he took me to dine in a restaurant of the neighbourhood. And then, you understand, he did not know how to be moderate. He was dead at the dessert.

"I had three months in prison, because I was not under superintendence Then I came to Paris. And, oh, sir, it is hard here! Hard to live! One cannot expect to eat every day; there are too many. But that is only so much the worse Each to his trouble, don't you say so?"

She was silent. I walked along by her side, my heart touched. Suddenly she began to be familiar with me, saying:

"So you will not go home with me, my dear?"

"No, I have told you so already."

"Oh well, good by, and thanks all the same, without any hard feeling, but assure you that you are wrong."

And she went away, plunging into the rain which was as fine as a veil. watched her pass under a gas jet and then disappear in a shadow. Poor girl!

THE MARQUIS DE FUMEROL

ROGER DE TOUMEVILLE was sitting astride a chair in the midst of his friends and talking; he held a cigar in his hand and from time to time took a whiff and blew out a small cloud of smoke.

"We were at dinner when a letter was brought in, and my

father opened it. You know my father who thinks that he is king to France *ad interim.* I call him Don Quixote, because for twelve years he has been running a tilt against the windmill of the Republic without quite knowing whether it was in the name of Bourbon or of Orleans. At present he is holding the lance in the name of Orleans alone, because there is nobody else left. In any case, he thinks himself the first gentleman in France, the best known, the most influential, the head of the party, and as he is an irremovable senator, he thinks that the meighboring kings' thrones are very insecure.

"As for my mother, she is my father's inspiration, the soul of the kingdom and of religion, the right arm of God on earth and the scourge of evil thinkers.

"Well, this letter was brought in while we were at dinner. My father opened and read it, and then he said to my mother: 'Your brother is dying.' She grew very pale. My uncle was scarcely ever mentioned in the house, and I did not know him at all; all I knew from public talk was that he had led and was still leading the life of a buffoon. After having spent his fortune with an incalculable number of women, he had only retained two mistresses, with whom he was living in small apartments in the Rue des Martyrs.

"An ex-peer of France and ex-colonel of cavalry, it was said that he believed in neither God nor devil. Having no faith, therefore, in a future life, he had abused that present life in every way and had become a living wound to my mother's heart.

" 'Give me that letter, Paul,' she said, and when she bad read it I asked for it in my turn. Here it is:

"Monsieur Le Comte: *I think I ought to let you know that your brother-in-law, Count Fumerol, is going to die. Perhaps you would make preparation and not forget that I told you.*

"Your servant, Melani."

" 'We must think, my father murmured. 'In my position I ought to watch over your brother's last moments."

"My mother continued:" I will send for Abbé Poivron and ask his advice. and then I will go to my brother's with him and Roger. Stop here, Paul, for you must not compromise yoursel, but a woman can and ought to do these things. For a politician in your position, it is another matter. It would be a fine thing for one of your opponents to be able to bring one of your most laudable actions up against you.

" 'You are right!' my father said. 'Do as you think best, my dear wife.'

"A quarter of an hour later the Abbé Poivron came into the drawing room, and the situation was explained to him, analyzed and discussed in all its bearings. If the Marquis de Fumerol, one of the greatest names in France, were to die without the succor of religion it would assuredly be a terrible blow to the nobility in general, to the Count de Toumeville in particular, and the freethinkers would be triumphant. The evilly disposed newspapers would sing songs of victory for six months; my mother's name would be dragged through the mire and brought into the slander of socialistic journals and my father's would be bespattered. It was impossible that such a thing should occur.

"A crusade was therefore immediately decided upon, which was to be led by the Abbé Piovron, a little fat, clean, slightly scented priest, the faithful vicar of a large chruch in a rich and noble quarter.

"The landau was ordered, and we three started, my mother, the cure and I, to administer the last sacraments to my uncle.

"It had been decided that first of all we should see Madame Meline who had written the letter and who was most likely the proter's wife or my uncle's servant, and I got down as a scout in front of a seven-storied house and went into a dark passage, where I had great difficulty in finding the porter's den. He looked at me distrustfully, and I said:

" 'Madame Melani, if you please.'

" 'Don't know her!'

" 'But I have received a letter from her.'

" 'That may be, but I don't know her. Are you asking for some kept woman?'

" 'No, a servant probably. She wrote me about a place.'

" 'A servant-a servant? Perhaps it is the marquis's. Go and see, the fifth story on the left.'

"As soon as he found I was not asking for a kept woman he became more friendly and came as far as the passage with me. He was a tall thin man with white whiskers, the manners of a beadle, and majestic in movement.

"I climded up a long spiral staircase whose balusters I did not venture to touch, and I gave three discreet knock at the left-hand door on the fifth story. It opened immediatedly, and an enormous dirty woman appeared before me, who barred the entrance with her open arms which she placed upon the two doorposts and grumbled out:

" 'What do you want?'

" 'Are you Madame Mélani?'

" 'Yes.'

" 'I am the Viscount de Toumeville.'

'"Ah! All right! Come in.'

" 'Well, the fact is, my mother is downstairs with a priest.'

" 'Oh! All right; go and bring them up, but take care of the porter.'

" 'I went downstairs and came up again with my mother who was followed by the abbe, and I fancied that I heard other foolsteps behind us. As soon as we were in the kitchen, Mélani offered us chairs, and we all four sat down to deliberate.

" 'Is he very ill?' my mother asked.

" 'Oh yes, madame; he will not be here long.'

" 'Does he seem disposed to receive a visit from a priest?'

" 'Oh! I do not think so.'

" 'Can I see him?'

" 'Well -yes-madame-only-only-those yound ladies are with him.'

" 'What young ladies?'

" 'Why-why-his lady friends of course.'

" 'Oh!' Mamma had grown scarlet, and the Abbé Poivron had lowered his eyes.

"The affair began to amuse me, and I said:" Suppose I go in first? I shall see how he receives me, and perhaps I shall be able to prepare his heart for you.'

"My mother, who did not suspect any trick, replied: 'Yes, go, my dear.'

"But a woman's voice cried out: 'Mélani!'

"The fat servant ran out and said: 'What do you want. Mademoiselle Claire?'

" The omelet, quickly.'

" 'In a minute, mademoiselle.' And coming back to us, she explained this summons.

" 'They ordered a cheese omelet at two o'clock as a slight collation.' And immediately she began to break eggs into a salad bowl and began to whip them vigorously, while I went out onto the landing and pulled the bell so as to announce my official arrival. Melani opened the door to me and made me sit down in an anteroom while she went to tell my uncle that I had come. Then she came back and asked me to go in, while the abbé hid behind the door so that he might appear at the first sign.

"I was certainly very much surprised at seeing my uncle, for he was very handsome, very solemn and very elegant-he old rake.

"Sitting, almost lying, in a large armchair, his legs wrapped in blankets, with his hands, his long white hands, over the arms of the chair, he was waiting for death with biblical dignity. His white beard fell on his chest, and his hair which was also white mingled with it on his cheeks.

"Standing behind his armchair as if to defend him against me were two young women, two stout young women, who looked at me with the bold eyes of prostitutes. In their petticoats and morning wrappers, with bare arms, with coal-black hair twisted up onto the napes of their necks, with embroidered oriental slippers which showed their ankles and silk stocking, they looked like the immoral figures of some symbolical painting by the side of the dying man. Between the easy chair and the bed there was a table covered with a white cloth on which two plates, two glasses, two forks and two knives were waiting for the cheese omelet which had been ordered some time before of Mélani.

"My uncle said in a weak, almost breathless, but clear voice: 'Good morning, my child; it is rather late in the day to come to see me; our acquaintanceship will not last long.'

"I stammered out: 'It was not my faunt. Uncle,' and he replied: 'No; I know that. It is your father's and mother's fault more than yours. How are they?"

" 'Pretty well, thank you. When they heard that you were ill they sent me to ask after you.'

" 'Ah! Why did they not come themselves?

"I looked up at the two girls and said gently: 'It is not their fault if they could not come. Uncle. But it would be difficult for my father and impossible for my mother to come in here.' The old man did not reply but raised his hand toward mine, and I took the pale, cold hand and kept it in my own.

"The door opened; Mélanli came in with the omelet and put it on the table, and the two girls immediately sat down in front of their plates and began to eat without taking their eyes off me.

"Then I said: 'Uncle, it would be a great pleasure for my mother to embrace you.'

" 'I also,' he murmured, 'should like-' He said no more. and I could think of nothing to propose to him, and nothing more was heard except the noise of the plates and the slight sound of eating mouths.

"Now the abbé, who was listening behind the door, seeing our embarrassment and thinking we had won the game, thought the time had come to interpose and showed himself. My uncle was so stupefied at that apparition that at first he remained motionless; then he opened his mouth as if he meant to swallow up the priest and cried out in a strong, deep, furious voice:" What are you doing here?'

"The abbé, who was used to difficult situations, came forward, murmuring: 'I have come in your sister's name, Monsieur le Marquis; she has sent me-she would be so happy, monsieur-"

"But the marquis was not listening. Raising one hand, he pointed to the door with a proud and tragic gesture and said angrily and gasping for hreath: 'Leave this room-go out-robber of souls. Go out from here, you violator of consciences! Go out from here, you picklock of dying men's doors!'

"The abbé went backward, and I, too, went to the door, beating a retreat with him, and the two little women who were avenged got up, leaving their omelet half eaten, and stood on either side of my uncle's armchair, putting their hands on his arms to calm him and to protect him against the criminal enterprises of the family and of religion.

"The abbé and I rejoined my mother in the kitchen, and Mélani again offered us chairs. 'I knew quite well that you would fail that way; we must try some other means, otherwise he will escape us.' And we began deliberating afresh, my mother being of one opinion and the abbe of another, while I held a third.

"We had been discussing the matter in a low voice for half an hour, perhaps, when a great noise of furniture being moved and of cries uttered by my uncle, more vehement and terible even than the former had been, made us all jump up.

"Through the doors and walls we could hear him shouting; 'Go out-out-rascals-humbugs; get out, scoundrels-get out-get out!'

"Mélani rushed in but came back immediately to call me to help her, and I hastened in. Opposite to my uncle who was terribly excited by anger, almost standing up and vociferating, two men, one behind the other, seemed to be waiting till he should be dead with rage.

"By his long, ridiculous coat, his pointed English shoes, by his manners-like those of a tutor out of a situation-by his high collar white necktie and straight hair, by his humble face. I immediately recognized the first as a Protestant minister.

"The second was the porter of the house who belonged to the Reformed religion and had followed us. Having known of our defeat, he had gone to fetch his own pastor in hope of a better fate. My uncle seemed mad with rage! If the sight of the Catholic priest of the priest of his ancestors, had irritated the Marquis de Fumerol, who had become a freethinker, the sight of his porter's minister made him altogether beside himself. I therefore took the two men by the arm and threw them out of the room so violently that they fell up against each other twice between the two doors which led to the staircase; then I disappeared in my turn and returned to the kitchen, which was our headquarters, in order to take counsel with my mother and the abbé.

"But Mélani came back in terror, sobbing out: 'He is dying-he is dying. Come immediately-he is dying.'

"My mother rushed out. My uncle had fallen onto the carpet, full length along the floor, and did not move. I fancy he was already dead. My mother was superb at that moment! She went straight up to the two girls who were kneeling by the body and trying to raise it up and. pointing to the door with irresistible authority, dignity and majesty, she said: 'Now it is for you to go out.'

"And they went out without a protest and without saying a word. I must add that I was getting ready to turn them out as unceremoniously as I had done the parson and the porter.

"Then the Abbé Poivron administered exterme unction to my uncle with all the customary prayers and remitted all his sins. while my mother sobbed, kneeling near her brother. Suddenly, however, she exclaimed: 'He recognized me; he pressed my hand; I am sure he recognized me and thanked me! O God, what happiness!'

"Poor Mamma! If she had known or guessed to whom those thanks ought to have heen addressed!

"They laid my mucle on his bed; he was certainly dead that time.

" 'Madame,' Mélani said, 'we have no sheets to bury him in; all the linen belongs to those two young ladies,' and when I looked at the omelet which they had not finished, I felt inclined to laugh and to cry at the same time. There are some strange moments and some strange sensations in life occasionally!

"We gave my uncle a magnificent funeral with five speeches at the grave. Baron de Croiselles, the senator, showed in admirable terms that God always returns victorious into well-born souls which have gone astray for a moment. All the members of the Royalist and Catholic party followed the funeral procession with triumphant enthusiasm, speaking of that beautiful death after a somewhat restless life."

Viscount Roger ceased speaking, and those around him laughed. Then somebody said: "Bah! That is the story of all conversions *in extremis.*"

THE SEQUEL TO A DIVORCE

CERTAINLY, although he had been engaged in the most extraordinary, most unlikely, most extravagant and funniest cases and had won legal games without a trump in his hand, although he had worked out the obscure law of divorce as if it had been a California gold mine, Maître Garrulier, the celebrated, the only Garrulier, could not check a movement of surprise, or a disheartening shake of the head or a smile when the Countess de Baudémont explained her affairs to him for the first time.

He had just opened his correspondence, and his slender hands on which he bestowed the greater attention buried themselves in a heap of female letters, and one might have thought oneself in the confessional of a fashionable preacher, so impregnated was the atmosphere with delicate perfumes.

Immediately, even before she had said a word, with the sharp glance of a practiced man of the world, that look which made beautiful Mme de Serpenoise say: "He strips your heart bare!" the lawyer had classed her in the third category. Those who suffer came into his first category; those who love, into the second, and those who are bored, into the third- and she belonged to the latter.

She was a pretty windmill, whose sails turned and flew round and fretted the blue sky with a delicious shiver of joy, as it were, and had the brain of a bird, in which four correct and healthy ideas cannot exist side by side and in which all dreams and every kind of folly are engulfed, like a great Kaleidoscope.

Incapable of hurting a fly, emotional, charitable, with a feeling of tenderness for the street girl who sells bunches of violets for a penny, for a cab horse which a driver is ill using, for melancholy pauper's funeral, when the body, without friends or relations to follow it, is being conveyed to the common grave, doing anything that might afford five minutes' amusement, not caring if she made men miserable for the rest of their days and taking pleasure in kindling passions which consumed men's whole being, looking upon life as too short to be anything else than one uninterrupted round of gaiety and enjoyment, she thought that people might find plenty of time for being serious and reasonable in the evening of life, when they are at the bottom of the hill and their looking glasses reveal a wrinkled face surrounded with white hair.

A thoroughbred Parisian whom one would follow to the end of the world like a poodle, a woman whom one adores with the head, the heart and the senses until one is nearly driven mad as soon as one has inhaled the delicate perfume that emanates from her dress and hair or touched her skin and heard her laugh, a woman for whom one would fight a duel and risk one's life without a thought, for whom a man would remove mountains and sell his soul to the devil several times over, if the devil were still in the habit of frequenting the places of bad repute on this earth.

She had perhaps come to see this Garrulier, whom she had so often heard mentioned at five o'clock teas, so as to be able to describe him to her female friends subsequently in droll phrases, imitating his gestures and the unctuous inflections of his voice in order, perhaps, to experience some new sensation or, perhaps, for the sake of dressing like a woman who ws going to try for a divorce, and certainly the whole effect was perfect. She wore a splendid cloak embroidered with jet-which gave an almost serious effect to her golden hair, to her small, slightly turned-up nose with its quivering nostrils and to her large eyes, full of enigma and fun-over a dark dress which was fastened at the neck by a sapphire and a diamond pin.

The barrister did not interrupt her but allowed her to get excited and to chatter, to enumerate her causes for complaint against poor Count de Baudémont, who certainly had no suspension of his wife's escapade and who would have been very much surprised if anyone told him of it at that moment, when he was taking his fencing lesson at the club.

When she had quite finished he said coolly, as if he were throwing a pail of water on some burning straw:

"But, madame, there is not the slightest pretext for a divorce in anything that you have told me here. The judges would ask me whether I took the law courts for a theater and intended to make fun of them."

And seeing how disheartened she was, that she looked like a child whose favorite toy had been broken, that she was so pretty that he would have liked to kiss her hands in his devotion, and as she seemed to be witty and very amusing, and as moreover, he had no objection to such visits being prolonged, when papers had to be looked over, while sitting close together, Maître Garrulier appeared to be considering. Taking his chin in his hand, he said:

"However, I will think it over; there is sure to be some dark spot that can be made out worse. Write to me and come and see me again."

In the course of her visits that black spot had increased so much, and Countess de Baudémont had followed her lawyer's advice so punctually and had played on the various strings so skillfully that a few months later, after a lawsuit which is still spoken of, in the course of which the president had to take off his spectacles and to use his pocket handkerchief noisily, the divorce was pronounced in favour of the Countess Marie Anne Nicole Bourn de Baudémont, née' de Tanchart de Peothus.

The count, who was nonplused at such an adventure turning out so seriously, first of all flew into a terrible rage, rushed off to the lawyer's office and threatened to cut off his knavish ears for him. But when his access of fury was over and he thought of it, he shrugged his shoulders and said:

"All the better for her if it amuses her!"

Then he bought Baron Silberstein's yacht and with some friends got up a cruise to Ceylon and India.

Marie Anne began by triumphing and felt as happy as a schoolgirl going home for the holidays; she committed every possible folly and soon tired, satiated and disfusted, began to yawn, cried and found out that she had sacrificed her happiness, like a millionaire who has gone mad and has cast his bank notes and shares into the river, and that she was nothing more than a disabled waif and stray. Consequently, she now married again, as the solitude of her home made her morose from morning till night; and then, besides, she found a woman requires a mansion when she goes into society, to race meetings or to the theater.

And so while she became a marchioness and pronounced her second "Yes" before a very few friends at the office of the mayor of the English urban district, malicious people in the Faubourg were making fun of the whole affair and affirming this and that, whether rightly or wrongly, and comparing the present husband with the former one, even declaring that he had partially been the cause of the former divorce. Meanwhile M. de Baude'mont was wandering over the four quarters of the globe, trying to overcome his homesickness and to deaden his longing for love, which had taken possession of his heart and of his body, like a slow poison.

He traveled through the most out-of-the-way places and the most lovely countries and spent months and months at sea and plunged into every kind of dissipation and debauchery. But neither the supple forms nor the luxurious gestures of the bayaderes, nor the large passive eyes of the Creoles, nor flirtations with English girls with hair the color of new cider, nor nights of waking dreams, when he saw new constellations in the sky, nor dangers during which a man thinks it is all over with him and mutters a few words of prayer in spite of himself, when the waves are high and the sky black, nothing was able to make him forget that little Parisian woman who smelled so sweet that she might have been taken for a bouquet of rare flowers; who was so coaxing, so curious, so funny; sho never had the same caprice, the same smile or the same look twice and who, at bottom, was worth more than many others, either saints or sinners.

He thought of her constantly during long hours of sleeplessness. He carried her portrait about with him in the breast pocket of his pea jacket-a charming portrait in which she was smiling and showing her white teeth between her half-open lips. Her gentle eyes with their magnetic look had an happy, frank expression, and from the mere arrangement of her hair one could see that she was fair among the fair.

He used to kiss that protrait of the woman who had been his wife, as if he wished to efface it, would look at it for hours and then throw himself down on the netting and sob like a child as he looked at the infinite expanse before him, seeming to see their lost happiness, the joys of their perished affections and the divine remembrance of their love in the monotonous waste of green waters. And he tried to accuse himself for all that had occurred and not to be angry with her, to think that his grievances were imaginary and to adore her in spite of everything and always.

And so he roamed about the world, tossed to and fro, suffering and hoping he knew not what. He ventured into the greatest dangers and sought for death just as a man seeks for his mistress, and death passed close to him without touching him, perhaps amused at his grief and misery.

For he was as wretched as a stonebreaker, as one of those poor devils who work and nearly break their backs over the hard flints the whole day long under the scorching sun or the cold rain, and Marie Anne herself was not happy, for she was pining for the past and remembered their former love.

At last, however, he returned to France, changed, tanned by exposure, sun and rain and transformed as if by some witch's philter.

Nobody would have recognized the elegant and effeminate clubman in this corsair with broad shoulders, a skin the color of tan, with very red lips, who rolled a little in his walk, who seemed to be stifled in his black dress coat but who still retained the distinguished manners and bearing of a nobleman of the last century, one of those who, when he was ruined, fitted out a privateer and fell upon the English wherever he met them, from St Milo to Calcutta. And wherever he showed himself his friends exclaimed:

"Why! Is that you? I should never have known you again!"

He was very nearly starting off again immediately; he even telegraphed orders to Havre to get the steam yacht ready for sea directly, when he heard that Marie Anne had married again.

He saw her in the distance at the Thréâtre Francais one Tuesday, and when he noticed how pretty, how fair, how desirable she was-looking so melancholy, with all the appearance of an unhappy soul that regrets something-his determination grew weaker, and he delayed his departure from week to week and waited, without knowing why, until at last, worn out with the struggle, watching her wherever she went, more in love with her than he had ever been before, he wrote her long, mad, ardent letters in which his passion overflowed like a stream of lava.

He altered his handwriting, as he remembered her restless brain and her many whims. He sent her the flowers which he knew she liked best and told her that she was his life, that he was dying of waiting for her, of longing for her, for her, his idol.

At last, very much puzzled and surprised, guessing-who knows? - from the instinctive beating of her heart and her general emotion that it must be he this time, he whose soul she had tortured with such cold cruelty, and knowing that she could make amends for the past and bring back their former love, she replied to him and granted him the meeting that he asked for. She fell into his arms, and they both sobbed with joy and ecstasy. Their kisses were those which lips give only when they have lost each other and found each other again at last, when they meet and exhaust themselves in each other's looks, thirsting for tenderness, love and enjoyment.

* * * * * *

Last week Count de Baudémount carried of Marie Anne quietly and coolly, just like one resumes possession of one's house on returning from a journey and drives out the intruders. And when Maître Garrulier was told of this unheard-of scandal he rubbed his hands- the long, delicate hands of a sensual prelate-and exclaimed:

"That is absolutely logical, and I should like to be in their place."

A USEFUL HOUSE

ROYAUMONT'S fat sides shook with laughter at the mere recollection of the funny story that he had promised to his friends, and, throwing himself back in the great armchair, which he completely filled, that confirmed gossip and busybody, as they called him at the club, at last said:

"It is perfectly true. Bordenave does not owe anyone a penny and can go through any street he likes and publish those famous memoirs of sheriff's officers, which he has been writing for the last ten years, when he did not dare to go out, and in which he carefully brought out the characters and peculiarities of all those generous distributors of stamped paper with whom he had had dealings— their tricks and wiles, their weaknesses, their jokes, their manner of performing their duties, sometimes with brutal rudeness and at others with cunning good nature, now embarrassed and almost ashamed of their work, and again ironically jovial—as well as the artifices of clerks to get a few crumbs from their employer's cake. The book will soon be published, and Machin, the vaudeville writer, has promised him a preface, so that it will be a most amusing work. You are surprised, eh? Confess that you are absolutely surprised, and I will lay you any bet you like that you will not guess how our excellent friend, whose existence is an inexplicable problem, has been able to settle with his creditors and suddenly produce the requisite amount."

"Do get to the facts, confound it," Captain Hardeur said, who was growing tired of all this verbiage.

"All right, I will get to them as quickly as possible," Royaumont replied, throwing the stump of his cigar into the fire. "I will clear my throat and begin. I suppose you all of you know that two better friends than Bordenave and Quillanet do not exist; neither of them could do without the other, and they have ended by dressing alike, by having the same gestures, the same laugh, the same walk and the same inflections of voice, so that one would think that some close bond united them and that they had been brought up together from childhood.

"There is, however, this difference between them, that Bordenave is completely ruined and that all that he possesses are bundles of mortgages, laughable parchments which attest his ancient race, and chimerical hopes of inheriting money someday, though these expectations are already heavily hypothecated. Consequently he is always on the lockout for some fresh expedient for raising money, though he is superbly indifferent about everything, while Sebastien Quillanet, of the banking house of Quillanet Brothers, must have an income of eight hundred thousand francs a year but is descended from an obscure labourer who managed to secure some of the national property. Then he becomes an army contractor, speculated on defeat as well as on victory, and does not know now what to do with his money.

"But as the millionaire is timid, dull and always bored, the spendthrift amuses him by his impertinent ways and jokes; he prompts him when he is at a loss for an answer, extricates him out of his difficulties, serves as his guide in the great forests of Paris which are strewn with so many pitfalls and helps him to avoid those vulgar adventures which socially ruin a man, no matter how well ballasted he may be. Then he points out to him what women would make suitable mistresses for him, who make a man noted and give the effect of some rare and beautiful flower pinned into his buttonhole. He is the confidant of his intrigues, his guest when he gives small, special entertainments, his daily, familiar table companion and the buffoon whose sly humour stimulates one and whose witticisms you tolerate,"

"Really, really," the captain interrupted him, "you have been going on for more than a quarter of an hour without saying anything."

But Royaumont shrugged his shoulders and continued:

Oh, you can be very tiresome when you please, my dear fellow! Last year, when he was at daggers drawn with his people, who were deafening him with recriminations, were worrying him and threatening him with a lot of annoyance, Quillanet got married. It was a marriage of reason, which apparently changed his habits and his tastes, more especially as the banker was at that time keeping a perfect little marvel of a woman, a Parisian jewel of unspeakable attraction and of bewitching delicacy, that adorable Suzette Marly, who is just like a pocket Venus and who in some prior stage of existence must have been Phryne or Lesbia. Of course he did not get rid of her, but as he was bound to take some judicious precautions, which are necessary for a man who is deceiving his wife, he rented and furnished a house with a courtyard in front and a garden at the back, which one might think had been built to shelter some amorous folly. It was the ideal that he had dreamed of, warm, snug, elegant, the walls covered with silk hangings of subdued tints, large pier glasses, allegorical pictures and filled with luxurious, low furniture that seemed to invite caresses and embraces.

"Bordenave occupied the ground floor, and the next floor served as a shrine for the banker and his mistress. Well, just a week ago, in order to hide the situation better, Bordenave asked

Quillanet and some other friends to one of those luncheons which he understands so well how to order, such a delicious luncheon, that before it was quite over every man had a woman on his lap and was asking himself whether a kiss from coaxing and naughty lips was not a thousand times more intoxicating than the finest old brandy or the choicest vintage wines, when the butler came in with an embarrassed look and whispered something to him.

" 'Tell the gentleman that he has made a mistake and ask him to leave me in peace,' Bordenave replied to him in an angry voice. The servant went out and returned immediately to say that the intruder was using threats, that he fused to leave the house and even spoke of having recourse to the commissary of police. Bordenave frowned, threw his napkin down, upset two glasses and swaggered out with a red face, swearing and ejaculating:

" 'This is rather too much, and the fellow shall find out what going out of the window means, if he will not leave by the door.' But in the anteroom he found himself face to face with a very cool, polite, impassive gentleman, who said very quietly to him:

" 'You are Count Robert de Bordenave, I believe, monsieur?'

" 'Yes, monsieur.'

" 'And the lease that you signed at the lawyer's, Monsieur Albin Calvert, in the Rue du Poissonnière is in your name, I believe?'

" 'Certainly, monsieur.'

'"Then I regret extremely to have to tell you that if you are not in a position to pay the various accounts which different people have entrusted to me for collection here, I shall be obliged to seize all the furniture, pictures, plate, clothes, etc., which are here in the presence of two witnesses who are waiting for me downstairs in the street.'

" 'I suppose this is some joke, monsieur?'

" 'It would be a very poor joke, Monsieur le Comte, and one which I should certainly not allow myself toward you!'

"The situation was absolutely critical and ridiculous, the more so, that in the dining room the women, who were slightly tipsy, were tapping the wineglasses with their spoons and calling for him. What could he do except explain his misadventure to Quillanet, who became sobered immediately and, rather than see his shrine of love violated, his secret sin disclosed and his pictures, ornaments and furniture sold, gave a check in due form for the claim there and then, though with a very wry face. And in spite of this, some people will deny that men who are utterly broke often have a stroke of luck!"

A VAGABOND

FOR more than a month Randel had been walking, seeking for work everywhere. He had left his native place, Ville-Avary, in the department of La Manche because there was no work to be had. He was a journeyman carpenter, twenty-seven years old, a steady fellow and good workman, but for two months he, the eldest son, had been obliged to live on his family, with nothing to do but loaf in the general stoppage of work. Bread was getting scarce with them; the two sisters went out as charwomen but earned little, and he, Jacques Randel, the strongest of them all, did nothing because he had nothing to do and ate the others' bread.

Then he went and inquired at the town hall, and the mayor's secretary told him that he would find work at the labor center. So he started, well provided with papers and certificates and carrying another pair of shoes, a pair of trousers and a shirt in a blue handkerchief at the end of his stick.

He had walked almost without stopping, day and night, along interminable roads, in the sun and rain, without ever reaching that mysterious country where workmen find work. At first he had the fixed idea that he must only work at his own trade, but at every carpenter's shop where he applied he was told that they had just dismissed men on accocut of work being so slack, and finding himself at the end of his resources, he made up his mind to undertake any job that he might come across on the road. And so by turns he was a navvy, stableman, stone sawyer; he split wood, lopped the branches of trees, dug wells, mixed mortar, tied up fagots, tended goats on a mountain, and all for a few pence, for he only obtained two or three days' work occasionally, by offering himself at a shamefully low price in order to tempt the avarice of employers and peasants.

And now for a week he had found nothing, and he had no money left. He was eating a piece of bread, thanks to the charity of some women from whom he had begged at house doors on the road. It was getting dark, and Jacques Randel, jaded, his legs failing him, his stomach empty and with despair in his heart, was walking barefoot on the grass by the side of the road, for he was taking care of his last pair of shoes, the other pair having already ceased to exist for a long time. It was a Saturday toward the end of autumn. The heavy gray clouds were being driven rapidly among the trees, and one felt that it would rain soon. The country was deserted at that time of the evening and on the eve of Sunday. Here and there in the fields there rose up stacks of thrashed-out corn like huge yellow mushrooms, and the fields looked bare, as they had already been for the next year.

Randel was hungry with the hunting of some wild animal, such a hunger as drives wolves to attack men. Worn out and weakened with fatigue, he took longer strides so as not to take so many steps, and with heavy head , the blood throbbing in his temples, with red eyes and dry mouth he grasped his stick tightly in his hand with a longing to strike the first passer-by whom he should meet, and who might be going home to supper, with all his force.

He looked at the sides of the road with the image of potatoes dug up and lying on the ground before his eyes; if he had found any he would have gathered some dead wood, made a fire in the ditch and have had a capital supper off the warm, round tubers, which he would first of all have held burning hot in his cold hands. But it was too late in the year, and he would have to gnaw a raw beetroot as he had done the day before, having picked one up in a field.

For the last two days he had spoken aloud as he quickened his steps, under the influence of his thoughts. He had never done much thinking hitherto, as he had given all his mind, all his simple faculties, to his industrial requirements. But now fatigue and this desperate search for work which he could not get, refusals and rebuffs, nights spent in the open air lying on the grass, long fasting, the contempt which he knew people with a settled abode felt for a vagabond, the question which he was continually asked: "Why did you not remain at home?" distress at not being able to use his strong arms which he felt so full of vigor, the recollection of his relations who had remained at home and who also had not a halfpenny, filled him by degrees with a rage which was accumulating every day, every hour, every minute, and which now escaped his lips in spite of himself in short growling sentences.

As he stumbled over the stones which rolled beneath his bare feet he grumbled: "How wretched! how miserable! A set of hogs, to let a man die of hunger, a carpenter. A set of hogs-not twopence-not twopence. And now it is raining-a set of hogs!"

He was indignant at the injustice of fate and cast the blame on men, on all men, because Nature, that great, blind mother, is unjust, cruel and perfidious, and he repeated through his clenched teeth, "A set of hogs," as he looked at the thin gray smoke which rose from the roofs, for it was the dinner hour. And without thinking about that other injustice, which is human and which is called robbery and violence, he felt inclined to go into one of those houses to murder the inhabitants and to sit down to table in their stead.

He said to himself: "I have a right to live, and they are letting me die of hunger- and yet I only ask for work-a set of hogs!" And the pain in his limbs, the gnawing in his heart, rose to his head like terrible intoxication and gave rise to this simple thought in his brain: "I have the right to live because I breathe and because the air is the common property of everybody, and so nobody has the right to leave me without bread!"

A thick, fine, icy- cold rain was coming down, and he stopped and murmured: "How miserable! Another month of walking before I get home." He was indeed returning home then, for he saw that he should more easily find work in his native town where he was known-and he did not mind what he did-than on the highroads where everybody suspected him. As the cerpentering business was not going well he would turn day laborer, be a mason's hodman, ditcher, break stones on the road. If he only earned tenpence a day, that would at any rate find him something to eat.

He tied the remains of his last pocket handkerchief round his neck to prevent the cold water from running down his back and chest, but he soon found that it was penetrating the thin material of which his clothes were made, and he glanced round him with the agonized look of a man who does not know where to hide his body and to rest his head and has no place of shelter in the whole world.

Night came on and wrapped the country in obscurity, and in the distance, in a meadow, he saw a dark spot on the grass; it was a cow, and so he got over the ditch by the roadside and went up to her without exactly knowing what he was doing. When he got close to her she raised her great head to him, and he thought: "If I only had a jug I could get a little milk." He looked at the cow, and the cow looked at him, and then suddenly, giving her a violent kick in the side, he said: "Get up!"

The animal got up slowly, letting her heavy udder hang down below her; then the man lay down on his back between the animal's legs and drank for a long time, squeezing the warm swollen teats which tasted of the cow stall with both hands, and drank as long as any milk remained in that living well. But the icy rain began to fall more heavily, and he saw no place of shelter on the whole of that bare plain. He was cold, and he looked at a light which was shining among the trees in the window of a house.

The cow had lain down again, heavily, and he sat down by her side and stroked her head, grateful for the nourishment she had given him. The animal's strong thick breath, which came out of her nostrils like two jets of steam in the evening air, blew onto the workman's face, who said: "You are not cold inside there!" He put his hands onto her chest and under her legs to find some warmth there, and then the idea struck him that he might pass the night against that large, warm stomach. So he found a comfortable place and laid his forehead against the great udder from which he had quenched his thirst just previously, and then, as he was worn out with fatigue, he fell asleep immediately.

He woke up, however several times, with his back or his stomach half frozen, according as he put one or the other to the animal's flank. Then he turned over to warm and dry that part of his body which had remained exposed to the night air, and he soon went soundly to sleep again.

The crowing of a cock woke him; the day was breaking, it was no longer raining and the sky was bright the cow was resting with her muzzle on the ground, and he stooped down, resting on his hands, to kiss those wide nostrils of moist flesh and said: "Good-by, my beauty, until next time. You are a nice animal! Good-by." Then he put on his shoes and went off, and for two hours he walked straight on before him, always following the same road, and then he felt so tired that he sat down on the grass. It was broad daylight by that time, and the church bells were ringing; men in blue blouses, women in white caps, some on foot, some in carts, began to pass along the road, going to the neighboring villages to spend Sunday with friends or relations.

A stout peasant came in sight, driving a score of frightened, bleating sheep in front of him whom an active dog kept together, so Randel got up and, raising his cap, he said: "You do not happen to have any work for a man who is dying of hunger?" But the other, giving an angry look at the vagabond, replied: "I have no work for fellows whom I meet on the road."

And the carpenter went back and sat down by the side of the ditch again. He waited there for a long time, watching the country people pass and looking for a kind, compassionate face before he renewed his request, and finally selected a man in an overcoat, whose stomach was adorned with a gold chain. "I have been looking for work," he said, "for the last two months and cannot find any, and I have not a halfpenny in my pocket."

But the semigentleman replied: "You should have read the notice which is stuck up at the beginning of the village: 'Begging is prohibited within the boundaries of this parish.' Let me tell you that I am the mayor, and if you do not get out of here pretty quickly, I shall have you arrested."

Randel, who was getting angry, replied: "Have me arrested if you like; I should prefer it, for at any rate I should not die of hunger." And he went back and sat down by the side of his ditch again, and in about a quarter of an hour two gendarmes appeared on the road. They were walking slowly, side by side, well in sight, glittering in the sun with their shining hats, their yellow accoutrements and their metal buttons, as if to frighten evildoers and to put them to flight at a distance. He knew that they were coming after him, but he did not move, for he was seized with a sudden desire to defy them, to be arrested by them and to have his revenge later.

They came on without appearing to have seen him, walking with military steps, heavily, and balancing themselves as if they were doing the goose step; and then suddenly, as they passed him, they noticed him and stopped, looking at him angrily and threateningly. The brigadier came up to him and asked:

" What are you doing here?"

"I am resting," The man replied calmly.

"Where do you come from?"

"If I had to tell you all the places I have been to, it would take me more than an hour."

"Where are you going to?"

"ToVille-Avary."

"Where is that?"

"In La Manche."

"Is that where you belong to?"

"It is."

"Why did you leave it?"

"To Try for work."

The brigadier turned to his gendarme and said in the angry voice of a man who is exasperated at last by the same trick: "They all say that, these scamps. I know all about it." And then he continued: "Have you any papers?"

"Yes, I have some."

"Give them to me."

Randel took his papers out of his pocket, his certificates, those poor wornout dirty papers which were falling to pieces, and gave them to the soldier, who spelled them through, hemming and hawing, and then, having seen that they were all in order, he gave them back to Randel with the dissatisfied look of a man whom someone cleverer than himself has tricked.

After a few moments' further reflection he asked him: "Have you any money on you?"

"No."

"None whatever?"

"None."

"Not even a sou?"

"Not even a sou?"

"How do you live then?"

"On what people give me."

"Then you beg?"

And Randel answered resolutely: "Yes, when I can."

Then the gendarme said: "I have caught you on the highroad in the act of vagabondage and begging, without any resources or trade, and so I command you to come with me."

The carpenter got up and said: "Wherever you please." And placing himself between the two soldiers, ever before he had received the order to do so, he added: "Come, lock me up; that will at any rate put a roof over my head when it rains."

And they set off toward the village, whose red tiles could be seen through the leafless trees, a quarter of a league off. Service was just going to begin when they went through the village. The square was full of people who immediately formed two hedges to see the criminal, who was being followed by a crowd of excited children, pass. Male and female peasants looked at the prisoner between the two gendarmes with hatred in their eyes and a longing to throw stones at him, to tear his skin with their nails, to trample him under their feet. They asked each other whether he had committed murder or robbery. The butcher, who was an ex-spahi, declared that he was a deserter. The tobacconist thought that he recognized him as the man who had that very morning passed a bad half-franc piece off on him, and the ironmonger declared that he was the murderer of Widow Malet, for whom the police had been looking for six months.

In the hall of the municipal council, into which his custodians took him, Randel saw the mayor again, sitting on the magisterial bench with the schoolmaster by his side.

"Ah! ah!" the magistrate exclaimed, "so here you are again, my fellow. I told you I should have you locked up. Well, Brigadier, what is he charged with?"

"He is a vagabond without house or home, Monsieur le

Maire, without any resources or money, so he says, who was arrested in the act of begging, but he is provided with good testimonials, and his papers are all in order."

"Show me his papers," the mayor said. He took them, read them, reread, returned them and then said: "Search him": they searched him but found nothing, and the mayor seemed perplexed and asked the workman:

"What were you doing on the road this morning?"

"I was looking for work."

"Work?" On the highroad?"

"How do you expect me to find any if I hide in the woods?"

They looked at each other with the hatred of two wild beasts which belong to different hostile species and the magistrate continued: "I am going to have you set at liberty, but do not be brought up before me again."

To which the carpenter replied: "I would rather you locked me up; I have had enough running about the country."

But the magistrate replied severely: "Be silent." And then he said to the two gendarmes: "You will conduct this man two hundred yards from the village and let him continue his journey."

"At any rate give me something to eat," the workman said, but the other grew indignant. "It only remains for us to feed you! Ah! ah! ah! that is rather strong!"

But Randel went on firmly: "If you let me nearly die of hanger again, you will force me to commit a crime, and then so much the worse for you other fat fellows."

The mayor had risen, and he repeated: " Take him away immediately, or I shall end by getting angry."

The two gendarmes thereupon seized the carpenter by the arms and dragged him out. He allowed them to do it without resistance, passed through the village again and found himself on the highroad once more; and when the men had accompanied him two hundred yards beyond the village the brigadier said:

"Now off with you, and do not let me catch you about here again, for if I do, you will know it."

Randel went off without replying or knowing where he was going. He walked on for a quarter of an hour or twenty minutes, so stupefied that he no longer thought of anything. But suddenly, as he was passing a small house where the window was half open, the smell of the soup and boiled meat stopped him suddenly in front of it, and hunger, fierce, devouring, maddening hunger, seized him and almost drove him against the walls of the house like a wild beast.

He said aloud, in a grumbling voice: "In heaven's name, they must give me some this time." And he began to knock at the door vigorously with his stick, and as nobody came he knocked louder and called out: "Hallo! you people in there, open the door!" And then, as nothing moved, he went up to the window and pushed it open with his hand, and the close warm air of the kitchen, full of the smell of hot soup, meat and cabbage, escaped into the cold outer air, and with a bound the carpenter was in the house. Two covers were laid on the table; no doubt the proprietors of the house, on going to church, had left their dinner on the fire, their nice Sunday boiled beef and vegetable soup while there was a loaf of new bread on the chimney piece between two bottles which seemed full.

Randel seized the bread first of all and broke it with as much violence as if he were strangling a man, and then he began to eat it voraciously, swallowing great mouthfuls quickly. But almost immediately the smell of the meat attracted him to the fireplace, and having taken off the lid of the saucepan, he plunged a fork into it and brought out a large piece of beef tied with a string. Then he took more cabbage, carrots and onions until his plate was full, and having put it on the table, he sat down before it, cut the meat into four pieces and dined as if he had been at home. When he had eaten nearly all the meat, besides a quantity of vegetables, he felt thirsty and took one of the bottles off the mantelpiece.

Scracely had he poured the liquor into his glass than he saw it was brandy. So much the better; it was warming, it would instill some fire into his veins, and that would be all right, after being so cold; and he drank some. He found it very good, certainly, for he had grown unaccustomed to it, and he poured himself out another glassful which he drank at two gulps. And then almost immediately he felt quite merry and light hearted from the effect of the alcohol, just as if some great happiness were flowing through his system.

He continued to eat, but more slowly, dipping his bread into the soup. His skin had become burning, and especially his forehead, where the veins were throbbing. But suddenly the church bells began to ring. Mass was over, and instinct rather than fear, the instinct of prudence which guides all beings and makes them clear-sighted in danger, made the carpenter get up. He put the remains of the loaf into one pocket and the brandy bottle into the other, and he furtively went to the window and looked out into the road. It was still deserted, so he jumped out and set off walking again, but instead of following the highroad he ran across the fields toward a wood which he saw a little way off.

He felt alert, strong, lighthearted, glad of what he had done and so nimble that he sprang over the inclosures of the fields at a single bound, and as soon as he was under the trees he took the bottle out of his pocket again and began to drink once more, swallowing it down as he walked, and then his ideas began to get confused, his eyes grew dim and his legs elastic as springs, and he started singing the old popular song:

"Oh! how nice, how nice it is,
To pick the sweet, wild strawberries. "

He was now walking on thick, damp, cool moss, and the soft carpet under his feet made him feel absurdly inclined to turn head over heels, like he used to do as a child; so he took a run, turned a somersault, got up and began over again. And between each time he began to sing again:

"Oh! how nice, how nice it is,
To pick the sweet, wild strawberries."

Suddenly he found himself on the edge of a sunken road, and in the road he saw a tall girl, a servant who was returning to the village with two pails of milk. He watched, stooping down and with his eyes as bright as those of a dog who scents a quail, but she saw him, raised her head and said: "Was that you singing like that?" He did not reply, however, but jumped down into the road, although it was at least six feet down, and when she saw him suddenly standing in front of her she exclaimed: "Oh dear, how you frightened me!"

But he did not hear her, for he was drunk, he was mad, excited by another requirement which was more imperative than hunger, more feverish than alcohol; by the irresistible fury of the man who has been in want of everything for two months and who is drunk, who is young, ardent and inflamed by all the appetites which nature has implanted in the flesh of vigorous men.

The girl strated back from him, frightened at his face, his eyes, his half-open mouth, his outstretched hands, but he seized her by the shoulders and without a word threw her down in the road.

She let her two pails fall, and they rolled over noisily and all the milk was spilt, and then she screamed, but comprehending that it would be of no use to call for help in that lonely spot and seeing that he was not going to make an attempt on her life, she yielded without much difficulty and not very angrily either, for he was a strong, handsome young fellow and really not rough.

When she got up the thought of her overturned pails suddenly filled her with fury, and taking off one of her wooden clogs she threw it, in her turn, at the man to break his head since he did not pay her for her milk.

But he, mistaking the reason for this sudden violent attack, somewhat sobered and frightened at what he had done, ran off as fast as he could while she threw stones at him, some of which hit him in the back.

He ran for a long time, very long, until he felt more tired than he had ever been before. His legs were so weak that they could scarcely carry him; all his ideas were confused; he lost the recollection of everything and could no longer think about anything, and so he sat down at the foot of a tree and in five minutes was fast asleep. He was soon awakened, however, by a rough shake, and on opening his eyes he saw two cocked hats of polished leather bending over him and the two gendarmes of the morning, who were holding him and binding his arms.

"I knew I should catch you again," said the brigadier jeeringly. But Randel got up without replying. The two men shook him, quite ready to ill-treat him if he made a movement, for he was their prey now; he had become a jailbird, caught by hunters of criminals who would not let him go again.

"Now, start!" the brigadier said, and they set off. It was getting evening, and the autumn twilight was settling, heavy and dark, over the land, and in half an hour they reached the village, where every door was open, for the people had heard what had happened. Peasants and peasant women and girls, excited with anger, as if every man had been robbed and every woman violated, wished to see the wretch brought back, so that they might overwhelm him with abuse. They hooted him from the first house in the village until they reached the mansion house, where the mayor was waiting for him. Eager to avenge himself on this vagabond as soon as he saw him, he cried:

"Ah! my fine fellow! Here we are!" And he rubbed his hands, more pleased than he usually was, and continued: "I said so. I said so the moment I saw him in the road." And then with increased satisfaction:

"Oh! you blackguard! Oh! you dirty blackguard! You will get your twenty years, my fine fellow!"

WAITER, A BOCK!'

WHY, on this particular evening, did I enter a certain beer shop? I cannot explain it. It was bitterly cold. A fine rain, a watery mist, floated about, veiling the gas jets in a transparent fog, making the pavements under the shadow of the shop fronts glitter, which revealed the soft slush and the soiled feet of the passers-by.

I was going nowhere in particular; was simply having a short walk after dinner. I had passed the Credit Lyonnais, the Rue Vivienne and several other streets. Suddenly I descried a large cafe', which was more than half full. I walked inside with no object in mind. I was not the least thirsty.

By a searching glance I detected a place where I would not be too much crowded. So I went and sat down by the side of a man who seemed to me to be old and who smoked a halfpenny clay pipe, which had become as black as coal. From six to eight beer saucers were piled up on the table in front of him, indicating the number of bocks he had already absorbed. With that same glance I had recognized in him a "regular toper," one of those frequenters of beerhouses who come in the morning as soon as the place is open and only go away in the evening when it is about to close. He was dirty, bald to about the middle of the cranium, while his long gray hair fell over the neck of his frock coat. His clothes, much too large for him, appeared to have been made for him at a time when he was very stout. One could guess that his pantaloons were not held up by braces and that this man could not take ten paces without having to pull them up and readjust them. Did he wear a vest? The mere thought of his boots and the feet they enveloped filled me with horror. The frayed cuffs were as black at the edges as were his nails.

As soon as I had sat down near him this queer creature said to me in a tranquil tone of voice:

"How goes it with you?"

I turned sharply round to him and closely scanned his features, whereupon he continued:

"I see you do not recognize me."

"No, I do not."

"Des Barrets."

I was stupefied. It was Count Jean des Barrets, my old college chum.

I seized him by the hand, so dumfounded that I could find nothing to say.

I at length managed to stammer out:

"And you, how goes it with you?"

He responded placidly:

"With me? Just as I like?"

He became silent. I wanted to be friendly and I selected this phrase:

"What are you doing now?"

"You see what I am doing ." he answered, quite resignedly.

I felt my face getting red. I insisted:

"But every day?"

"Every day is alike to me," was his response, accompanied

with a thick puff of tobacco smoke.

He then tapped on the top of the marble table with a sou to attract the attention of the waiter and called out:

"Waiter, two bocks."

A voice in the distance repeated:

"Two bocks instead of four."

Another voice, more distant still, shouted out:

"Here they are, sir, here they are."

Immediately there appeared a man with a white apron carrying two bocks, which he set down foaming on the table, the foam running over the edge onto the sandy floor.

Des Barrets emptied his glass at a single draught and replaced it on the table, sucking in the drops of beer that had been left on his mustache. He next asked:

"What is there new?"

"I know of nothing new, worth mentioning really," I stammered. "But nothing has grown old for me; I am a commercial man."

In an equable tone of voice he said:

"Indeed-does that amuse you?"

"No, but what do you mean by that? Surely you must do something!"

"What do you mean by that?"

"I only mean, how do you pass your time?"

"What's the use of occupying myself with anything? For my part, I do nothing at all, as you see, never anything. When one has not got a sou one can understand why one has to go to work. What is the good of working? Do you work for yourself or for others? If you work for yourself you do it for your own amusement, which is all right; if you work for others you reap nothing but ingratitude."

Then, sticking his pipe into his mouth, he called out anew:

"Waiter, a bock! It makes me thirsty to keep calling so. I am not accustomed to that sort of thing. Yes, I do nothing; I let things slide and I am growing old. In dying I shall have nothing to regret: If so, I should remember nothing outside this public house. I have no wife, no children, no cares, no sorrows, nothing.

That is the very best thing that could happen to one."

He then emptied the glass which had been brought him, passed his tongue over his lips and resumed his pipe.

I looked at him, stupefied, and asked him:

"But you have not always been like that?"

"Pardon me, sir; ever since I left college."

"It is not a proper life to lead, my dear sir; it is simply horrible. Come, you must indeed have done something; you must have loved something; you must have friends."

"No, I get up at noon; I come here; I have my breakfast; I drink my bock; I remain until evening; I have my dinner; I drink bock. Then about one in the morning I return to my couch, because the place closes up. And it is this latter that embitters me more than anything. For the last ten years I have passed six tenths of my time on this bench in my corner and the other four tenths in my bed, never changing. I talk sometimes with the habitues."

"But on arriving in Paris what did you do at first?"

"I paid my devoirs to the Café de Medicis."

"What next?"

"Next? I crossed the water and came here."

"Why did you take even that trouble?"

"What do you mean? One cannot remain all one's life in the Latin Quarter. The students make too much noise. But I do not move about any longer. Waiter, a bock."

I now began to think that he was making fun of me, and I continued:

"Come now, be frank. You have been the victim of some great sorrow; despair in love, no doubt! It is easy to see that you are a man whom misfortune has hit hard. What age are you?

"I am thirty years of age, but I look to be forty-five at least."

I looked him straight in the face. His shrunken figure, badly cared for, gave one the impression that he was an old man. On the summit of his cranium a few long hairs shot straight up from a skin of doubtful cleanness. He had enormous eyelashes, a large mustache and a thick beard. Suddenly I had a kind of vision-I know not why-the vision of a basin filled with noisome water, the water which should have been applied to that poll. I said to him:

"Verily, you look to be more than that age. Of a certainty you must have experienced some great disappointment." He replied:

"I tell you that I have not. I am old because I never take air. There is nothing that vitiates the life of a man more than the atmosphere of a cafe." I could not believe him.

"You must surely have been married as well? One could not get baldheaded as you are without having been much in love."

He shook his head, sending down his back little hairs from the scalp. "No, I have always been virtuous."

And, raising his eyes toward the luster which beat down on our heads , he said:

"If I am bald-headed it is the fault of the gas. It is the enemy of hair. Waiter, a bock. You must be thirsty also?"

"No, thank you. But you certainly interest me. When did you have your first discouragement? Your life is not normal; is not natural. There is something under it all."
:

"Yes, and it dates from my infancy. I received a heavy blow when I was very young. It turned my life into darkness, which will last to the end."

" How did it come about?"

"You wish to know about it? Well then, listen. You recall, of course, the castle in which I was brought up, seeing that you used to visit it for five or six months during the vacations. You remember that large gray building in the middle of a great park and the long avenues of oaks, which opened toward the four cardinal points? You remember my father and my mother, both of whom were ceremonious, solemn and severe ?

"I worshiped my mother; I was suspicious of my father, but I respected both, accustomed always as I was to see everyone bow before them. In the country they were Monsieur le Comte and Madame la Comtesse, and our neighbors, the

Tannemares, the Ravelets, the Brennevilles, showed the utmost consideration for them.

"I was then thirteen years old, happy, satisfied with everything, as one is a that age, and full of joy and vivacity.

"Now toward the end of September, a few days before entering the lycée while I was enjoying myself in the mazes of the park, climbing the trees and swinging on the branches, I saw crossing an avenue my father and mother, who were walking together.

"I recall the thing as though it were yesterday. It was a very windy day. The whole line of trees bent under the pressure of the wind, moaned and seemed to utter cries-cries dull, yet deep-so that the whole forest groaned under the gale "Evening had come on, and it was dark in the thickets. The agitation of the wind and the branches excited me, made me skip about like an idiot and howl in imitation of the wolves.

"As soon as I perceived my parents I crept furtively toward them under the branches, in order to surprise them, as though I had been a veritable wolf. But suddenly seized with fear, I stopped a few paces from them. My father, a prey to the most violent passsion, cried:

" 'Your mother is a fool; moreover, it is not your mother that is the question; it is you. I tell you that I want money, and I will make you sign this.'

My mother responded in a firm voice:

" 'I will not sign it. It is Jean's fortune: I shall guard it for him and I will not allow you to devour it with strange women, as you have your own heritage.'

"Then my father, full of rage, wheeled round and seized his wife by the throat and began to slap her full in the face with the disengaged hand.

"My mother's hat fell off; her hair became disheveled and fell down her back; she essayed to parry the blows but could not escape from them. And my father, like a madman, banged and banged at her. My mother rolled over on the ground , covering her face in both her hands. Then he turned her over on her back in order to batter her still more, pulling away the hands which were covering her face.

"As for me, my friend, it seemed as though the world had

come to an end, that the eternal laws had changed. I experienced the overwhelming dread that one has in presence of things supernatural, in presence of irreparable disaster. My boyish head whirled round and soared. I began to cry with all my might without knowing why, a prey to terror, to grief, to a dreadful bewilderment. My father heard me I believed that he wanted to kill me, and I fled like a hunted animal, running straight in front of me through the woods.

"I ran perhaps for an hour, perhaps for two; I know not. Darkness had set in; I tumbled over some thick herbs, exhausted, and I lay there lost, devoured by terror, eaten up by a sorrow capable of breaking forever the heart of a child. I became cold; I became hungry. At length day broke. I dared neither get up, walk, return home or save myself, fearing to encounter my father whom I did not wish to see again.

"I should probably have died of misery and of hunger at the foot of a tree if the guard had not discovered me and led me by force.

"I found my parents wearing their ordinary aspect. My mother alone spoke tome:

" How you have frightened me, you naughty boy; I have been the whole night sleepless.'

"I did not answer but began to weep. My father did not utter a single word.

"Eight days later I entered the lycée.

"Well, my friend, it was all over with me. I had witnessed the other side of things, the bad side; I have not been able to perceive the good side since that day. What things have passed in my mind, what strange phenomena have warped my ideas, I do not know. But I no longer have a taste for anything, a wish for anything, a love for anybody, a desire for anything whatever, no ambition, no hope. And I always see my poor mother lying on the ground in the avenue while my father was maltreating her. My mother died a few years after; my father lives still. I have not seen him since. Waiter, a bock."

A waiter brought him his bock, which he swallowed at a gulp. But in taking up his pipe again, trembling as he was, he broke it. Then he made a violent gesture:

"Zounds! This is indeed a grief, a real grief. I have had it for a month, and it was coloring so beautifully!"

Then he went off through the vast saloon which was now full of smoke and of people drinking, calling out:

"Waiter, a bock-and a new pipe."

A COCK CROWED

MME BERTHA d'Avancelles had up till that time resisted all the prayers of her despairing adorer, Baron Joseph de Croissard. He had pursued her ardently in Pans during the winter, and now he was giving fetes and shooting parties in her honor at his chateau at Carville, in Normandy.

M. d'Avancelles, her husband, saw nothing and knew nothing, as usual. It was said that he lived apart from his wife on account of a physical weakness for which Mme d'Avancelles would not pardon him. He was a short, stout, bald man, with short arms, legs, neck, nose, and very ugly; while Mme d'Avancelles, on the contrary, was a tall, dark and determined young woman who laughed in her husband's face with sonorous peals while he called her openly "Mrs Housewife." She looked at the broad shoulders, strong build and fair mustaches of her titled admirer, Baron Joseph de Croissard, with a certain amount of tenderness.

She had not, however, granted him anything as yet. The baron was ruining himself for her, and there was a constant round of feting, hunting parties and new pleasures to which he invited the neighboring nobility. All day long the hounds gave tongue in the woods as they followed the fox or the wild boar, and every night dazzling fireworks mingled their burning plumes with the stars while the illuminated windows of the drawing room cast long rays of light onto the wide lawns where shadows were moving to and fro.

It was autumn, the russet-colored season of the year, and the leaves were whirling about on the grass like flights of birds. One noticed the smell of damp earth in the air, of the naked earth, like one scents the odor of the bare skin when a woman's dress falls off her after a ball.

One evening in the previous spring, during an entertainment, Mme d'Avancelles had said to M. de Croissard, who was worrying her by his importunities: "If I do succumb to you, my friend, it will not be before the fall of the leaf. I have too many things to do this summer to have any time for it." He had not forgotten that bold and amusing speech, and every day he became more pressing, every day he pushed his approaches nearer-to use a military phrase-and gained a hold on the heart of the fair, audacious woman who seemed only to be resisting for form's sake.

It was the day before a large wild-boar hunt, and in the evening Mme Bertha said to the baron with a laugh: "Baron, if you kill the brute, I shall have something to say to you." And so at dawn he was up and out, to try and discover where the solitary animal had its lair. He accompanied his huntsmen, settled the places for the relays and organized everything personally to insure his triumph. When the horns gave the signal for setting out he appeared in a closely fitting coat of scarlet and gold, with his waist drawn in tight, his chest expanded, his eyes radiant and as fresh and strong as if he had just got out of bed. They set off; the wild boar bolted through the underwood as soon as he was dislodged, followed by the hounds in full cry, while the horses set off at a gallop through the narrow side-cuts in the forest. The carriages which followed the chase at a distance drove noiselessly along the soft roads.

From mischief Mme d'Avancelles kept the baron by her side, lagging behind at a walk in an interminably long and straight drive, over which four rows of oaks hung so as to form almost an arch, while he, trembling with love and anxiety, listened with one ear to the young woman's bantering chatter and with the other to the blast of the horns and to the cry of the hounds as they receded in the distance.

"So you do not love me any longer?" she observed.

"How can you say such things?" he replied.

And she continued: " But you seem to be paying more attention to the sport than to me."

He groaned and said: "Did you not order me to kill the animal myself?"

And she replied gravely: "Of course I reckon upon it. You must kill it under my eyes."

Then he trembled in his saddle, spurred his horse until it reared and, losing all patience, exclaimed: "But, by jove, madame, that is impossible if we remain here."

Then she spoke tenderly to him, laying her hand on his arm or stroking his horse's mane, as if from abstraction, and said with a laugh; "But you must do it-or else so much the worse for you."

Just then they turned to the right into a narrow path which was overhung by trees, and suddenly, to avoid a branch which barred their way, she leaned toward him so closely that he felt her hair tickling his neck. Suddenly he threw his arms brutally round her, and putting his heavily mustached mouth to her forehead, he gave her a furious kiss.

At first she did not move and remained motionless under that mad caress; then she turned her head with a jerk, and either by accident or design her little lips met his, under their wealth of light hair, and a moment afterward, either from confusion or remorse, she struck her horse with her riding whip and went off at full gallop, and they rode on like that for some time, without exchanging a look.

The noise of the hunt came nearer; the thickets seemed to tremble, and suddenly the wild boar broke through the bushes, covered with blood and trying to shake off the hounds who had fastened onto him, and the baron, uttering a shout of triumph, exclaimed: "Let him who loves me follow me!" And he disappeared in the copse as if the wood had swallowed him up.

When she reached an open glade a few minutes later he was just getting up, covered with mud, his coat torn and his hands bloody, while the brute was lying stretched out at full length with the baron's hunting knife driven into its shoulder up to the hilt.

The quarry was cut at night by torchlight. It was a warm and dull evening, and the wan moon threw a yellow light onto the torches which made the night misty with their resinous smoke. The hounds devoured the wild boar's entrails and snarled and fought for them, while the prickers and the gentlemen, standing in a circie round the spoil, blew their horns as loud as they could. The flourish of the hunting horns resounded beyond the woods on that still night and was repeated by the echoes of the distant valleys, awakening the timid stags, rousing the yelping foxes and disturbing the little rabbits in their gambols at the edge of the rides.

The frightened night birds flew over the eager pack of hounds, while the women, who were moved by all these strangely picturesque things, leaned rather heavily on the men's arms and turned aside into the forest rides before the hounds had finished their meal. Mme d'Avancelles, feeling languid after that day of fatigue and tenderness, said to the baron: "Will you take a turn in the park, my friend?" And without replying, but trembling and nervous, he went with her, and immediately they kissed each other. They walked slowly under the almost leafless trees through which the moonbeams filtered, and their love, their desires, their longing for a closer embrace became so vehement that they nearly yielded to it at the foot of a tree.

The horns were not sounding any longer, and the tired hounds were sleeping in the kennels. "Let us return," the young woman said, and they went back.

When they got to the chateau and before they went in she said in a weak voice: "I am so tired that I shall go to bed, my friend." And as he opened his arms for a last kiss she ran away, saying as a last good-by: "No-I am going to sleep. Let him who loves me follow me!"

An hour later, when the whole silent chateau seemed dead, the baron crept stealthily out of his room and went and scratched at her door. As she did not reply he tried to open it and found that it was not locked.

She was in a reverie, resting her arms against the window ledge. He threw himself at her knees, which he kissed madly through her dress. She said nothing but buried her delicate fingers caressingly in his hair, and suddenly, as if she had formed some great resolution, whispered with a daring look: "I shall come back; wait for me." And, stretching out her hand, she pointed with her finger to an indistinct white spot at the end of the room; it was her bed.

Then with trembling hands, and scarcely knowing what he was doing, he quickly undressed, got into the cool sheets and, stretching himself out comfortably, almost forgot his love in the pleasure he found, tired out as he was, in the contact of the linen. She did not return, however, no doubt finding amusement in making him languish. He closed his eyes with a feeling of exquisite comfort and reflected peaceably while waiting for what he so ardently longed for. But by degrees his limbs grew languid and his thoughts became indistinct and fleeting, until his fatigue gained the upper hand and he fell asleep.

He slept that unconquerable heavy sleep of the worn-out hunter, slept through until daylight. Then, as the window had remained half opened, the crowing of a cock suddenly woke him. The baron opened his eyes, and feeling a woman's body against his- finding himself, much to his surprise, in a strange bed, and remembering nothing for the moment-he stammered:

"What? Where am I? What is the matter?"

Then she, who had not been asleep at all, looking at this unkempt man with red eyes and swollen lips, replied in the haughty tone of voice in which she occasionally spoke to her husband:

"It is nothing; it is only a cock crowing. Go to sleep again, monsieur, it has nothing to do with you."

A DUEL

THE war was over. The Germans occupied France. The country was panting like a wrestler lying under the knee of his successful opponent.

The first trains from Paris, after the city's long agony of famine and despair, were making their way to the new frontiers, slowly passing through the country districts and the villages. The passengers gazed through the windows at the ravaged fields and burned hamlets. Prussian soldiers, in their black hamlets with brass spikes, were smoking their pipes on horseback or sitting on chairs in front of the houses which were still left standing. Others were working or talking just as if they were members of the families. As you passed through the different towns you saw entire regiments drilling in the squares, and in spite of the rumble of the carriage wheels you could, every moment, hear the hoarse words of command.

M. Dubuis, who during the entire siege had served as one of the National Guard in Paris, was going to join his wife and daughter, whom he had prudently sent away to Switzerland before the invasion.

Famine and hardship had not diminished the big paunch so characteristic of the rich, peace-loving merchant. He had gone through the terrible events of the past year with sorrowful resignation and bitter complaints at the savagery of men. Now that he was journeying to the frontier at the close of the war he saw the Prussians for the first time, although he had done duty at the ramparts and stanchly mounted guard on cold nights.

He stared with mingled fear and anger at those bearded armed men installed all over French soil as if in their own homes, and he felt in his soul a kind of fever of impotent patriotism even while he yielded to that other instinct of discretion and self-preservation which never leaves us. In the same compartment two Englishmen, who had come to the country as sight-seers, were gazing around with looks of stolid curiosity. They were both stout also and kept chattering in their own language, sometimes referring to their guide book and reading in loud tones the names of the places indicated.

Suddenly the train stopped at a little village station, and a Prussian officer jumped up with a great clatter of his saber on the double footboard of the railway carriage. He was tall, wore a tight-fitting uniform, and his face had a very shaggy aspect. His red hair seemed to be on fire, and his long mustache and beard, of a paler color, was stuck out on both sides of his face, which it seemed to cut in two.

The Englishmen at once began staring at him with smiles of newly awakened interest, while M. Dubuis made a show of reading a newspaper. He sat crouched in a comer, like a thief in the presence of a gendarme.

The train started again. The Englishmen went on chatting and looking out for the exact scene of different battles, and all of a sudden, as one of them stretched out his arm toward the horizon to indicate a village, the Prussian officer remarked in French, extending his long legs and lolling backward:

"We killed a dozen Frenchmen in that village and took more than a hundred prisoners."

The Englishmen, quite interested, immediately asked:

"Ha! And what is the name of this village?"

The Prussian replied:

"Pharsbourg."

He added: "We caught these French blackguards by the ears."

And he glanced toward M. Dubuis, laughing into his mustache in an insulting fashion.

The train rolled on, always passing through hamlets occupied by the victorious army. German soldiers could be seen along the roads, on the edges of fields, standing in front of gates or chatting outside cafés. They covered the soil like African locusts.

The officer said with a wave of his hand:

"If I were in command I'd take Paris, bum everything and kill everybody. No more France!"

The Englishmen, through politeness, replied simply:

"Ah yes."

He went on:

"In twenty years all Europe, all of it, will belong to us. Prussia is more than a match for all of them."

The Englishmen, getting uneasy, said nothing in answer to this. Their faces, which had become impassive, seemed made of wax behind their long whiskers. Then the Prussian officer began to laugh. And then, lolling back, he began to sneer. He sneered at the downfall of France, insulted the prostrate enemy; he sneered at Austria which had been recently conquered; he sneerede at the furious but fruitless defense of the departments; he sneered at the Garde Mobile and at the useless artillery. He announced that Bismarck was going to build a city of iron with the captured cannons. And suddenly he pushed his boots against the thigh of M. Dubuis, who turned his eyes away, reddening to the roots of his hair.

The Englishmen seemed to have assumed an air of complete indifference, as if they had found themselves all at once shut up in their own island, far from the din of the world.

The officer took out his pipe and, looking fixedly at the Frenchman, said:

"You haven't got any tobacco-have you?"

M. Dubuis replied:

"No, monsieur."

The German said:

"You might go and buy some for me when the train stops next."

And he began laughing afresh as he added:

"I'll let you have the price of a drink."

The train whistled and slackened its pace. They had reached a station which had been burned down, and here there was a regular stop.

The German opened the carriage door and, catching M. Dubuis by the arm, said:

"Go and do what I told you-quick, quick!"

A Prussian detachment occupied the station. Other soldiers were looking on from behind wooden grating. The engine was already getting up steam in order to start off again. Then M. Dubuis hurriedly jumped on the platform and, in spite of the warnings of the station master, dashed into the adjoining compartment.

He was alone! He tore open his waistcoat, so rapidly did his heart beat, and, panting for breath, he wiped the perspiration off his forehead.

The train drew up at another station. And suddenly the officer appeared at the carriage door and jumped in, followed close behind by the two Englishmen, who were impelled by curiosity. The German sat facing the Frenchman and, laughing still, said:

"You did not want to do what I asked you."

M. Dubuis replied: "No, monsieur."

The train had just left the station when the officer said:

"I'll cut off your mustache to fill my pipe with." And he put out his hand toward the Frenchman's face.

The Englishmen kept staring in the same impassive fashion with fixed glances. Already the German had caught hold of the mustache and was tugging at it, when M. Dubuis, with a backstroke of his hand, threw back the officer's arm and, seizing him by the collar, flung him down on the seat. Then, excited to a pitch of fury, with his temples swollen and his eyes glaring he kept throttling the officer with one hand while with the other, clenched, he bagan to strike him violent blows in the face. The Prussian struggled, tried to draw his saber and to get a grip, while lying back, on his adversary. But M. Dubuis crushed him with the enormous weight of his stomach and kept hitting him without taking breath or knowing where his blows fell. Blood flowed down the face of the German, who, choking and with a rattling in his throat, spat forth his broken teeth and vainly strove to shake off this infuriated man who was killing him.

The Englishmen had got on their feet and came closer to see better. They remained standing, full of mirth and curiosity, ready to bet for or against each of the combatants.

And suddenly M. Dubuis, exhausted by his violent efforts, went and resumed his seat without uttering a word.

The Prussian did not attack him, for the savage assault had scared and terrified the officer. When he was able to breathe freely he said:

"Unless you give me satisfaction with pistols I will kill you."

M. Dubuis replied:

"Whenever you like. I'm quite ready."

The German said:

"Here is the town of Strasbourg. I'll get two officers to be my seconds, and there will be time before the train leaves the station."

M. Dubuis, who was puffing as much as the engine, said to the Englishmen:

"Will you be my seconds?" They both answered together: "Oh yes."

And the train stopped.

In a minute the Prussian had found two comrades who carried pistols, and they made their way toward the ramparts.

The Englishmen were continually looking at their watches,

shuffling their feet and hurrying on with the preparations, uneasy lest they should be too late for the train.

M. Dubuis had never fired a pistol in his life. They made him stand twenty paces away from his enemy. He was asked:

"Are you ready?"

While he was answering "Yes, monsieur," he noticed that one of the Englishmen had opened his umbrella in order to keep off the rays of the sun.

A voice gave the word of command.

"Fire!"

M. Dubuis fired at random without minding what he was doing, and he was amazed to see the Prussian staggering in front of him, lifting up his arms and, immediately afterward, falling straight on his face. He had killed the officer.

One of the Englishmen ejaculated: "Ah!" quivering with delight, satisfied curiosity and joyous impatience. The other, who still kept his watch in his hand, hurried him in double-quick time toward the station, his fellow country-man counting their steps with his arms pressed close to his sides: "One, two! One, two!"

And all three marching abreast, they rapidly made their way to the station like three grotesque figures in a comic newspaper.

The train was on the point of starting. They sprang into their carriage. Then the Englishmen, taking off their traveling caps, waved them three times over their heads, exclaiming:

"Hip! hip! hip! hurrah!"

Then gravely, one after the other, they stretched out their right hands to M. Dubuis and then went back and sat in their own corner.

THE DEVIL

THE peasant was standing opposite the doctor, by the bedside of the dying old woman, and she, calmly resigned and quite lucid, looked at them and listened to their talking. She was going to die and she did not rebel at it, for her life was over-she was ninety-two.

The July sun streamed in at the window and through the open door and cast its hot flames onto the uneven brown clay floor which had been stamped down by four generations of clodhoppers. The smell of the fields came in also, driven by the brisk wind and parched by the noontide heat. The grass-hoppers chirped themselves hoarse, filling the air with their shrill noise, like that of the wooden crickets which are sold to children at fair time.

The doctor raised his voice and said: "Honore', you cannot leave your mother in this state; she may die at any moment." And the peasant, in great distress, replied: "But I must get in my wheat, for it has been lying on the ground a long time, and the weather is just right for it; what do you say about it. Mother?" And the dying woman, still possessed by her Norman avariciousness, replied yes with her eyes and her forehead and so urged her son to get in his wheat and to leave her to die alone. But the doctor got angry and, stamping his foot, he said: "You are no better than a brute; do you hear? And I will not allow you to do it. Do you understand? And if you must get in your wheat today, go and fetch Rapet's wife and make her look after your mother. *I will* have it. And if you do not obey me I will let you die like a dog when you are ill in your turn; do your hear me?"

The peasant, a tall thin fellow with slow movements who was tormented by indecision, by his fear of the doctor and his keen love for saving, hesitated, calculated and stammered out: "How much does La Rapet charge for attending sick people?"

"How should I know?" the doctor cried. "That depends

upon how long she is wanted for. Settle it with her, by Jove! But I want her to be here within an hour; do you hear?"

So the man made up his mind. "I will go for her," he replied; "don't get angry, Doctor." And the latter left, calling out as he went: "Take care, you know, for I do not joke when I am angry!" And as soon as they were alone the peasant turned to his mother and said in a resigned voice: "I will go and fetch La Rapet, as the man will have it. Don't go off while I am away."

And he went out in his turn.

La Rapet, who was an old washerwoman, watched the dead and the dying of the neighborhood, and then as soon as she had sewn her customers into that linen cloth from which they would emerge no more, she went and took up her irons to smooth the linen of the living. Wrinkled like a last year's apple, spiteful, envious, avaricious with a phenomenal avarice, bent double, as if she had been broken in half across the loins by the constant movement of the iron over the linen, one might have said that she had a kind of monstrous and cynical affection for a death struggle. She never spoke of anything but of the people she had seen die, of the various kinds of deaths at which she had been present, and she related, with the greatest minuteness, details which were always the same, just like a sportsman talks of his shorts.

When Honore' Bontemps entered her cottage he found her preparing the starch for the collars of the village women, and he said: "Good evening; I hope you are pretty well. Mother Rapet."

She turned her head round to look at him and said: "Fairly well, fairly well, and you?"

"Oh, as for me, I am as well as I could wish, but my mother is very sick."

"Your mother?"

"Yes, my mother!"

"What's the matter with her?"

"She is going to turn up her toes; that's what's the matter with her!"

The old woman took her hands out of the water and asked with sudden sympathy: "Is she as bad as all that?"

"The doctor says she will not last till morning."

"Then she certainly is very bad!" Honore' hesitated, for he wanted to make a few preliminary remarks before coming to his proposal, but as he could hit upon nothing, he made up his mind suddenly.

"How much are you going to ask to stop with her till the end? You know that I am not rich, and I cannot even afford to keep a servant girl. It is just that which has brought my poor mother to this state, too much work and fatigue! She used to work for ten, in spite of her ninety-two years. You don't find any made of that stuff nowadays!"

La Rapet answered gravely: "There are two prices: forty sous by day and three francs by night for the rich, and twenty sous by day and forty by night of the others. You shall pay me the twenty and forty." But the peasant reflected, for he knew his mother well. He knew how tenacious of life, how vigorous and unyielding she was. He knew, too, that she might last another week, in spite of the doctor's opinion, and so he said resolutely: "No, I would rather you would fix a price until the end. I will take my chance one way or the other. The doctor says she will die very soon. If that happens, so much the better for you and so much the worse for me, but if she holds out till tomorrow or longer, so much the better for me and so much the worse for you!"

The nurse looked at the man in astonishment, for she had never treated a death as a speculative job, and she hesitated, tempted by the idea of the possible gain. But almost immediately she suspected that he wanted to juggle her. I Can say nothing until I have seen your mother," she replied.

"Then come with me and see her."

She washed her hands and went with him immediately. They did not speak on the road; she walked with short, hasty steps, while he strode on with his long legs, as if he were crossing a brook at every step. The cows lying down in the fields, overcome by the heat, raised their heads heavily and lowed feebly at the two passers-by, as if to ask them for some green grass.

When they got near the house Honore' Bontemps murmured: "Suppose it is all over?" And the unconscious wish that it might be so showed itself in the sound of his voice.

But the old woman was not dead. She was lying on her back on her wretched bed, her hands covered with a pink cotton counterpane, horrible thin, knotty paws, like some strange animal's or like crabs' claws, hands closed by rheumatism, fatigue and the work of nearly a century which she had accomplished.

La Rapet went upto the bed and looked at the dying woman, felt her pulse, tapped her on the chest, listened to her breathing and asked her questions so as to hear her speak; then, having looked at her for some time longer, she went out of the room, followed by Honore'. His decided opinion was that the old woman would not last out the night, and he asked: "Well?" And the sick nurse replied:

"Well, she may last two days, perhaps three. You will have to give me six francs, everything included."

"Six francs! Six francs!" he shouted. "Are you out of your mind? I tell you that she cannot last more than five or six hours!" And they disputed angrily for some time, but as the nurse said she would go home as the time was slopping away, and as his wheat would not come to the farmyard of its own accord, he agreed tc her terms at last.

"Very well then, that is settled; six francs, including everything, until the corpse is taken out."

"That is settled, six francs."

And he went away with long strides to the wheat which was lying on the ground under the hot sun which ripens the grain, while the sick nurse returned to the house.

She had brought some work with her, for she worked without stopping by the side of the dead and dying, sometimes for herself, sometimes for the family who employed her as seamstress also, paying her rather more in that capacity. Suddenly she asked:

"Have you received the last sacrament. Mother Bontemps?"

The old peasant woman said no with her head, and La Rapet, who was very devout, got up quickly. "Good heavens, is it possible? I will go and fetch the cure'," and she rushed off to the parsonage so quickly that the urchins in the street thought some accident had happened when they saw her trotting off like that.

The priest came immediately in his surplice, preceded by a

choirboy, who rang a bell to announce the passage of the Host through the parched and quiet country. Some men, working at a distance, took off their large hats and remained motionless until the white vestment had disappeared behind some farm buildings; the women who were making up the sheaves stood up to make the sign of the cross; the frightened black hens ran away along the ditch until they reached a well-known hole through which they suddenly disappeared, while a foal, which was tied up in a meadow, took fright at the sight of the surplice and began to gallop round at the length of its rope, kicking violently. The choirboy. in his red cassock, walked quickly, and the priest, the square biretta on his bowed head, followed him, muttering some prayer. Last of all came La Rapet, bent almost double, as if she wished to prostrate herself; she walked with folded hands, as if she were in chruch.

Honore' saw them pass in the distance, and he asked: "Where is our priest going to?" And his man, who was more acute, replied: "He is taking the sacrament to your mother, of course!"

The peasant was not surprised and said: "That is quite possible," and went on with his work.

Mother Bontemps confessed, received absolution and extreme unction, and the priest took his departure, leaving the two women alone in the suffocating cottage. La Rapet began to look at the dying woman and to ask herself whether it could last much longer.

The day was on the wane, and a cooler air came in stronger puffs, making a view of Epinal, which was fastened to the wall by two pins, flap up and down. The scanty window curtains, which had formerly been white but were now yellow and covered with flyspecks, looked as if they were going to fly off and seemed to struggle to get .'way, like the old woman's soul.

Lying motionless, with her eyes open, the old mother seemed to await the death which was so near and which yet delayed its coming, with perfect indifference. Her short breath whistled in her throat. It would stop altogether soon, and there would be one woman less in the world, one whom nobody would regret.

At nightfall Honore' returned, and when he went up to the bed and saw that his mother was still alive he asked: "How is she?" just as he had done formerly when she had been sick. Then he sent La Rapet away, saying to her: "Tomorrow morning at five o'clock without fail." And she replied: "Tomorrow at five o'clock."

She came at daybreak and found Honore' eating his soup, which he had made himself, before going to work.

"Well, is you mother dead?" asked the nurse. "She is rather better, on the contrary," he replied with a malignant look out of the corners of his eyes. Then he went out.

La Rapet was seized with anxiety and went up to the dying woman, who was in the same state, lethargic and impassive, her eyes open and her hands clutching the counterpane. The nurse perceived that this might go on thus for two days, four days, eight days, even, and her avaricious mind was seized with fear. She was excited to fury against the cunning fellow who had tricked her and against the woman who would not die.

Nevertheless, she began to sew and waited with her eyes fixed on the wrinkled face of Mother Bontemps. When Honore' returned to breakfast he seemed quite satisfied and even in a bantering humor, for he was carrying in his wheat under very favorable circumstances.

La Rapet was getting exasperated; every passing minute now seemed to her so much time and money stolen from her. She felt a mad inclination to choke this old ass, this headstrong old fool, this obstinate old wretch-to stop that short, rapid breath, which was robbing her of her time and money, by squeezing her throat a little. But then she reflected on the danger of doing so, and other thoughts came into her head, so she went up to the bed and said to her: "Have you ever seen the devil?"

Mother Bontemps whispered: "No."

Then the sick nurse began to talk and to tell her tales likely to terrify her weak and dying mind. "Some minutes before one dies the devil appears," she said, "to all. He has a broom in his hand, a saucepan on his head, and he utters loud cries. when anybody has seen him all is over, and that person has only a few moments longer to live"; and she enumerated all those to whom the devil had appeared that year: Josephine Loisel, Eulalie Ratier, Sophie Padagnau, Se'raphine Grospied.

Mother Bontemps, who was at last most disturbed in mind, moved about, wrung her hands and tried to turn her head to look at the other end of the room. Suddenly La Rapet disappeared at the foot of the bed. She took a sheet out of the cupboard and wrapped herself up in it; then she put the iron pot onto her head so that its three short, bent feet rose up like horns, took a broom in her right hand and a tin pail in her left, which she threw up suddenly so that it might fall to the ground noisily.

Certainly when it came down it made a terrible noise. Then, climbing onto a chair, the nurse showed herself, gesticulating and uttering shrill cries into the pot which covered her face, while she menaced the old peasant woman, who was nearly dead, with her broom.

Terrified, with a mad look on her face, the dying woman made a super-human effort to get up and escape; she even got her shoulders and chest out of bed; then she fell back with a deep sigh. All was over, and La Rapet calmly put everything back into its place; the broom into the corner by the cup-board, the sheet inside it, the pot onto the hearth, the pail onto the floor and the chair against the wall. Then with a professional air she closed the dead woman's enormous eyes, put a plate on the bed and poured some holy water into it, dipped the twig of boxwood into it and, kneeling down, she fervently repeated the prayers for the dead, which she knew by heart, as a matter of business.

When Honore' returned in the evening, he found her praying. He calculated immediately that she had made twenty sous out of him, for she had only spent three days and one night there, which made five francs altogether, instead of the six which he owed her.

AN UNFORTUNATE LIKENESS

IT WAS during one of those sudden changes of the electric light, which at one time throws rays of exquisite pale pink, of a liquid gold filtered through the light hair of a woman, and at another, rays of bluish hue with strange tints, such as the sky assumes at twilight, in which the women with their bare shoulders looked like living flowers—it was, I say, on the night of the first of January at Montonirail's, the dainty painter of tall, undulating figures, of bright dresses of Parisian prettiness—that tall Pescarelle, whom some called Pussy, though I do not know why, suddenly said in a low voice:

"Well, people were not altogether mistaken, in fact, were only half wrong when they coupled my name with that of pretty Lucy Ponelle. She had caught me, just as a bird-catcher on a frosty morning catches an imprudent wren on a limed twig—in fact, she might have done whatever she liked with me.

"I was under the charm of her enigmatical and mocking smile, that smile in which her teeth gleamed cruelly between her red lips and glistened as if they were ready to bite and to heighten the pleasure of the most delightful, the most voluptuous kiss by pain.

"I loved everything in her—her feline suppleness, her languid looks which emerged from her half-closed lids, full of promises and temptation, her somewhat extreme elegance and her hands, those long, delicate white hands, with blue veins, like the bloodless hands of a female saint in a stained-glass window, and her slender fingers, on which only the large blood drop of a ruby glittered.

"I would have given her all my remaining youth and vigour to have laid my burning hands upon the back of her cool, round neck and to feel that bright, silk, golden mane enveloping me and caressing my skin. I was never tired of hearing her disdainful, petulant voice, those vibrations which sounded as if they proceeded from clear glass, whose music at times became hoarse, harsh and fierce, like the loud, sonorous calls of the Valkyries.

"Good heavens! To be her lover, to be her chattel, to belong to her, to devote one's whole existence to her, to spend one's last halfpenny and to sink in misery, only to have the glory and the happiness of possessing her splendid beauty, the sweetness of her kisses, the pink and the white of her demonlike soul all to myself, if only for a few months!

"It makes you laugh, I know, to think that I should have been caught like that—I who give such good, prudent advice to my friends—I who fear love as I do those quicksands and shoals which appear at low tide and in which one may be swallowed up and disappear!

"But who can answer for himself, who can defend himself against such a danger as the magnetic attraction that inheres in such a woman? Nevertheless. I got cured and perfectly cured, and that quite accidentally. This is how the enchantment, which was apparently so infrangible, was broken.

"On the first night of a play I was sitting in the stalls close to Lucy, whose mother had accompanied her, as usual. They occupied the front of a box side by side. From some insurmountable attraction I never ceased looking at the woman whom I loved with all the force of my being. I feasted my eyes on her beauty; I saw nobody except her in the theatre and did not listen to the piece that was being performed on the stage.

"Suddenly, however, I felt as if I had received a blow from a dagger in my heart, and I had an insane hallucination. Lucy had moved, and her pretty head was in profile, in the same attitude and with the same lines as her mother. I do not know what shadow or what play of light had hardened and altered the colour of her delicate features, effacing their ideal prettiness, but the more I looked at them both, at the one who was young and the one who was old, the greater the distressing resemblance became.

"I saw Lucy growing older and older, striving against those accumulating years which bring wrinkles in the face, produce a double chin and crow's feet and spoil the mouth. *They almost looked like twins.*

"I suffered so that I thought I should go mad. Yet in spite of myself, instead of shaking off this feeling and making my escape out of the theatre, far away into the noise and life of the boulevards, I persisted in looking at the other, at the old one, in examining her, in judging her, in dissecting her with my eyes. I got excited over her flabby cheeks, over those ridiculous dimples that were half filled up, over that treble chin, that dyed hair, those lustreless eyes and that nose which was a caricature of Lucy's beautiful, attractive little nose.

"I had a prescience of the future. I loved her, and I should love her more and more every day, that little sorceress who had so despotically and so quickly conquered me. I should not allow any participation or any intrigue from the day she gave herself to me, and once intimately connected, who could tell whether, just as I was defending myself against it most, the legitimate termination—marriage—might not come?

"Why not give one's name to a woman whom one loves and whom one trusts? The reason was that I should be tied to a disfigured, ugly creature with whom I should not venture to be seen in public. My friends would leer at her with laughter in their eyes and with pity in their hearts for the man who was accompanying those remains.

"And so as soon as the curtain had fallen, without saying good day or good evening, I had myself driven to the Moulin Rouge."

"Well," Florise d'Anglet exclaimed, I shall never take Mamma to the theatre with me again, for the men are really going crazy!"

A FISHING EXCURSION

PARIS was blockaded, desolate, famished. The sparrows were few, and anything that was to be had was good to eat.

On a bright morning in January, Monsieur Morissot, a watchmaker by trade, but idler through circumstances was walking along the boulevard, sad, hungry, with his hands in the pockets of his uniform trousers, when he came face to face with a brother-in-arms whom he recognized as an old-time friend.

Before the war, Morrissot could be seen at daybreak every Sunday, trudging along with a cane in one hand and a tin box on his back. He would take the train to Colombes and walk from there to the Isle of Marante where he would fish until dark.

It was there he had met Monsieur Sauvage who kept a little notion store in the Rue Notre Dame de Lorette, a jovial fellow and passionately fond of fishing like himself. A warm friendship had sprung up between these two and they would fish side by side all day, very often without saying a word. Some days, when everything looked fresh and new and the beautiful spring sun gladdened every heart, Monsieur Morissot would exclaim :

"How delightful!" and Monsieru Sauvage would answer:

"There is nothing to equal it."

Then again on a fall evening, when the glorious setting sun, spreading its golden mantle on the already tinted leaves, would throw strange shadows around the two friends, Sauvage would say:

"What a grand picture!"

"It beats the boulevard!" would answer Morissot. But they understood each other quite as well without speaking.

The two friends had greeted each other warmly and had resumed their walk side by side, both thinking deeply of the past and present events. They entered a *cafe* and when a glass of absinthe had been placed before each Sauvage sighed:

"What terrible events, my friend!"

"And what weather!" said Morissot sadly; "this is the first nice day we have had this year. Do you remember our fishing excursion?"

"Do I! Alas! when shall we go again!"

After a second absinthe they emerged from the *cafe,* feeling rather dizzy— that light-headed effect which alcohol has on an empty stomach. The balmy air had made Sauvage exuberant and he exclaimed:

"Suppose we go!"

"Where?"

"Fishing."

"Fishing! Where?"

"To our old spot, to Colombes. The French soldiers are stationed near there and I know Colonel Dumoulin will give us a pass."

"It's a go; I am with you."

An hour after, having supplied themselves with their fishing tackle, they arrived at the colonel's villa. He had smiled at their request and had given them a pass in due form.

At about eleven o'clock they reached the advance guard, and after presenting their pass, walked through Colombes and found themselves very near their destination. Argenteuil, across the way, and the great plains toward Nanterre were all deserted. Solitary the hill of Orgemont and Sannois rose clearly above the plains; a splendid point of observation.

"See," said Sauvage pointing to the hills, "the Prussians are there."

Prussians! They had never seen one, but they knew that they were all around Paris, invisible and powerful; plundering, devastating, and slaughtering. To their superstitious terror they added a deep hatred for this unknown and victorious people.

"What if we should meet some?" said Morissot.

"We would ask them to join us," said Sauvage in true Parisian style.

Still they hesitated to advance. The silence frightened them. Finally Sauvage picked up courage.

"Come, let us go on cautiously."

They proceeded slowly, hiding behind bushes, looking anxiously on every side, listening to every sound. A bare strip of land had to be crossed before reaching the river. They started to run. At last, they reached the bank and sank into the bushes; breathless, but relieved.

Morissot thought he heard some one walking. He listened attentively, but no, he heard no sound. They were indeed alone! The little island shielded them from view. The house where the restaurant used to be seemed deserted; feeling reassured, they settled themselves for a good day's sport.

Sauvage caught the first fish, Morissot the second; and every minute they would bring one out which they would place in a net at their feet. It was indeed miraculous! They felt that supreme joy which one feels after having been deprived for months of a pleasant pastime. They had forgotten everything; even the war!

Suddenly, they heard a rumbling sound and the earth shook beneath them. It was the cannon on Mont Valérien. Morissot looked up and saw a trail of smoke, which was instantly followed by another explosion. Then they followed in quick succession.

"They are at it again," said Sauvage shrugging his shoulders. Morissot, who was naturally peaceful, felt a sudden uncontrollable anger.

"Stupid fools! What pleasure can they find in killing each other!"

"They are worse than brutes!"

"It will always be thus as long as we have governments."

"Well, such is life!"

"You mean death!" said Morissot laughing.

They continued to discuss the different political problems, while the cannon on Mont Valérien sent death and desolation among the French.

Suddenly they started. They had heard a step behind them. They turned and beheld four big men in dark uniforms, with guns pointed right at them. Their fishing-lines dropped out of their hands and floated away with the current.

In a few minutes, the Prussian soldiers had bound them, cast them into a boat, and rowed across the river to the island which our friends had thought deserted. They soon found out their mistake when they reached the house, behind which stood a score or more of soldiers. A big burly officer, seated astride a chair, smoking an immense pipe, addressed them in excellent French:

"Well, gentlemen, have you made a good haul?"

Just then, a soldier deposited at his feet the net full of fish which he had taken care to take along with him. The officer smiled and said:

"I see you have done pretty well; but let us change the subject. You are evidently sent to spy upon me. You pretended to fish so as to put me off the scent, but I am not so simple. I have caught you and shall have you shot. I am sorry, but war is war. As you passed the advance-guard you certainly must have the password; give it to me, and I will set you free."

The two friends stood side by side, pale and slightly trembling, but they answered nothing.

"No one will ever know. You will go back home quietly and the secret will disappear with you. If you refuse, it is instant death! Choose!"

They remained motionless; silent. The Prussian officer calmly pointed to the river.

"In five minutes you will be at the bottom of this river! Surely, you have a family, friends waiting for you?"

Still they kept silent. The cannon rumbled incessantly. The officer gave orders in his own tongue, then moved his chair away from the prisoners. A squad of men advanced within twenty feet of them, ready for command.

"I give you one minute; not a second more!"

Suddenly approaching the two Frenchmen, he took Morissot aside and whispered:

"Quick; the password. Your friend will not know; he will think I changed my mind." Morissot said nothing.

Then taking Sauvage aside he asked him the same thing, but he also was silent. The officer gave further orders and the men leveled their guns. At that moment, Morissot's eyes rested on the net full of fish lying in the grass a few feet away. The sight made him faint and, though he struggled against it, his eyes filled with tears. Then turning to his friend:

"Farewell! Monsieur Sauvage!"

"Farewell! Monsieur Morissot."

They stood for a minute, hand in hand, trembling with emotion which they were unable to control.

"Fire!" commanded the officer.

The squad of men fired as one. Sauvage fell straight on his face. Morissot, who was taller, swayed, pivoted and fell across his friend's body, his face to the sky; while blood flowed freely from the wound in the breast. The officer gave further orders and his men disappeared. They came back presently with ropes and stones, which they tied to the feet of the two friends, and four of them carried them to the edge of the river. They swung them and threw them in as far as they could. The bodies weighted by stones sank immediately. A splash, a few ripples and the water resumed its usual calmness. The only thing to be seen was a little blood floating on the surface. The officer calmly retraced his steps toward the house muttering :

"The fish will get even now."

He preceived the net full of fish, picked it up, smiled, and called:

"Wilhelm!"

A soldier in a white uniform approached. The officer handed him the fish saying:

"Fry these little things while they are still alive; they will make a delicious meal."

And having resumed his position on the chair, he puffed away at his pipe.

THE VENDETTA

THE widow of Paolo Saverini lived alone with her son in a poor little house on the ramparts of Bonifacio. The town, built upon the side of the mountain, suspended in spots above the sea, overlooks, through defile bristling with rocks, the lowest part of Sardinia. At its foot, on the other side, and almost entirely surrounding it, is a cut in the cliff, which resembles a gigantic corridor and serves as a port; it leads up to the first houses (after a long circuit between the two abrupt walls), the little Italian or Sardinian fishing-boats, and, every two weeks, the old, broken-winded steamer that plies between there and Ajaccio.

Upon the white moutains, the bunch of houses makes a spot whiter still. They have the appearance of nests of wild birds, fastened thus upon this rock, overlooking this terrible passageway where ships scarcely dare venture. The wind, without repose, harasses the sea, harasses the bare coast, which is nibbled by it until it has but little vegetation; it rushes into the defile, whose two sides it strips bare. The track of pale foam, fastened to black points on the innumerable rocks which pierce the waves, has the look of bits of cloth floating and palpitating upon the surface of the water.

The house of the widow Saverini, soldered to the edge of the cliff, had three windows opening upon this wild and desolate horizon.

She lived there alone, with her son Antoine and their dog Semillante, a great, thin beast with long, coarse hair, of a race that watches the herds. This dog served the young man for hunting.

One evening, after a dispute, Antoine Saverini was killed traitorously with a blow of a knife by Nicholas Ravolati who, the same night, went over to Sardinia.

When the old woman received the body of her child, which some passers-by brought to her, she did not weep but remained a long time motionless, looking at him. Then, extending her wrinkled hand upon the dead body, she promised revenge. She did not wish anyone to remain with her, and she shut herself up with the body and the dog.

The dog howled. She howled, this beast, in a continuous fashion, at the foot of the bed, her head extended toward her master, her tail held fast between her legs. She no more stirred than did the mother, who, hanging now upon the body, her eyes fixed, was weeping great tears while gazing at him.

The young man, upon his back, clothed in his coat of gray cloth, torn and bloody about the breast, seemed to be asleep. And there was blood everywhere: on his shirt, drawn up in the first moments, on his waistcoat, his trousers, upon his face, and his hands. Little clots of blood had coagulated in his beard and in his hair.

The old mother began to speak to him. At the sound of her voice, the dog was silent.

"Come, come," she said, "you shall be avenged, my little one, my boy, my poor child. Sleep, sleep, you shall be avenged, do you hear? It is your mother who promises! And she always keeps her word, does your mother, as you know well."

And gently she bent over him, gluing her cold lips to his dead mouth. Then Semillante began to groan again. She uttered a long, plaintive monotone, harrowing and terrible.

There they remained, the corpse, the woman and the beast, until morning.

Antoine Saverini was buried the next day, and soon no one spoke of him more in Bonifacio.

He had left no brother, no near relatives. There was no man to follow up the revenge. Alone, the mother thought of it, the old woman.

On the other side of the defile she saw, each morning and evening, a white spot on the coast. It was the little Sardinian village Longosardo, where Corsican bandits took refuge when too closely pursued. They almost peopled this hamlet, opposite the shore of their own country, and awaited there the moment of returning, of going back again to the brakes. It was in this village, she knew, that Nicholas Ravolati had taken refuge.

All alone, the whole day long, seated before her window, she would look down there and think of vengeance. How could she do it without anyone to help, infirm as she was and so near death? But she had promised, she had sworn it upon his dead body. She could not forget, she must not delay. How should she accomplish it? She could not sleep at night; she had no repose, no ease; she sought obstinately. The dog slept at her feet, and, sometimes raising her head, howled to the distance. Since her master was no longer there, she often howled thus, as if she were calling him, as if her soul, that of an inconsolable beast, had preserved a remembrance of him that nothing could efface.

One night, as Semillante began to howl in this way, the mother suddenly had an idea, a savage, vindictive, ferocious idea. She meditated upon it until morning; then, rising at the approach of day, she betook herself to the church. She prayed, prostrate upon the floor, humbled before God, supplicating him to aid her, to sustain her, to give to her poor, spent body force that would be sufficient to avenge the death of her son.

Then she returned. She had in her yard an old barrel with the head knocked in, which caught the rain from the gutters.

She emptied it and turned it over, making it fast to the soil by means of some stakes and stones; then she chained Semillante in this niche and went into her house.

Now she walked about constantly in her room, without repose, her eye fixed upon the coast of Sardinia. He was down there, was that assassin.

The dog howled all day and all night. The old woman carried her some water in the morning, in a bowl. But nothing more; no soup, no bread.

The day slipped away. Semillante, weakened from want of food, slept. The next day she had shining eyes and bristling hair; she pulled desperately at her chain.

Still the old woman gave her nothing to eat. The beast became furious, baying with raucous voice. The night passed away thus. Then, at the break of day, Mother Saverini went to the house of a neighbor and begged him to give her two bundles of straw. She took some old clothes that her husband had formerly worn and filled them full of the fodder, to simulate a human body.

Having stuck a stick in the ground before Semillante's niche, she bound the manikin to it, giving him the appearance of standing. Then she formed a head by means of a package of old linen.

The dog, surprised, looked at the straw man and was silent, although devoured with hunger.

Then the old woman went to the butcher's and bought a long piece of black pudding. She returned home, lighted a wood fire in her yard, and cooked this pudding. Semillante, excited, bounded about and frothed at the mouth, her eyes fixed upon the meat, the fumes of which entered her stomach.

Next the woman made a cravat for the straw man of this smoking sausage. She wound it many times about his neck, as if to make it penetrate him. When this was done, she unchained the dog.

With a formidable leap, the beast reached the manikin's throat, and, her paws upon his shoulders, began to tear him to pieces, she fell back, a piece of her prey in her mouth, then leaped upon him again, sinking her teeth in the cords, snatching some particles of nourishment, fell back again, and rebounded enraged. She tore away the face with great blows of the teeth, tearing into shreds the whole neck.

The old woman, mute and motionless, looked on, her eyes lighting up. She rechained the beast, made her fast two days again, and repeated this strange operation.

For three months, she accustomed the dog to this kind of struggle, to a repast conquered by tooth and claw. She did not chain her now, but set her upon the manikin with a gesture.

She taught her to tear him, to devour him, even without anything eatable hung around his throat. She would give her afterward, as a recompense, the pudding she had cooked for her.

Whenever she perceived the manikin, Semillante growled and turned her eyes toward her mistress, who would cry: "Go! in a whistling tone, at the same time raising her finger.

When she thought the right time had come, Mother Saverini went to confession and to communion one morning in ecstatic fervor ; then, having clothed herself in male attire, so that she looked like a feeble, old man, she went with a Sardinian fisherman, who took her and her dog to the other side of the defile.

She had, in a sack of cloth, a large piece of pudding. Semillante had fasted for two days. Every few moments the old woman made her smell of the pleasant food and endeavored to excite her.

They entered into Longosardo. The Corsican went into a wine-shop. She presented herself at a baker's and asked where Nicholas Ravolati lived. He had taken his old trade, that of a carpenter. He was working alone at the back of his shop.

The old woman opened the door and called:

"Hey, Nicholas!"

He turned around; then, loosing the dog, she cried out:

"Go! go! Devour him! devour him!"

The animal, excited, threw herself upon him and seized him by the throat. The man extended his arms, clinched her, and rolled upon the floor. For some minutes he twisted himself, beating the soil with his feet; then he remained motionless, while Semillante dug at his neck until it was in shreds.

Two neighbors, seated before their doors, recalled perfectly having seen an old man go out of the shop, with a black dog at his side, which was eating, as he went along, something brown that his master gave him.

That evening, the old woman returned to her house. She slept well that night.

THE RELICS

THEY had given him a grand public funeral, like they do to victorious soldiers who have added some dazzling pages to the glorious annals of their country, who have restored courage to desponding hearts and cast over other nations the proud shadow of their country's flag, like a yoke under which those go who are no longer to have a country or liberty.

During a whole bright, calm night, when falling stars made people think of unknown metamorphoses and the transmigration of souls, tall cavalry soldiers in their cuirasses, sitting as motionless as statues on their horses, had watched by the dead man's coffin, which was resting, covered with wreaths, under the porch of the heroes, every stone of which is engraved with the name of a brave man and of a battle.

The whole town was in mourning, as if it had lost the only object that had possession of its heart and love. The crowd went silently and thoughtfully down the avenue of the Champs Elysées and almost fought for the commemorative medals and the common portraits which hawkers were selling, or climbed upon the stands which street boys had erected here and there, from which they could see over the heads of the crowd.

The Place de la Concorde had something solemn about it, with its circle of statues hung from head to foot with long crape coverings which looked in the distance like widows; weeping and praying.

According to his last wish, Jean Ramel had been conveyed to the Pantheon in the wretched paupers' hearse which takes them to the common grave behind the shambling trot of some thin and broken-winded horse.

That dreadful, black conveyance without any drapery, without plumes and without flowers, followed by ministers and deputies, by several regiments with their bands, with their flags flying above the helmets and the sabres, by children from the national schools, by delegates from the provinces and by an innumerable crowd of men in blouses, of women, of shopkeepers from every quarter, had a most theatrical effect. Standing on the steps of the Pantheon, at the foot of the massive columns of the portico, the orators successively on Ramel's apotheosis, tried to make their voices dominate over the noise, emphasized their pompous periods and finished the performance by a poor third act, making people yawn and gradually dispersing the audience. People remembered who that man had been on whom such posthumous honours were being bestowed and who was having such a funeral: it was Jean Ramel.

Those three sonorous syllables called up a leonine head with white hair thrown back in disorder like a mane, with features that looked as if they had been cut out with a billhook but which were so powerful and in which there flamed such life as to make one forget their vulgarity and ugliness, with black eyes under bushy eyebrows, eyes which dilated and flashed like lightning, now veiled as if in tears and then filled with serene mildness, a voice which now growled so as almost to terrify its hearers and would have filled the hall of some working man's club, full of the thick smoke from strong pipes, without being affected by it, and then would be soft, coaxing, persuasive and unctuous as that of a priest who is holding out promises of Paradise or giving absolution for our sins.

He had had the good luck to be persecuted, to be in the eyes of the people the incarnation of that lying formula which appears on every public edifice, those three words of the Golden Age which make those who think, those who suffer and those who govern smile somewhat sadly: "Liberty, Fraternity, Equality." Luck had been kind to him, had sustained, had pushed him on by the shoulders and had set him up on his pedestal again when he had fallen as all idols do.

He spoke and he wrote, and always in order to announce the good news to all the multitudes who suffered—no matter to what grade of society they might belong—to hold out his hand to them and to defend them, to attack the abuses of the *Code,* that book of injustice and severity, to speak the truth boldly, even when it lashed his enemies as if it had been a whip.

His books were like Gospels which are read, chapter by chapter, and warmed the most despairing and the most sorrowing hearts, bringing comfort, hope and dreams to each.

He had lived very modestly until the end and appeared to spend nothing and had only kept one old servant, who spoke to him in the Basque dialect.

That chaste philosopher, who had all his life long feared women's snares and wiles, who had looked upon love as a luxury made only for the rich and idle, which unsettles the brain and interferes with acuteness of thought, had allowed himself to be caught like an ordinary man—late in life-when his hair was white and his forehead deeply wrinkled.

It was not, however, as happens in the visions of solitary ascetics, some strange queen or female magician, with stars in her eyes and witchery in her voice, or some loose woman who holds up the symbolical lamp immodestly to light up her radiant nudity and the pink-and-white bouquet of her sweet-smelling skin, or some woman in search of voluptuous pleasures whose lascivious appeals it is impossible for any man to listen to without being excited to the very depths of his being. Neither a princess out of some fairy tale, nor a frail beauty who was expert in reviving the ardour of old men and of leading them astray, nor a woman disgusted with her ideals, finding them all alike, who dreams of awakening the heart of one of those men who suffer, who afford so much alleviation to human misery, who seem to be surrounded by a halo and who never know anything but the true, the beautiful and the good.

It was only a little girl of twenty who was as pretty as a wild flower, had a ringing laugh, white teeth and a mind that was as spotless as a new mirror in which no figure has been reflected as yet.

He was an exile at the time for having given public expression to what he thought and was living in an Italian village which was buried in chestnut trees and situated on the shores of a lake so narrow and so transparent that it might have been taken for some nobleman's fishpond, an emerald in a large park. It consisted of about twenty red-tiled houses; steep paths paved with flint led up the side of the hills among the vines, where the Madonna, full of grace and goodness, extended her indulgences from shrines which contained dusty tinsel nosegays.

For the first time in his life Ramel remarked that there were some lips that were more desirable, more smiling than others, that there was hair in which it must be delicious to bury the fingers as in fine silk and which it must be delightful to kiss, and that there were eyes which contained an infinitude of caresses. He wandered right through the eclogue, which at length revealed true happiness to him, and he had a child, a son, by her.

This was the only secret that Ramel jealously concealed and of which no more than two or three of his oldest friends knew aught. While he hesitated about spending twopence on himself and went to the Institute and to the Chamber of Deputies outside an omnibus, Pepa led the happy life of a millionaire who is not frightened of the tomorrow and brought up her son like a little prince, with a tutor and three servants, who had nothing to do but to look after him.

All that Ramel made went into his mistress's hands, and when he felt that his last hour was approaching and that there was no hope of his recovery, in full possession of his faculties and with joy in his dull eyes, he gave his name to Pepa and made her his lawful widow in the presence of all his friends. She inherited everything that her former lover left behind, a considerable income from the royalties on his books and also his pension, which the state continued to pay to her.

Little Ramel throve wonderfully amid all this luxury and gave free scope to his instincts and his caprices without his mother ever having the courage to reprove him in the least, and he did not bear the slightest resemblance to Jean Ramel.

Full of pranks, effeminate, a superfine dandy and precociously vicious, he suggested the idea of those pages at the court of Florence, whom we meet with in the *Decameron* and who were the playthings for the idle hands of patrician ladies.

He was very ignorant, lived at a great rate, bet on races and played cards for heavy stakes with seasoned gamblers old enough to be his father. It was distressing to hear this lad joke about the memory of him whom he called *the old* man and persecute his mother because of the worship and adoration which she felt for Jean Ramel, whom she spoke of as if he had become a demigod when he died, as in the Roman theogony.

He would have liked altogether to have altered the arrangement of that sanctuary, the drawing room, where Pepa kept some of her husband's manuscripts, the furniture that he had most frequently used, the bed on which he had died, his pens, his clothes and his weapons. And one evening, not knowing how to dress himself up more originally than the rest for a masked ball that stout Toinette Danicheff was going to give as a house wanning, without saying a word to his mother, he took down the academician's dress, the sword and cocked hat that had belonged to Jean Ramel, and put it on as if it had been a disguise on Shrove Tuesday.

Slightly built and with thin arms and legs, the wide clothes hung on him. He was a comical sight with the embroidered skirt of his coat sweeping the carpet and his sword knocking against his heels. The elbows and the collar were shiny and greasy from wear, for the master had worn it until it was threadbare, to avoid having to buy another, and had never thought of replacing it.

He made a tremendous hit, and fair Liline Ablette laughed so at his grimaces and his disguise that that night she threw over Prince Noureddin for him, although he had paid for her house, her horses and everything else and allowed her six thousand francs a month for extras and pocket money.

THE RABBIT

OLD Leacacheur appeared at the door of his house at his usual hour, between five and a quarter past five in the morning, to look after his men who were going to work.

With a red face, only half awake, his right eye open and the left nearly closed, he was buttoning his braces over his fat stomach with some difficulty, all the time looking into every comer of the farmyard with a searching glance. The sun was darting his oblique rays through the beech trees by the side of the ditch and the apple trees outside, making the cocks crow on the dunghill and the pigeons coo on the roof. The smell of the cow stalls came through the open door, mingling In the fresh morning air with the pungent odor of the stable where the horses were neighing, with thier heads turned toward the light.

As soon as his tousers were properly fastened Lecacheur came out and went first of all toward the hen house to count the morning's eggs, for he had been suspecting thief's for some time. But the servant girl ran upto him with lifted arms and cried:

"Master! Master! They have stolen a rabbit during the night."

"A rabbit?"

"Yes, master, the big gray rabbit, from the hutch on the left." Whereupon the farmer quite opened his left eye and said simple:

"I must see that."

And off he went to inspect it. The hutch had been broken open and the rabbit was gone. Then he became thoughtful, closed his left eye again, scratched his nose and after a little consideration said to the frightened girl who was standing stupidly before him:

"Go and fetch the gendarmes; say I expect them as soon as possible."

Lecacheur was mayor of the village, Pairgry-le Gras, and ruled it like a tyrant on account of his money and position. As soon as the servant had disappeared in the direction of the village, which was only about five hundred yards off, he went his wife. He found her on her knees in front of the fire, trying to get it to bum up quickly. As soon as he got to the door he said:

"Somebody has stolen the gray rabbit."

She turned round so quickly that she found herself sitting on the floor and, looking at her husband with distress eyes, she said:

"What is it, Cacheux! Somebody has stolen a rabbit?"

"The big gray one."

She sighed. "How sad! Who can have done it?"

She was a little, thin, active, neat woman, who knew all about farming.

But Lecacheur had his own ideas about the matter.

"It must be that fellow Polyte."

His wife got up suddenly and said in a furious voice:

"He did it! He did it! You need not look for anyone else. He did it! You have said it, Cacheux!"

All her peasant's fury, all her avarice, all the rage of saving woman against the man of whom she had always been suspicious and against the girl whom she had always suspected, could be seen in the contraction of her mouth, in the wrinkles in her cheeks and in the forehead of her thin, exasperated face.

"And what have you done?" she asked.

"I have sent for the gendarmes."

This Polyte was a laborer who had been employed on the farm for a few days and had been dismissed by Lecacheur for an insolent answer. He was an old soldier and was supposed to have retained his habits of marauding and debauchery from his campaigns in Africa. He did anything for a livelihood, but whether working as a mason, a navy, a reaper, whether he broke stones or lopped trees, he was always lazy. So he remained in no position long and had, at times, to change his neighborhood to obtain work.

From the first day that he came to the farm Lecacheur's wife had detested him, and now she was sure that he had committed the robbery.

In about half an hour the two gendarmes arrived. Brigaedier Se'nateur was very tall and thin, and Gendarme Lenient, short and fat. Lecacheur made them sit down and told them the affair, and then they went and saw the scene of the theft, in order to verify the fact that the hutch had been broken open and to collect all the proofs they could. When they got back to the kitchen the mistress brought in some wine, filled their glasses and asked with a distrustful look:

"Shall you catch him?"

The brigadier, who had his sword between his legs, appeared thoughtful.

Certainly he was sure of taking him if he was pointed out to him, but if not, he could not himself answer for being able to discover him. After reflecting for a long time he put this simple question:

"Do you know the thief?"

And Lecacheur replied with a look of Normandy slyness in his eyes:

"As for knowing him, I do not, as I did not see him commit the robbery. If I had seen him I should have made him eat it raw, skin and flesh, without a drop of cider to wash it down. As for saying who it is, I cannot, although I believe it is that good-for-nothing Polyte."

Then he related at length his troubles with Polyte. his leaving his service, his bad reputation, things which had been told him, accumulating insignificant and minute proofs. Then the brigadier, who had been listening very attentively while he emptied his glass and filled it again, turned to his gendarme with as indifferent air and said:

"We must go and look in the cottage of Severin's wife." At which the gendarme smiled and nodded three times.

Then Mme Lecacheur came to them and very quitely, with all a peasant's cunning, questioned the brigadier to her turn. The shepherd Serverin, a simpleton, a sort of brute who had been brought up from youth among his bleating flocks and who knew of scarcely anything besides them in the world, had nevertheless preserved the peasant's instinct for saving at the bottom of his heart. For years and years he had hidden in hollow trees and crevices in the rocks all that he earned, either as shepherd or by curing the fractures of animals (for the bonesetter's secret had been handed down to him by the old shepherd whose place he took) by touch or advice, for one day he bought a small property consisting of a cottage and a field for three thousand francs.

A few months later it became known that he was going to marry a servant notorious for her bad morals the innkeeper's servant. The young fellows said that the girl, knowing that he was pretty well off, had been to his cottage every night and had taken him, bewitched him, led him on to matrimony litle by little, night by night.

And then having been to the mayor's office and to church, she lived in the house which her man had bought, while he continued to tend his flocks day and night on the plains.

And the brigadier added:

"Polyte has been sleeping with her for three weeks, for the thief has no place of his own to go to!"

The gendarme made a little joke:

"He takes the shepherd's blanket."

Mme Lecacheur, seized by a fresh access of rage, of rage increased by a married woman's anger against debauchery, exclaimed:

"It is she, I am sure. Go there. Ah! The blackguard thieves!"

But the brigadier was quite unmoved.

"A minute," he said. "Let us wait until twelve o'clock; as Polyte goes and dines there every day, I shall catch them with it under their noses."

The gendarme smiled, pleased at his chiefs idea, and Lecacheur also smiled now, for the affair of the shepherd struck him as very funny: deceived husbands are always amusing.

* * * * *

Twelve o'clock had just struck when the brigadier, followed by his man, knocked gently three times at the door of a small, lonlely house situated at the corner of a wood, some five hundred yards from the village.

They stood close against the wall so as not to be seen from within and waited. As nobody answered, the brigadier knocked again in a minute or two. It was so quiet that the house seemed uninhabited but Lenient, the gendarme, who had very quick ears, said that he heard somebody moving about inside. Se'nateur got angry. He would not allow anyone to resist the authority of the law for a moment and, knocking at the door with the hilt of his sword, he cried out:

"Open the door in the name of the law."

As this order had no effect, he roared out:

"If you do not obey I shall smash the lock. I am the brigadier of the gendarmery, by God! Here, Lenient."

He had not finished speaking when the door opened and Senateur saw before him a fat girl with a very red color, blowzy, with pendent breasts, big stomach and broad hips, sort of sanguine and sensual female, the wife of the shepherd Serverin. He entered the cottage.

"I have come to pay you a visit, as I want to make a little search," he said, and he looked about him. On the table there was a plate, jug of cider and a glass half full, which proved that a meal had been going on. Two knives were lying side by side. and the shrewd gendarme winked at his superior officer.

"It smells good," the latter said.

"One might swear that it was stewed rabbit," Lemient added much amused.

"Will you have a glass of brandy?" the peasant woman asked.

"No, thank you; I only want the skin of the rabbit that you are eating." She pretended not to understand, but she was trembling.

"What rabbit?"

The brigadier had taken a seat and was calmly wiping his forehead.

"Come, come, you are not going to try and make us believe that you live on couch grass. What were you eating there all by yourself for your dinner?"

"I? Nothing whatever, I swear to you. A mite of butter on my bread."

"You are a novice, my good woman – *a mite of butter on your bread.* You are mistaken; you ought to have said: amite of butter on the rabbit. By God, your better smells good! It is a special butter, extra-good butter, butter fit for a wedding, certainly not household butter!"

The gendarme was shaking with laughter and repeated:

"Not household butter, certainly."

As Brigadier Senateur was a joker, all the gendarmes had grown facetious, and the officer continued:

"Where is your butter?"

"Mybuter?"

"Yes, your butter."

"In the Jar."

"Then where is the butter jar?"

"Here it is."

She brought out an old cups, at the bottom of which there was a layer of rancid salt butter. The brigadier smelled it and said with a shake of his head:

"It is not the same. I want the butter that smell of the rabbit. Come, Lenient, open your eyes; look under the sideboard, my good fellow and I will look under the bed."

Having shut the door, he went up to the bed and tried to move it, but it was fixed to the wall and had not been moved for more than half a century, apparently. Then the brigadier stooped and made his uniform crack. A button had flown off.

"Lenient," he said.

"Yes, Brigadier.

"Come here, my lad, and look under the bed; I am too tall. I will look after the sideboard." –

He got up and waited while his man executed his orders.

Lenient, who was short and stout, took off his kepi, laid

himself on his stomach and, putting his face on the floor, looked at the black cavity under the bed. Then suddenly he exclaimed:

"All right, here we are!"

"What have you got? The rabbit?"

"No, the thief."

"The thief! Pull him out, pull him out!"

The gendarme had put his arms under the bed and laid hold of something. He pulled with all his might, and at last a foot shod in a thick boot appeared, which he was holding in his right hand. The brigadier grabbed it, crying:

"Pull, pull!"

And Lenient, who was on his knees by that time, was pulling at the other leg. But it was a hard joy, for the prisoner kicked out hard and arched up his back across the bed.

"Courage! Courage! Pull! Pull!" Senateur cried, and they pulled with all their strength-so hard that the wooden bar gave way and the victim came out as far as his head. At last they got that out also and saw the terrified and furious face of Polyte, whose arms remained stretched out under the bed.

"Pull away!" the brigadier kept on exclaiming. Then they heard a strange noise as the arms followed the shoulders and the hands the arms. In the hands was the handle of a saucepan and at the end of the handle the pan itself, which contained stewed rabbit.

"Good lord! Good lord!" the brigadier shouted in his delight, while Lenient took charge of the man. The rabbit's skin, an overwhelming proof, was discovered under the mattress, and the gendarmes returned in triumph to the village with their prisoner and their booty.

* * * * * *

A week later, as the affair had made much stir, Lecacheur, on going into the *mairie* to consult the schoolmaster, was told that the shepherd Severin had been waiting for him for more than an hour. He found him sitting on a chair in a corner with his stick between his legs. When he saw the mayor he got up, took off his cap and said :

"Good morning, Maitre Cacheux," and then he remained standing, timid and embarrassed.

"What do you want?" the former said.

"This is it, monsieur. Is it true that somebody stole one of your rabbits last week?"

"Yes, it is quite true, Severin."

"Who stole the rabbit?"

"Polyte Ancas, the laborer."

"Right! Right! And it is also true that it was found under my bed?"

"What do you mean, the rabbit?"

"The rabbit and then Polyte."

"Yes, my poor Severin, quite true, but who told you?"

"Pretty well everybody. I understand! And I suppose you know all about marriages, as you marry people?"

"What about marriage?"

"With regard to one's rights."

"What rights?"

"The husband's rights and then the wife's rights."

"Of course I do."

"Oh! Then just tell me, M'sieu Cacheux, has my wife the right to go to bed with Polyte?"

"What do you mean by going to bed with polyte?"

"Yes, has she any right before the law, and seeing that she is my wife, to go to bed with Polyte?"

"Why, of course not, of course not."

"If I catch him there again shall I have the right to thrash him and her also?"

"Why-why-why, yes."

"Very well, then; I will tell you why I want to know. One night last week, as I had my suspicions, I came in suddenly, and they were not behaving properly. I chucked Polyte out to go and sleep somewhere else, but that was all, as I did not know what my rights were. This time I did not see them; I only heard of it from others. That is over, and we will not say any more about it; but if I catch them again-by God! if I catch them again-I will make them lose all taste for such nonsense, Maitre Cacheux, as sure as my name is Severin.